The Mule Tamer: The Case of the Silver Republicans

The Mule Tamer: The Case of the Silver Republicans

John C. Horst

FIVE STAR
A part of Gale, Cengage Learning

Farmington Hills, Mich • San Francisco • New York • Waterville, Maine
Meriden, Conn • Mason, Ohio • Chicago

All scripture quotations, unless otherwise noted, are taken from the King James Bible.
Five Star™ Publishing, a part of Cengage Learning, Inc.

LIBRARY OF CONGRESS CATALOGING-IN-PUBLICATION DATA

Names: Horst, John C. author.
Title: The mule tamer : the case of the silver republicans / by John C. Horst.
Description: First edition. | Waterville, Maine : Five Star, 2016.
Identifiers: LCCN 2016024463 | ISBN 9781432832780 (hardcover) | ISBN 1432832786 (hardcover) | ISBN 9781432832728 (ebook) | ISBN 1432832727 (ebook) | ISBN 9781432833701 (ebook) | ISBN 1432833707 (ebook)
Subjects: LCSH: Frontier and pioneer life—Arizona—Fiction. | GSAFD: Western stories. | Historical fiction
Classification: LCC PS3608.O7724 M85 2016 | DDC 813/.6—dc23
LC record available at https://lccn.loc.gov/2016024463

First Edition. First Printing: December 2016
Find us on Facebook– https://www.facebook.com/FiveStarCengage
Visit our website– http://www.gale.cengage.com/fivestar/
Contact Five Star™ Publishing at FiveStar@cengage.com

Printed in the United States of America
1 2 3 4 5 6 7 20 19 18 17 16

For Harlan

That which has been is what will be, that which is done is what will be done, and there is nothing new under the sun.

—Ecclesiastes 1:9

Chapter 1

The report from Arvel Walsh's Henry rifle shattered the stillness of the desert afternoon in a place that defined loneliness. Three chickens flushed as the Mexican dropped like a pole-axed beef, dead before he hit the hard red earth, Dick Welles cursing as he made it to his feet. Free of the hill's crest, he beat his dirty shirt front and trousers clean of the Arizona sand.

"*Damn it all to hell,* Arvel, will you *please* quit killing every hombre we track down!" Reaching out, he whacked his partner across the back with his dusty hat brim. Dan George quietly worked on a cigarette, daring not to intervene, as the Indian had seen this play acted out more than a few times. Nothing he could say would improve his boss's mood or mitigate his sense of exasperation.

Walsh shrugged indifferently. "Sorry, Dick." Levering another round, he watched for further movement a hundred yards down the sloping ravine. The body lay crumpled, in the attitude of dead men.

They picked their way to the shack, a godforsaken hovel in a godforsaken bit of desolation just south of Tombstone. None of them hopeful, and directly, their worst fears realized, as none of the family of homesteaders had survived.

Dan George worked on building a pot of coffee, first washing the percolator and stovetop and table clean of blood and gore, as the Mexican had been creative in carrying out his unholy deeds. A fire was lit, the Rangers worked together and by evening, the departed were arranged, with as much dignity as the aftermath would allow, in an outbuilding just behind the homestead's cabin. The undertaker would be summoned in the morning.

Arvel Walsh watched his partner pace. He'd do what he could to make the best of it, simultaneously doing what he could to hide his trademark ubiquitous smirk and irreverent attitude, as Dick Welles was in no mood for frivolity. They sat and smoked and watched the sun go down.

"I'm sorry as hell, Dick."

"No you're not, Arvel. You're never goddamned sorry, never, goddamn it, so stop acting like you are."

Dan George nodded. "The bastard needed killing, Dick." He cast his gaze to the cabin's open door, considering the evidence of the miscreant's labors. Blood splatters covered the walls, curtains, doors. It was evident when he'd tended to the dead that the woman and children had been defiled. The stench of the place, despite their ministrations, still unbearable.

"Of course he needed killing." He sneered at both his partner and secretary. "They always need killing, not doubting it, Dan, but Jesus Christ, boys, it's getting out of hand, with the papers and the like. It's all getting out of hand. And, and why'd you have to shoot 'im in the eye? Goddamn it, Arvel, his mug'll be plastered all over the papers looking like that. Eye gone, back of his head gone. They're going to have a field day. It's all perfect fodder."

"Sorry, Dick, I pulled the shot a little."

Welles craned his neck. "*Pulled the shot a little!* Pulled the shot a little! Well, that's just grand! What the hell were you aiming for?"

"The bridge of his nose." Arvel searched the air. It was as still as a tomb, he could not blame his errant marksmanship on the wind. "Maybe that front sight moved again. Son of a gun does that on occasion. Drifts." He fiddled with his saddle, lying on the porch nearby. Pulling it from the scabbard, he checked the Henry. "Nope, nope, just as it should be. Maybe I'm getting old. Chica says I need spectacles just to wipe my ass."

Dick was spot-on of course, and with the election looming, the newly formed Ranger team could not afford bad publicity. It was difficult enough as they'd been appointed by the Republican governor Murphy, and all the dead men they'd piled up in their time on duty seemed to be mostly Democrats or friends of Democrats, or folks Democrats thought did not deserve killing. The *Tombstone Democrat* all but reserved the first page of its paper to the terrible actions of the Arizona Rangers. They were featured constantly. Even Cleveland's Democrat-appointed replacement could not deflect his own party's ire, when it came to the Rangers. They had a reputation they simply could not live down.

Dick stood, slapping his chaps with the backs of his hands. "I'm going to go check on our mounts."

Arvel lit a fresh cigarette from his dying stub and blew smoke at the porch roof. "What's got him so riled, Dan? He's a hundred times worse than usual. Man's going to give himself an apoplectic fit."

"He's nervous, Arvel. You know, if McKinley doesn't win, it's damned likely a Democrat's going to be appointed governor, and not the kind of Democrat we have in Hughes. Hughes is a good man, good as Murphy, but if Bryan's elected, well, it's more likely than not that that'll be the end of us as Rangers. We'll be dissolved, certain as the turning of the earth."

"Well, it's not like this devil was important. He *was* just a Mexican."

Dan's face contorted. "*Just* a Mexican?"

"You know what I mean. He wasn't *politically* connected, like those damned cowboys or some rancher's ne'er-do-well son or the like. Don't think too many Arizonans are going to shed many tears for this bastard from the south. Hell, he's less important than those turd Dunstable brothers, and look, we never did have any fallout from that."

Dan considered the carnage. He certainly remembered the Dunstables well enough. How could anyone forget them?

Arvel stood and stretched, as a man readying himself for bed. "And besides, Dan, you know I'll never risk friends or Rangers trying to take such filth alive. If we'd have tried to arrest him, take him alive, he'd just hole up in here"—Arvel patted the thick adobe wall behind him—"and shoot at us. I'm too goddamned old for that. Too damned old to leak any more blood. It's just not worth it, Dan, not worth it by a long shot."

He rummaged in the war bag at his feet. Retrieving a bottle, he poured for both of them. He found Dick's cup and emptied it, refilling it generously. He began making up his sleeping bag outside, as it was not going to be a cold night.

Dick was soon among them and Arvel read his mind. "Not sleeping in there, Dick. Too damned depressing *and* it still stinks of the dead." Glancing at the Mexican's corpse, he said, "Worthless son of a bitch."

They were in the regular habit of reading each other's minds, as working together over the years had led to a friendship, a bond stronger than either man had known. Not even in the war, among their brothers in arms, had they known such comradery. Arvel Walsh and Dick Welles were partners in law work and friends for life.

"Dick, my friend," he chose his words carefully. "We can't be worried over things we can't control. If they disband us, then they disband us. It's not worth all the bother."

"Maybe not to you!"

Welles loved his work. Knew he and Arvel did it well, and nothing, to his mind, would ever replace it. Sure he could become a US marshal or a town deputy, even run for sheriff and likely win, at least in his local county, but the Arizona Rangers were different. What he and Arvel Walsh had built was the crowning achievement of his life. The Rangers were special. He loved them.

In the short three years they'd existed, they'd done some grand and stellar work. Work to be proud of, work that needed doing and work that needed to continue, Welles was convinced of that.

"Goddamn it, Arvel, I'm sorry for being cross with you, really I am. I know you're always in the right, know you don't kill for no reason, but son of a bitch, I also know what'll be written in the damned papers as soon as we deliver this hombre to the court." He laughed using a cynical tone. "I thought, when we started, that me being a life-long Democrat and you a Republican would balance things out. But no! The sons of bitches can't find anything right about us."

"Amen to that, Dick. Amen to that."

"And why the hell do you have to be such a good goddamned shot! Jesus Christ, man, every time, right in the goddamned forehead."

Dan interjected, "That boy was shot through the eye, remember, Dick?"

Arvel grinned as he winked at the Indian. "Jerked the trigger a smidgen. Too much coffee for lunch, maybe."

"Very funny. You two ought to take this show on the road, make a fine Vaudeville act. But goddamn it, every time we bring a dead fellow in, every goddamned time, it's all about us, all about how we don't follow the due course of law. How we execute the prisoners, and shooting them with the precision of a surgeon, well, I don't know. To tell the truth, I'm about sick of it."

Arvel drained the bottle into Dick's cup, motioning for him

to sit on the upended barrel beside him. They watched Dan George put the finishing touches on a small campfire.

The Indian rejoined them, all three soon half mesmerized by the dancing flames.

"I think Arvel's right, Dick. You'll never find any logic or justice in the workings of politics. Try to play with them, and you'll only end up burned or sacrificed or used up." He nodded at his bosses. "Neither one of you is worth any of that, and Arvel's right. That Mexican bastard would have given us hell, and he'd have still ended up dead, no doubt in my mind about it. Arvel saved everyone a lot of time, grief and trouble, and not a little bit of lead to duck." He turned his attention to the corpse lying a few yards beyond the corral. "Bastard like that'll never give up, and he'd like nothing more than to take a few law dogs with him."

Dan swallowed hard to get the whiskey down. He yawned into the back of his hand. It was time for bed and he'd have difficulty getting off as the visions of the dead weighed heavily in his mind's eye. "And at the end of the day, there's not a politician alive, Democrat or Republican, that gives more than a squirt of piss for how many lives it takes to keep him on top."

He awoke at three and could not sleep as Dan and Dick seemed hell-bent on beating each other in a snoring contest. He lit a smoke and watched a skinny coyote chew on the Mexican's face. He didn't stop it for a while, then thought better of it, chucking a stone and then another until the animal sauntered away. The newspapers would like that certain enough, could take up an entire column on how the evil Rangers not only executed the man, but then didn't even have the decency to keep his corpse safe from the ravages of vermin.

His thoughts drifted to his family. Chica and his baby Rebecca were safely tucked away, at least he hoped, back at his mule ranch not ten miles from where he was camped. He considered the hovel roof shimmering in the moonlight, remembered every detail about the family who'd moved into it not long ago. He liked them. He'd given them the galvanized metal for that roof. They were nice people. Poor as dirt and nice, decent, hardworking. They'd moved west to escape the terrible economic panic. Chica used to bring them deer and javelina she'd killed on her little adventures around the ranch land. She'd be heartbroken when he told her what happened.

He never worried about his girls. Between his wife and Uncle Bob and the men and women on his spread, there was little to worry over. Every miscreant with half a brain knew, it was not conducive to good health to tangle with anyone associated with the Walsh clan.

Dick Welles coughed and snored a great loud snore and changed positions and was soon back to his normal rhythm. Arvel grinned at the memory of his surly partner whacking him on the back with his dirty old hat brim. He didn't like to annoy him.

He'd never change and Dick knew that well enough, nor would his partner ever stay angry with him for any length of time, as Arvel had a way of getting under everyone's skin, and most certainly not in a bad way. Most who knew him couldn't help but like him. Even those who hated him respected him. He was a force, had a presence that was nothing less than extraordinary. The Indian secretary called him one in a million, and no one would give the Sioux an argument on that point.

He thought about Dan George and his new love. He'd never be able to face the diminutive Chinese if he'd gotten the Indian killed. No, he wouldn't do that. He'd never do that and well, if the Republicans or the Silver Republicans or the Democrats or socialists or prohibitionists or anarchists couldn't live with that, well, then, they'd have to not live with that. It made no difference to Arvel Walsh whom he pleased and whom he annoyed.

Except, of course, for Chica. But the politicians, they mattered not a whit to him, as they weren't the ones traipsing around the territory dealing with the lowest of the low. They had no business judging him or his partner or men, and as far as he was concerned, they could all go to hell. Not a one of his people would ever be sacrificed or put in undue danger for the sake of politics.

Truth was, he wouldn't be heartbroken over the dissolution of the Rangers, anyway. He'd had a belly full of the nonsense over the past three years and now he wanted to enjoy his new bride and baby girl a little. At his age he'd never imagined he'd be starting a new family, but there it was. He could imagine no other life now. He took a deep breath and settled the flutter in his heart as his heart fluttered whenever he thought of Chica and his darling Rebecca. He loved them more than life itself.

They'd made him reborn. They'd given him a life that he loved and a life that made him happy and made everything worthwhile and all the mundane and inconsequential things of it seemed, frankly, no longer a bother. In fact, nothing seemed to bother or irritate Arvel Walsh. In that regard, he was a blessed and lucky man. Being on the trail, being in danger, living rough and uncomfortable reminded him of it every time.

But he also appreciated that it wouldn't go well for Dick if the Rangers ceased to exist. He knew that, had really done all this for his friend in the first place. It made the man happy. Even Dick's tenuous relationship with his son Michael, the reformed addict, had been improved since Dick found solace, found purpose in the rangering business.

Dan George snored himself awake and joined Arvel for a smoke in the dark. Arvel inquired as he watched the handsome Indian's face glow in the match light. "How's Ging Wa?"

"Good, Arvel. She's damned well. Finishing her studies and she'll be home soon. Hope to set up a practice in Bisbee and start working on a family." He grinned with pride. "She'll be the first woman and I guess first Chinese doctor in the whole damned territory, by God."

"That's mighty fine, Dan. You don't know how much it pleased Chica when you married her."

"All thanks to Uncle Bob." He rummaged in Arvel's war bag and opened another bottle.

"And your law studies?"

"Not much time for them, Arvel, you know." He pointed with the end of his cigarette at Dick's sleeping form. "He keeps me pretty busy with this Ranger nonsense."

"He's something, isn't he?"

"That he is, Arvel. Like a damned nervous cat with this election on the horizon. Jesus, Arvel, he worries more about all that than about the danger he's in most of the time."

"Oh, how I know it, Dan!" Arvel considered it as he held out his cup for Dan to fill.

"How much longer are you going to stay in it?"

"Not much, likely retire next year. I want to see what happens with the election. Can't load too many burdens on Dick at one time. He might explode if we push him too hard. But he'll be all right without me. You boys did fine when Chica and I were away in Europe, hell, that was ten months." He grinned. "And you, when will you bail on the old boy?"

"Oh, no rush." It was evident to everyone that Dan George enjoyed his vocation more than he'd ever let on. "Besides, might as well try to become a US senator as much as becoming a lawyer in this damned territory. Indians need not apply."

"Stupid, stupid, Dan. That's all I got to say. You're better read, better versed in the law than most attorneys I've known, and I can assure you, I've known my share of the bastards." He thought of his old dead father, his life back east in Maryland and laughed. "It's ridiculous, Dan. I'm sorry about that."

The Indian stood and stretched. He looked at his watch and then the horizon. "Wish you hadn't mentioned Ging Wa, Arvel. Damn it, now I'm thinking about her." He tossed his cigarette butt into the fire. "Thinking thoughts a man in the middle of the desert in the middle of the night has no business thinking." He winked. "If you get my meaning."

"Sorry, friend. You're sure right about all that. Ranger work's no vocation for happily married men."

CHAPTER 2

She was the most beautiful whore seen in the territory for many years and some hoped that she might help revitalize the dying town. Something had to. The fires, the mine floods, the collapse of the price of silver, the economic depression, had all taken its toll. No one seemed much interested in Tombstone or, for that matter, the territory of southern Arizona.

Robert Craster admired her as he waited for his assistant to finish tuning the upright now that they'd moved it into place. The laird went into a lively polka as he turned to regard what had his young boss's attention. The Scotsman nodded, smiling. "Good evening, young lady."

"If it would ever stop this rainin'." She smiled her business smile as she didn't know if they'd be staying.

Craster lit a cigar, pulling on it with enthusiasm as the laird watched him.

"Not taking a smoke break, Alasdair"—he pointed—"there's a big scratch on the top, not from us, but we best rub it out, so's there's no question." He nodded. "Go on, keep playin'."

Lori the cat lady, as she was known, sidled over to see what he was about. She was a curious woman, despite her trade, and she liked to learn new things.

Craster smiled as he worked. "Oldest trick in the book, ma'am, use a little cigar ash and spit, and a soft cloth, take a scratch out so's you'll never know it was there."

She watched as, if by magic, the blemish disappeared.

"I'll be."

The sleigh bells hanging from the doorknob jingled and Lori prepared to take her leave. She was alone this night, and despite feeling poorly, had to tend to any customers that might have braved the deluge. "You men need anything before I go?"

"No, ma'am, we're nearly finished." Craster nodded at the laird who'd broken into a melancholy piece, the laird winking at his boss's reddening face, as the young man was not used to dealing with pretty ladies of the evening. "You go on about your business. The madam's paid up in full. We'll let ourselves out."

Though she was no spring chicken, more likely sliding down the backside of thirty, she possessed a quality, a beauty that transcended youth. She was exotic, unusual in her appearance and attitude and the way she carried herself. She was sweet and kind. Had the mind, it seemed, of a child, though no one could ever say she was stupid. Ignorant, perhaps, but not stupid. Her innocence was her most appealing quality. She was adored, revered by men and women alike.

She was exotic to look at, almost oriental, though no one would ever mistake her for anything but a white. One might say catlike, with almond-shaped eyes, a small, well-formed nose, thin lips framing a diminutive, delicate mouth, and skin the color of porcelain, without so much as a blemish or freckle or scar. She blushed easily, and when aroused, had cheeks as rosy as a newborn's.

Her ginger hair reflected spun gold when the light touched it, her ample bosom never encumbered by more than the sheerest of petticoats. She rarely wore stockings and never underwear. She smelled nice, too, never of sweat or liquor or tobacco or sex. She was the cleanest whore anyone had known in all of the territory and this freshness, purity even, translated into an ability to entrance, not unlike some mythological creature, a shapeshifter perhaps, or at the minimum something unnatural, protean, and with this gift seemed able to transform herself into whatever the client wanted or desired at the moment.

A Brazilian who once had her, declared that she was an *encantado,* from the folklore of his land. He even ran his fingers through her hair, convinced he'd find a blowhole. He seemed a little disappointed both when he found nothing and in her lack of comprehension, appreciation of the compliment. Her overall cluelessness was often vexing, as a deep thinker she certainly wasn't.

But despite this lack of awareness, or even control over the gift, this power to transform into what her client wanted, or at least thought he wanted, was also the quality that had permitted her for so long to endure, even thrive in a business that consumed women by the bushel load. Her lack of awareness protected her mind from despondency, anxiety, depression, helplessness and hopelessness. She never needed, never succumbed to the mind killers that destroyed the victims of her trade, and this was all a sort of perverse blessing. She could live in the love trade without love or hope or any expectation of enduring happiness.

Her current madam had wisely set her up in the most opulent room of a house which in itself was out of the ordinary, as it was no brothel anyone from the region had known. It had started out as a respectable abode in a decent part of town, a home built for one of the early prospectors who'd made good and eventually found, due to his new wealth, the rustic environment tedious and boring. He'd moved on north to seek other distractions and fortunes. Shortly after his departure, the madam set up house.

The cat lady's bedroom was decorated in cheerful colors with flowered wallpaper and trimmed in white and pink, something more akin to a fairytale setting than a bordello, and it all added to the harpy mystique. The bedclothes were changed at least weekly, more frequently as required.

The madam had furnished it with a nice dressing table, replete with three-sided mirror and upholstered chair, all gilt in gold leaf, or at the least, gold paint. On this vanity, the pretty woman arranged her cat collection, which totaled more than fifty.

She loved cats and from the time she left the orphanage always had a real one. She had one for several years until it was killed by a dog in some town where she worked for a little while. She couldn't remember the name of the place, but never forgot the cat.

The other cats were glass or porcelain, some handmade of fabric, others carved from wood or bone or peach stones, according to the skill and sophistication of the customer. Some of her more dedicated clients brought them to her as extra payment. Actually more as tribute. More than a few treated her, worshiped her, as one would a goddess. One dedicated client, a bookish man who lived with his mother, had given her a pedigree cat, a Siamese informing her that such cats befit royalty and most certainly a kind she deserved. It was the one killed by the dog and many said the man took his own life when he found out that the death of the animal had broken his whore's heart.

She'd had many repeat clients in her last place of employment and would have stayed there indefinitely, despite the suicide of the bookish man, had she not been the cause of a prominent judge and his wife's murder and suicide. Intrigue constantly seemed to find her, and that is why she stayed in no place for very long.

She was presently one of eight whores and they all got along well enough. No one gave her a hard time, as they knew perfection when they saw it, and perfection, even in a whore, was something to be respected and appreciated and admired. Besides, as she was only one person, there were plenty she'd drawn in who'd rather be serviced than pass up an opportunity, or wait an inordinate amount of time for her to become available. The girls were all good to her. She seemed happy in her new home.

On this night the young man who'd fallen under her spell was smitten and acted accordingly. As the weather was bad there was no other commerce, the piano haulers clearly not interested, as evidenced by their behavior and actions. He'd been able to buy her for the entire night, and as the madam had decided to take advantage of the inclement weather, she let the others out for an evening's entertainment. He'd have her all to himself.

She was even better than he'd imagined, far superior to all the stories he'd heard. He trembled, as if it was his first time. Yet despite her allure and pleasant demeanor and attention, he could not perform. This enraged him. He was further put out by her kindness and understanding. It would have been better had she laughed or ridiculed him. But she'd never do that. It was not in her nature to be mean to anyone.

He ultimately blamed her, of course, and not the four shots of spirits washed down with beer or his own cowardice, lack of manliness, lack of ability to live as a human being, and when she tried to further comfort him, he backhanded her, causing her head to jerk, striking the heavy brass headboard. She gagged then sputtered, spitting a mouthful of blood and one tooth into his lap. Never, in all her life, had she known such brutality.

This, of course, further enraged him. He pointed to his soiled lap. "Clean that up, you bitch!"

She could not comprehend, felt like vomiting, resisted the urge, became dreamy as he pulled her by the long auburn tresses when she did not respond quickly enough to his demands. Her inactivity was vexing to both of them.

"I *said*, clean that up!"

He shook and punched her until the almond eyes swelled shut. Falling back on the soft pillow, she steadily lost most of her senses, drifted in and out of reality and consciousness. Out of the corner of one rapidly closing eye, she saw the glint of the blade, she felt, heard the cutting. And then, strangely an animal began wailing, away off in the distance. A long plaintive cry. Never had she heard such heartbreaking utterances in all her life.

She was floating, not in her body, looking down at the spectacle unfolding, uncontrollably, before her eyes. He was a large man and suddenly no longer a man, more a deranged creature, a great wild beast, perhaps a bear or some kind of monster from mythology. He was savaging the poor creature, a creature detached, a creature whom she could not identify. Warm liquid poured into and burned her eyes. Red sticky blood and then she mercifully lost consciousness.

Arvel slipped into bed and found her awake. She'd been hoping, waiting for him since dark. She rolled toward his body, kissing him on the cheek and mouth.

"Pendejo, where have you been so long?"

"Rangering." He wanted her and was soon distracted enough to put off the news of the neighbor settlers' demise. "You feel nice, Chica."

Afterward they reclined together, sharing a whiskey and cigarette.

"Everyone's all right? Rebecca's all right?"

"She is, my love. They are all good." She turned. "Oh, and Billy Livingston is with us. He has come for a visit."

"Billy! I haven't seen him in an age. How is he, Chica?"

"He has been sick, Pendejo. He got some bad water and was not able to move from his camp for more than a week." She smiled. "He said he could do nothing but shit. He is thinner than ever, but much better now. He is up at Rebecca Place, staying in the cabin. He is happy there."

"I'll go see him tomorrow."

"Did you catch the bad man?"

"The Hudsons are dead, Chica. I'm sorry to tell you, they're all dead."

She became quiet, blessed herself and said a prayer. "I am sorry. They were so happy there. Who did this terrible thing?"

"A drifter. A Mexican, a nobody."

"Did you send him to hell?"

"I did, Chica." He finished his drink, got up to pour another and crawled back under the covers to his love. "Got Dick's back up to boot. I provoked him again."

"He needs to get a grip on himself, Pendejo. He is always mad, always unhappy about something you do or say or act. What is his problem this time, my darling?"

He could always rely on her to understand him. He shrugged. "He's not like us, Chica. He's too, too damned civilized."

"You are funny." She stretched, running a bare foot up his thigh. "Dick Welles does not even like Mexicanos, what does he care if you send one to the grave?"

"He doesn't *dislike* Mexicans, Chica, not really."

"He does not like *me*. Does not approve of our marriage and look how he treats his only boy who married a Mexicana." She turned her head solemnly. "No, Pendejo, he does not like us, but you are right, he would go to his own grave defending a Mexican or an Anglo, or even an Indio. Dick Welles is a lot of annoying things, but one thing that must be respected about him, he is an honorable and just man."

She sprang from their bed, flitting to the desk. "Pendejo, I almos' forgot, the new Greener came from England!" She tossed it onto Arvel's lap, the candlewick bedspread doing little to protect him from the weight of the double.

"Ouch!" He pulled the gun up, reached for his reading glasses and had a look, smiling at Chica's grin as she admired it in his hands. He was happy when she looked such a way, like a child at Christmastime, as he knew Chica had known so few happy moments in her life. They were well overdue for her now. He'd do his best to make up for the lost Christmases.

"How does it fit you?"

"Like a nice glove, Pendejo. Ben Wallace is a good gunsmith, a good gun fitter. It is *muy bien.* I shot one hundred and fifty-six discs in a row with it."

Arvel handed the shotgun back, beckoning her to bed. He pulled her in close and kissed her, breathing in the scent of her hair. "That's a lot of shooting."

"*Sí,* we got a flinger and Uncle Bob and I shot it almost all day. It is a little short for him, though. It look like a toy when he was shooting it."

"A flinger?"

"*Sí,* it is *muy bien,* it flings the clay discs. We got Juan to work it for us, it is like back in England, Pendejo. Uncle Bob enjoyed it very much."

She held him close, wanting him again. "I do not like when you are away so long. I miss you all the time."

"I don't like it, either, Chica. I miss you more and more, too. I think about you constantly." He pulled her onto his body. Soon in their happy place, they slept until three.

"Pendejo, are you awake?"

He opened his eyes, remembering where he was. "I am now, Chica."

"Pendejo, we need to help Ben Wallace and some others. This bad *depresión,* it has made business so poor. I am worried for so many of them."

It was a significant problem and had hung heavily on the Walshes' minds. They'd avoided its effects, both he and Uncle

Bob on the mule ranch, and his mother back home in Maryland, as they'd invested in cash, none had ever fallen victim to the get-rich quick schemes that had decimated so many fortunes, and while they lived well, none were prey to opulence or carrying on with a lifestyle beyond their means.

"What did you have in mind, Chica?"

"I want to start a club for shooting, like that place that had the clay targets and flingers, like what we did in England. There is not such things here, Pendejo, and many would like it I think. Señor Wallace would be helped as well as other businessmen."

"How much do you suppose it would cost, Chica?"

She jumped from bed and turned up a light. She was extra beautiful when engaged in such enterprises, and she had so many going on, often at the same time. She pulled a file folder from the desk, full of her scribbling and cyphering, a quaint, almost childlike scrawl.

"Here, Pendejo, I worked it all out. I have not told the gunsmith any of it, though." She smiled. "Why are you looking at me in such a way, Pendejo?"

"Because I love you and am always so pleased to see you happy. You're happy when you are helping others, aren't you, darling?"

"I am, Pendejo. I am, and we needa talk about some other things as well. The Ramirezes have had their baby since you were gone. A little girl."

"She's all right?"

"She is well, Pendejo, both mother and baby are good and now we have more than twenty children on the ranch and we need a proper school. I do not like the way it is now and I want to build a proper schoolhouse and hire a teacher, for our ranch babies and our Rebecca."

She retrieved another packet of papers from the desk. "It is all figured out, Pendejo. I made all the plans, it will not cost too much money, either, but it will be good and right."

"Good and right."

"Sí."

Arvel looked the plans over. "Did you find time to sleep at all, Chica, while I was gone?"

"Oh, *sí*, I did sleep, and this did not take me so much time."

"How did I get such a smart and kind wife?"

"Oh, you were jus' lucky, I think."

"As do I. I think I am very lucky, Chica."

"Pendejo, what are we to do about this business? This Ranger job. I do not like it any more."

"You have never liked it."

"*Sí,* that is true. But now, I many times lie in bed at night and worry about you. I don't want you to die. I am too happy and we have too much, too many people to take care of for you to be dead. I am sorry if that sound selfish, but there are many men who can be Rangers, but there is no one who could replace you. It is time for you to stop."

"I couldn't agree more, Chica. After the election. It's only fair to Dick, and once it's decided who will be in the White House, then we can move on. That'll decide the fate of the Rangers, and if they survive, it'll be easier for Dick to handle. And if they don't, well, there's no need for me to quit. It'll all be decided for us."

"That is a good plan, Pendejo." She turned, pressing her back, until she was, like a nested spoon, against his belly. "Now, go to sleep, darling. I'm tired, and we have much to do tomorrow."

Chapter 3

Dick Welles kept vigil in a chair next to the bed occupied by the pretty whore. He held the diminutive hand and dared not do more as the blood had coagulated, gluing the terrible wounds shut. Any movement would surely cause her to bleed again. At least she was in no apparent distress or pain. Dr. Gillespie had already been to call, deeming her case a hopeless one. The sawbones declaring that he'd never seen a body take such abuse and survive and even gone so far as to suggest not cleaning her. She'd not last the day and any movement would most certainly set off a cascade of events that would do nothing but hasten her demise and worse, further her torment. It was his considered opinion that leaving her lie unmolested was more of a kindness, to just let her sleep her way into oblivion.

Jack the Ripper was the only thing that would come to mind for Dick as he surveyed the terrible scene surrounding him. Everything was soaked in blood. Perhaps the bastard had come to Arizona. Rumors had circulated for years that he'd escaped to America. No local, he was convinced, not even an Apache or a Mexican could have carried out such brutality. It made the Dunstable brothers' work look like that of amateurs. At least they put their victims out of their misery, once they'd finished tormenting them.

Arvel was soon with him, quietly pulling up a chair next to his old friend, felt him tremble as he placed a hand on a sinewy shoulder. Dick looked into his eyes and smiled.

"You ever seen her, Arvel, I mean, out and about?"

"I have."

"She was probably the most beautiful woman I've ever laid eyes on, and that counts your Maria and Michael's Salvatora."

Arvel smiled. "Hold on, you've never even met Salvatora."

"I'll take your word on how pretty she is." He reached over and brushed a lock of hair from her eyes. "And soon, mercifully, she'll be gone from this shitty existence."

Arvel peered at her. "You mean, you mean to say, she's, she's not *dead*?"

"No, no, but Doc Gillespie said she's not long for this world. No use trying to save her, Arvel. Moving her'll certainly finish her off and with more pain than she deserves."

"For Christ's sake, Dick, Gillespie's a fool and a drunk!" He moved around his Ranger partner, looking the battered woman over, he pressed his ear to her breast.

"Her heart's going strong. Her lungs are working." He pulled her eyelids open. "Jesus, man, this girl'll survive!"

Arvel shouted for the madam who, like a scolded child, stood, waiting in the doorway. "Ye—yes, Mr. Walsh?"

"Get me bandages, gauze, clean sheets, whatever you've got."

"But, but she's gone, Captain, she's gone."

Arvel turned on her, fury in his eyes. "Do it!" He stopped her. "Wait! What's her name? Her Christian name?"

"L—Lori, Captain."

Arvel whispered into her ear. "Lori, can you hear me?"

She nodded.

"Sweetheart, you've been hurt very badly, but we're going to get you help, do you understand?" He pressed his hand to her forehead. "Don't move, my dear, don't try to talk, just squeeze Dick's hand if you understand."

"Arvel, she has!"

"Dick, telephone the ranch, the bank's got a phone. Tell

Uncle Bob to have one of the boys ride to Rebecca's Place, fetch Billy Livingston, he's camping there. Have Billy to go to my hacienda, set up a hospital room, quick as he can."

Dick rushed for the door. "Got it, Arvel." He turned. "Arvel, I'm damned sorry."

"It's okay, Dick, now, go on and come back, soon as you can."

In an hour he had her plastered up like an Egyptian mummy and Dick ready with the madam's six-passenger surrey out front. Arvel wandered about the house, found what he was seeking, and pulled the madam's mattress from its frame. He carried it out to make up a proper ambulance. He unceremoniously tore the backseats from the vehicle, tossing them into the front yard, fitting the mattress to make the whore as comfortable as possible. Wisely the old madam did not object. One of his Rangers would drive Billy's patient to the Walsh ranch.

He turned his attention to the madam. "Who did this?"

"I don't know, Captain. I swear, I don't know."

"Bullshit! More like you won't tell!" He absentmindedly fingered the grip of his six-shooter.

Dick turned to the madam. He was worried for her, as, though he'd seen Arvel agitated many times, he'd never seen him in such a state as this. Something about the victim had gotten to him. He appeared manic, wild-eyed, nearly deranged, and for the first time in his rangering career, Welles worried that his partner might carry things too far. He interjected. "What's got you so scared, Hortense? You know us, you know we'll take care of you. Now, tell us what bastard did this?"

"I honestly don't know, Mr. Welles. I swear to you. I was gone. I went out. It was raining so hard and nothing was happening. No one was coming in. I went and had a tea with a, a friend. I swear. When I come back, Lori was like you saw."

Arvel spoke through gritted teeth. "And none of the others

saw anything. No one, not one of your bevy of whores saw anything!"

"No, Mr. Walsh, I swear to you. They was all out too, to a show, 'cause I give 'em the night off. They was out and Lori stayed. She didn't feel good and didn't want to go. They went to a show. I swear it. We can prove it, I swear!"

Billy Livingston unwrapped the bandages, swallowing hard as he'd never seen anything like it. He regarded Pilar who stood, stone-faced by the aborigine's side, and then to Chica at the foot of the bed, the women prepared to render whatever aid they could to the healer. He took a deep breath and continued, speaking as he worked.

"She's likely got a concussion, no brain swellin', at least on how her eyes look." He gave Chica a knowing nod. At least he'd not have to drill a hole through her skull, as he'd done to Arvel back at his camp. "Throat's been slashed, but obviously not deep enough to be fatal. Missed the jugular *and* carotid. Windpipe's intact. She's been cut from the corners of her mouth to each ear. Likely going to be significant nerve damage." He gently opened her mouth. "Two teeth have been knocked out, her tongue's lacerated." He pulled back the sheet covering her body. "Contusions to the breasts, right nipple's been lacerated, appears to be from a human bite." He turned to his volunteer nurse. "We gotta keep an eye on that, Miss Pilar, human bite's the nastiest kind."

He continued his assessment, moving down her body. Parting her thighs, he squinted, motioning for a wash pan. Pilar held it ready. "One—two—three—four shards of glass"—he counted as he extracted each piece—"in the vaginal canal. Looks like from the neck of a whiskey bottle." He looked up and swallowed hard. "Likely broke it from the outside after it was put inside her body."

"Oh, Dios!" Chica cried out.

Pilar blessed herself.

"*Ay Chingao,* what kind of *animale* would do such a thing!"

Billy pressed a clean towel to staunch the bleeding triggered by his ministrations. He nodded again to Pilar. "Miss Pilar, you have any of little Rebecca's old diapers?"

"Oh, *sí.*"

"Please boil some. Once they're clean we'll pack her with 'em." He shook his head from side to side, looking to Chica as if just remembering her question. "I don't know, Chica. I've never, in all my days, seen anything like it."

They bathed her, replacing her bedclothes with clean ones. Billy applied cold compresses to her eyes to bring the swelling down in hopes of easing her pain. She coughed and cleared her throat. She was awake.

"Hello, Miss Lori." He held her hand. "Don't try to move and don't try to talk, you're pretty sick. You're at the Walsh mule ranch not too far from town. You're safe and we're going to take good care of you."

She nodded, mouthing a thank-you.

"I need you to drink some medicine, Miss Lori." He rummaged in his bag and pulled out a funnel. "Then we need you to breathe when I hold this contraption over your nose." He smiled. "It looks silly but it won't hurt a bit. It'll just make you sleep. Need to stitch you up some and it won't feel good if you're awake."

She nodded and complied. After a dose of laudanum she was ready.

He soaked a cotton rag in chloroform, then wedged it in the bottom of the funnel. He upended it, holding the widest part of the cone above Lori's nose and mouth. She breathed steadily as

Pilar waved, with a church palm fan, the fumes from Billy's face. The girl was soon insensible. The healer went to work.

Billy Livingston sat in a rocker on the porch and watched the night pass. He was a hermit and a wolfer and a healer who'd come to Arizona from Australia as an attendant of camels, as some entrepreneur had the theory that they'd be useful in the American desert. It never caught on. Now he was the most respected unofficial *doctor* in the region, mostly owing to the endorsement of the Walsh clan.

Chica joined him, handing him a generous glass of scotch. "How is she, Billy?"

"Don' know, Chica. Don' know." He shifted in his chair then twisted and lit both of them cigarettes. The work helped to steady his trembling hands. "How's Arvel?"

She half grinned, half frowned. "You know what he gets like when women have been savaged, Billy. Dios help the bastard who did this thing. I jus' hope, for the devil's sake, Arvel is not the first one to fin' him."

"Any clues yet?"

"None, Billy." She took a long drink. "I was told that she was even more *bonita* than me. Now, look at her, Billy. Even your great skill will not be enough. She will never, ever be right, not in mind or body I guess."

Billy shrugged. "She's dyin', anyway."

"What do you mean, Billy? She looks horrible, but she does not seem to be dying to me."

"She's got a cancer, Chica. It's killin' her. She'd have probably been dead by Christmastime, even if she hadn't been attacked."

Chica looked on him with reverence. She'd never doubt him. "How do you know this thing, Billy?"

"She got tumors, you know, up there." He looked into his

glass, embarrassed to speak to her of such things. "You know, where we pulled the bits of bottle out. And her lungs, I can hear it in her lungs, they're riddled with dead spots, Chica." He turned his head. "Poor thing's consumed with it. She'll soon die."

He waited for Chica to finish a prayer. He worked on twisting another cigarette. "She kept goin' on about cats, Chica. Said she wanted her cats."

"Dick Welles is going back to the brothel. I will tell him to look for them."

"Thanks, and, Chica, don't say anything about the cancer. Don't tell anyone, please." He stared at the tip of his cigarette. "Don't know why, Chica, but I don't want anyone, aside from you and Miss Pilar, to know about it just yet. Don't know if we should even tell the poor girl about it."

She squeezed his arm. "Don' worry, Billy. I promise, I will say nothing."

Uncle Bob watched his love work in the kitchen, and, as they were alone, enveloped her with his arms, pressing their bodies together in a desperate embrace. She did not resist. Her trembling alarmed him. Pilar was the toughest woman he'd ever known, at least before Chica. It took a lot to elicit such trembling.

"Bad business, Pilar." He looked over her shoulder, observing that she'd been drying the shards of bottle after washing them. "What's this?"

"This was taken from the body of the poor girl, Roberto." She turned, burying her face into his old boney chest. "What could cause a person to be so wicked, Roberto, tell me, what could that poor creature ever do to make a man behave in a way such as this?"

"Nothing, nothing." He held her tightly. He'd seen his share of cruelty in his time, knew that Pilar had as well, but something about the prostitute, some certain innocence, made the act all the more reprehensible. "There's no figuring out a reason, darling. No sense in trying. Plain evil, that's all. Just plain evil." He pulled her face by the chin from his chest, kissing her tear-streaked cheeks.

She smiled and held up a hand. "I'm being too emotional, Roberto, please forgive me."

"Nothing to forgive." He considered her work. "Why are you saving them?"

She pieced them together. "Do you remember, Roberto, the new whiskey that you and Arvel love so much, what that salesman was peddling last winter? The drink from Scotland?"

"Sure, the Dewar's. Grand stuff."

"Look, look at this, Roberto." She put the pieces together, holding them next to a bottle retrieved from Arvel's liquor cabinet. "They are the same. This is the special whiskey, and if you remember, it was *muy caro.* Do you remember, I told Arvel that it was a waste of money when he bought so much?"

"I do remember, Pilar." Uncle Bob rubbed his chin, it was a significant clue. He kissed her on the temple. "You're a clever old gal."

Tears once again ran down the housekeeper's face. "I hope it will help, Roberto, I only hope that it will help. My guess is that the evil person is a man of means. At least it is *something* to go on."

Chapter 4

Francis O'Higgins sat in a rocker next to the locked door and read a dime novel, stroking the ears of the cat sleeping on his lap. He'd just turned twenty-seven and had been a Ranger going on six months. Dick Welles hired him after the lad helped him arrest a rather bad hombre in the Birdcage saloon one late winter night. O'Higgins had no business intervening, it was the act of a Good Samaritan, and his actions had most certainly saved the Ranger captain's life.

It had been Francis's first brush with law work, though not his first fight, as he was a handsome fellow with boyish features, unruly black curls and a slight build. He stood a little over five foot five. He was also gregarious, prone to teasing much larger and typically humorless, mostly ill-tempered, often unintelligent men, and though he was not educated, Francis was smarter than most whose company he kept. His shenanigans, wavy locks and good looks, more often than not led to the steady loss of temper in the baser sort and, almost invariably, fisticuffs. He could not help himself. Francis O'Higgins enjoyed a good fight.

He was an easterner and the lore of the West brought him, first to Texas, then New Mexico, and finally Arizona. He hoped to make his fortune prospecting. He immediately discovered that gold and silver did not lie about in great chunks to be picked up and stuffed into pockets by handsome dudes from the East and soon found other ways to make a living, as most people liked him, he could read, and had a good work ethic.

Women adored him as he treated them well, with respect and kindness, and because of this, many had a hand in hiring him.

But he never stayed in any job very long. It was the Irish in him, his mother would say, he was one of those race of men who could not settle down, those race of men who simply didn't fit in. He wandered constantly, and he'd likely never stop. It was both a curse and a blessing.

The madam would rather have had an older or at least uglier man posted as guard as she was growing weary of being banned from one of her own rooms, but Francis could neither be resisted nor defied. He was too gorgeous and pleasant to argue with, and because of these qualities, he was the perfect sentry.

He sat up straighter in his chair when she sauntered by. He nodded respectfully, motioning as if he were tipping his hat. "Mornin', ma'am."

"Good morning to you, Francis. Any news on when I might clean up?"

"None, ma'am." He went back to his reading and remembered something. "Thank you kindly for the meal and beers, ma'am. You have the best cookin' since home."

"The girls treating you all right?"

"Oh, sure, ma'am. They're mighty friendly." Francis couldn't help teasing her. "They keep inviting me for a lie down, ma'am, even keep sayin' *no charge.* I tell 'em, ain't tired, plus the captain'll pay my room *and* board while I'm here, and they all giggle." He gave a coy smile, knitting his brow as if all of it confused him. "Can't understand why everyone wants to put me up in their room, you know, them bein' in the trade an' all. Seems I'd be a considerable nuisance. Don't even think you could fit more than two in those narrow beds." He shrugged. "Besides, I don't think I'd get a wink a sleep with some fellow bouncin' like they do all the time. Squeaking beds, need oilin' I guess."

Hortense pinched his cheek. "I wish you were as ignorant and dumb as you acted, Francis. You'd be the ideal man."

Dick Welles interrupted the banter, inspiring Francis to spring to his feet, which the sleeping cat did not appreciate. The young Ranger did not joke with Dick Welles.

He nodded. "Morning, Captain."

"Morning." He glared at the madam. "No trouble, I trust."

"Oh, no, no, sir. Hortense and I were just talking about the sleepin' arrangements." He gave her a quick wink. "All is well, not a soul's been inside, sir."

"Good lad." He opened the door. His stomach churned at the sight, the memory of the victim lying in her blood-drenched bed. The stench of the gore still palpable.

Dick had taken his law-enforcement business seriously, studying and reading as much as he could about the science of detective work from every source he could find. He'd learned early on to secure crime scenes, and this is what he'd done here. He'd even had the photographer in immediately after discovering the scene and had it documented in this way.

He cautioned Francis to stand by the door as he began a careful survey of the room.

"How's the girl, Captain?"

Dick looked back at the young man, and then at Hortense hovering nearby. She was all ears, and he thought he'd give her something to think and talk about.

"She's dead, Francis. She lost too much blood, and I guess the ride to the ranch was too much. Died yesterday."

Francis looked genuinely affected. "Damn, Captain. I'm mighty sorry about that."

"I know, Francis. So am I." He nodded. "Go on out to my wagon, lad. I've got some empty cartridge crates. Fetch them in here, I need to take some things back to the office."

Dick was alone and began observing, as he'd read and

learned. Every inch of the room, first the ceiling, then walls, then floor, carefully gleaning all for clues, anything that might help track down the monster. He examined the pattern of the blood splatter. He wrote notes in a diary, adding sketches. He measured bloody footsteps, then placed newspapers over each one, tracing the shape and outline.

He got down on hands and knees, looked under the bed and found the remains of a whiskey bottle. The cat trilled in his ear, rubbing her head under his chin as he retrieved the evidence. He looked at her and smiled, patting her head. "Pilar's a genius, by God, a genius, little cat."

"What's that, Captain?"

"Nothing, Francis, just talking to myself." He nodded. "Francis, take all those cats"—he pointed to the dressing table—"put 'em in boxes for me, carefully so they don't get broken on the ride back." He handed the young fellow the remains of the scotch bottle now securely wrapped in cloth. "And this. Put everything in my wagon and wait for me."

"Yes, sir." He tried to tame a lock of hair with his hand, which he did often, absentmindedly, especially when he had a lot on his mind. "What's it all, clues, Captain?"

"Yes, Francis, clues." He spoke a little loudly, ensuring Hortense could hear. "No witnesses, Francis, so it's all up to us to find the murderer of this poor wretched girl."

When he was finished he walked out, lit a smoke and regarded Francis, sitting at the reins. The wagon packed and ready. The young fellow grinned and smiled at the cat, its head poking out of one of the crates. She trilled again when she saw the captain. "What we do with her, Captain?"

"Bring her along, Francis, bring her along."

Arvel clapped the young Ranger on the back. "Francis, it's good to see you again, lad. Don't think you've ever been to the ranch, have you, son?"

"Good to be here, Captain, and no, my first visit, sir." He took the cigar from Arvel's proffered hand, allowing his captain boss to light it for him. He nodded to Dan George and began to offer the Indian a greeting when Chica made her entrance. She took his breath away in mid-inhale. He sputtered, dropping the cigar in his lap. He immediately began beating the dislodged glowing tip, burning its way through his trousers.

Dan George, patting him on the back to clear his airway, said, "Careful, lad."

Arvel winked as he relit the Cubano, holding it until Francis recovered. "It's okay, son, Chica has that effect on most everyone, first time you see her."

He stood at attention, then bowed at the neck, red-faced from embarrassment and coughing. "*Lo siento mucho,* señora. Mighty sorry, folks."

Chica smiled. "Oh, Pendejo, I like *him*!"

Arvel turned his attention to his Ranger partner. "What have you got for us, Dick?"

Francis spoke up. "Oh, Captain, he's got all kinds of clues." His face reddened. "Sorry, seem to be running on and on, folks. I'll just shut my yap."

Arvel patted him on the back. He liked the boy's enthusiasm.

Dick smiled. "Well, one thing's for certain, Hortense took it all, hook, line and sinker. By now, everyone in Tombstone'll think the girl's dead." He glanced at Francis. "Sorry for doing that to you, lad, but you helped fool her. The busybody is certain little Lori's dead." He hesitated. "How *is* she?"

"Good, Dick, but she won't be any help. She can't remember anything. Billy seems to think it's a sort of fugue. Her tortured mind's way of coping with the calamity."

"Well, no matter." He pulled the remains of the bottle from the box. "Miss Pilar, may I have those pieces you saved?"

"Oh, *sí*."

She retrieved them from the kitchen and on returning, handed them over in a cigar box.

Dick began piecing them together. "There, a perfect fit."

Arvel shrugged. "So now we know he drinks Dewar's, how's that help?"

"Oh, but look at this little beauty, Arvel." He held the bottle to the light.

Arvel nodded. "A bloody fingerprint!"

"Ay chingao!"

"Yes, Miss Pilar, thanks to you." He returned his attention to Arvel. "And we know he's right-handed, wears size-ten congress gaiters that have Star heel plates and heel stiffeners, and a worn area on the sole, at the right big toe. He trod in a pool of Lori's blood, then tracked it on the carpet as he made his escape."

"Bloody bastard. The gore he created will help to catch him." Arvel looked at Chica who gave him a knowing nod.

Arvel sat in the same comfy chair he'd brought from Maryland, the same chair he'd sat in when reading stories to his little Katherine, the child he'd lost to typhoid fever, the child whose death convinced him his life was over, too many years ago, but never enough to keep her from his memory. He recalled every detail about his little girl, as if she'd passed only yesterday. Thoughts of his dead wife and daughter visited him constantly.

He felt Chica behind him as she pulled the shawl from the back of the rocker, down over his shoulders. She reached out and grasped his hands.

Whispering in his ear, she said, "You are as cold as ice, Pendejo. Why are you not in bed?"

Arvel nodded toward his little Rebecca, sleeping soundly. "I like to listen to her breathe." He reached over and kissed her temple, brushing the raven hair from her eyes. Her mother's hair. He smiled at Chica. "If that doesn't prove there's an Almighty, I don't know what does, Chica. I simply don't know what does."

He followed his love out into the parlor. She lit them cigarettes. "You are sad, my darling?"

He wandered to the porch and gazed into the desert night. The sky so littered with stars it was difficult to make out any one in particular. Chica wrapped her arms around him, squeezing him tightly, pressing his back against her breast.

"Sometimes I don't know whether I'm sad or angry." He looked off toward the room occupied by the prostitute. "Sometimes, Chica, sometimes, I don't know of which I have more, sadness or anger."

"At least she is safe now."

"Well, I guess." He turned, framing her face with his palms. He kissed the scar given to her by the Apache who'd nearly done him in. "Dick was going to let her just die, and, now, Chica, now I wonder if that wouldn't have been more of a kindness."

"I do not think so, Pendejo. I think she has some life ahead of her and soon she will be healed. Maybe the scars on her face will be a blessing."

"A blessing?"

"*Sí*, she will no longer be able to make a living in such a way, and I think that is a good thing, my love."

He ran his hands through her raven locks, then kissed her forehead. "How am I so lucky to have found you, Chica? Tell me, how?"

"You never did find, me, Pendejo. I found *you.*" She hugged him. "Now, please try to stop being so sad. I like it much better when you are happy and funny."

He smiled. "I'm a selfish devil."

"How so?"

"I have all this, you and little Rebecca and all my friends and family and good health and still I can't stop feeling so angry and sad all the time. I feel an ass being that way, Chica. Just a regular selfish ass."

"Well, you are not these things. You are sad and angry because you are a good man and take so much to heart all the wickedness of the world. I know these feelings, too. It is why we were made for each other, my love, and together, we will help each other to stop being too angry and too sad all the time."

"I love you, Chica."

"I know you do. You must not let these feelings too much take over your life. We will never stop getting angry and sad, my Arvel, and the evil will never stop being done, but we can try to make it not so hard on those whose lives we touch." She pulled him by the hand toward bed. "Come, I have something to make you stop being sad and angry." She winked devilishly. "I think you will like it very much."

David Gold paced the carpeted parlor floor and blew clouds of smoke as he drew on the cigar, clenched between his teeth, the air thick and rank with the acrid stuff, moving past him like water around the bow of a vessel under full power. He had an ironic name as he'd made his fortune in silver, not gold. And the name itself, at least as it concerned him, was Anglo-Saxon in origin, not Germanic. This was an important point as he felt constantly compelled to defend against any supposition that he might be a Jew. He was *not* a Jew and would fight a man to prove the point, the implication that repugnant to him.

As he paced, he glared at his secretary, an ugly man by the name of Dobbs who could have been the model for Dubois's missing link. He wore the same suit always, a loud checkered outfit reserved for men much younger and he looked extra ugly in it as the pattern accentuated the head too large for the squat, ape-like body. He was vulgar and uneducated and without any sense of propriety, making him wholly unsuitable for the position of secretary. He was more a henchman than anything else, the title a poor attempt at hiding his true purpose in the enterprise. His love of money kept him devoted to Gold and his various enterprises.

He sat, slumped in a leather chair, picking his fingernails with a folding knife. He spoke little, and only when required to do so, in a kind of guttural, primitive way, as if his brain would not allow him to process complex thoughts or articulate them, an incongruity, as Dobbs was not stupid.

Gold was a nervous sort of man and for good reason. He was self-made, had come from nothing and by the age of fifty-seven, amassed a significant fortune through various business dealings, mostly silver and other mining endeavors. Those who knew him said he could smell the stuff in the ground. The economic panic and his worthless sons were a constant threat to this fortune, the boys especially adept at squandering money, or getting into the kind of trouble that cost lots of it to make whatever mess they'd gotten into right. And this is why David Gold was nervous mostly all the time.

He, like Arvel Walsh, had outlived a wife and daughter. Unlike Walsh, however, Gold took the tragedy more as a relief rather than a crisis, as he did not love his wife, and as far as he was concerned, daughters were little more than a liability, almost certain to cost him a significant dowry. His in particular was spoilt and unpleasant. She fought with him constantly. He did not lament either woman's departure.

He was now in Tombstone to revive the flooded mines and hopefully continue with the extraction of silver and copper as well as manganese, a material that was becoming more desirable as steel construction and technology merited it. Gold was, if nothing else, a visionary. He hoped to get the mines going again for silver extraction, but was perhaps more enthused by the prospect of obtaining the abundant lesser valued element, which he was certain would be the future in the quickly approaching twentieth century.

What he needed were sharp and like-minded partners, and he had invested heavily in the education of his twin sons. From an early age he groomed them, anticipating, and fully expecting them to learn the finer points of mine engineering and metallurgy so that they would continue his legacy.

What he got was a pair of wastrel dolts who managed nothing more than to run up bill after bill and disgrace him, both ejected from the most prestigious universities in the East and ensure that the entire clan would be treated as pariahs by the elite of society. No one of consequence would have anything to do with them. Secretly he hated them both, and the constant trouble they caused him occupied his mind as he awaited their arrival.

Damian was most certainly the worst of the two, though Dennis was little better. The names were his wife's idea. She was Darla, and thought it clever that everyone should have a name that started with the letter D. His dead daughter was Debra. So, when it came to writing Christmas or greeting cards, she'd place a great D at the signature, followed by each name in turn. Thus it would read; "Greetings from the Golds; D—avid,—arla,—amian,—ennis, and—ebra." He *hated* that. Hated the sappiness, the sentimentality of it.

He'd seen neither of his sons for three days but knew, from the stories about the whore's demise, that at least one of them had been up to no good. Digging them out of such predicaments was nearly a full-time job, but this little indiscretion was different, for up until now, at least as far as David Gold knew, neither boy had taken a life.

At the completion of his third cheroot, they both sauntered

in. Like a pair of scolded dogs, he cuffed each on the ear by turns as they slunk past him. They took a position across from Dobbs, who did not bother taking his eyes from the fingernail picking project.

"Stop it, Dad. That hurts!"

"Good." He glared at Damian and pointed. "It's supposed to. Now, sit!"

The younger complied.

The older did his best to not look so pleased. He'd nonetheless enjoyed seeing his reprobate brother tortured, even if it meant he'd have to subject himself to a slap or two about the ears now and again. It was worth it. He was older by ten minutes and the more sensible of the two which could never remotely be taken as a suggestion of virtue. He was simply less evil and slightly more intelligent than his brother.

They were both handsome men, taking after their mother. Though not identical, they were tall, athletically built with chiseled features, dusty brown hair and blue eyes. They dressed well always, drank the finest spirits, smoked the best tobacco, dined on the finest cuisine. They were clever in their casual speech and engaging, at least initially, to everyone they met. They knew how to turn pretty women's heads, yet neither could hold one's attentions for very long as they were lecherous and had certain interests, proclivities that were abhorrent to even the most world-weary prostitute. Certainly no decent female, or really indecent female, for that matter, would have anything to do with them once they'd shown themselves in their natural form.

Gold lost his temper, as was often his wont when involved with anything having to do with his sons. He beat the youngest Gold again and again about the face and chest.

The boy, sobbing like a child, cried out.

Gold ignored him. "What have you done! What on earth have you done?"

"Nothing, Daddy, nothing, nothing, I swear, she, she attacked *me* with"—he pointed at Dobbs's blade—"with a knife like that when I didn't pay her enough. I, I had to *defend* myself. And that's all I did, I swear to you that's all I did!"

The patriarch glared at the older sibling. "Is it true?"

Dennis shrugged. "Don't know, wasn't with him. I was up in Jerome, Pa, nowhere near Damian that night."

Gold looked both of them over, sensing the typical lie. "I heard she was *butchered.* Butchered! Go to hell, what kind of goddamned monster are you?"

"That's a lie, Daddy. That's a lie. Someone must have gone in after, or maybe those law dogs cut her face like that. She was breathing when I left her. I cut her once, only once and that wasn't a terrible wound. It was just enough to make her stop fighting me, I swear, I swear!"

Dennis spoke up, wearing a satisfied smirk. "No one mentioned her face being cut up, Damian."

The old man backhanded the young Gold, knocking him from the sofa. He kicked him hard across the nose, opening up a torrent of blood. Dobbs moved his feet, making certain to stay clear of the flying gore. The elder Gold kicked his boy again and again until he was pulled away by Dennis.

"This is going to ruin our plans. God damn you, boy. God damn you, I should turn you over to those Rangers and let them string you up!"

Dennis interjected. His miscreant brother had, to his mind, suffered enough. "She was only a whore, Pa. Not like she was important or anything. Wasn't like that girl back in Vermont." He smiled at his brother working to staunch the blood. Dennis turned his head from side to side, whistling through his teeth. "Only fifteen years old! My God, brother, what could you have been thinking?"

"Shut up, Dennis. I never cut her up."

"No! *You* shut up!"

Gold kicked him in the leg. He turned his attention to Dennis. "That's not the goddamned point. I don't give a hoot in hell about a whore. What I care about is the success of the mining operation and these Rangers, well, from what I've learned, they're not like any police we've ever encountered. It's going to cost a fortune to extricate ourselves from this. And *that*"—he turned and kicked the young man again, this time in the side—"will cut into the goddamned bottom line!"

Dobbs interjected, "You mean *if* you extricate yourselves from it. You're right. Those Rangers can't be bought, so's I've heard."

Damian began sobbing. He groveled, hugging the old man's legs. "I'm sorry, Daddy, I'm sorry, I'm sorry. She got me so, so worked up. She didn't do what she was supposed to do and then she looked like she might laugh and I was drinking and I lost my temper."

"Get off me and get up!" Gold kicked himself free.

The lad crouched, red-faced and crying, he dare not look up. "What, what are we going to do, Daddy? What are we going to do? Jesus, I don't want to go to prison."

Dennis harrumphed. "Prison, brother, you won't go to prison. Hell, you'd be lucky to go to prison. This is murder. This is a hanging affair."

Damian ignored him. His tortured mind wouldn't let him think such thoughts. He went on. "I don't want to be put away. I swear I'm sorry. I'll never do it again. I don't know what gets into me, honest I don't."

Dennis suppressed a grin. "Supposedly she was not only the prettiest whore in the territory, but sweet as a little angel." He waited for the words to sink in, then continued. "That's what I think they called her, you know, as a nickname. *The angel.* She might as well have had wings, that's how pretty and sweet she was, Pa." He smiled at his groveling brother. "The *angel*, yes, that's what she was called."

Gold turned to his blubbering son. He was many things, but a misogynist he was not. He'd himself had many whores in his time and never once did any of them an unkindness. In fact, he was known for his tenderness and generosity with the soiled doves.

"You piece of trash!" He had a thought. "Who saw you?"

Damian thought on it. "No, no one, Pa." He sat up, grinning like an imbecile, as if the answer to the question would lead to his exoneration, or at least a reprieve. "It was that night, remember, the night it was pissing rain. All the other whores were out, and so was the madam. They had no other customers. Business was dead. That girl, she was the only one in. She stayed in alone, she was feeling poorly."

Dennis grinned. "Business was *dead.* Nice choice of words, little brother."

"Shut up, Dennis."

"No, *you* shut up, damned fool."

"Both of you shut up." Gold turned his attention to Dobbs. "No witnesses."

Dobbs shrugged.

Damian went pale. "Except . . ."

Gold looked on him. "Except *what*?"

"Two men, a freight hauler and a piano tuner. They were delivering a new upright. They were there, but, but, I don't think they paid any notice of me. When I left, they were gone, Daddy, they were gone, and no one saw me leave."

Dennis once again blew air through his teeth. "Only *two* witnesses, brother? You're slipping." He nodded at him, stretched out on the floor between them. "I know one thing," he pointed at his brother's feet, "I wouldn't bother having those gaiters resoled any time soon. Where you're going, brother, you won't be needing 'em."

"You worthless little goddamned runt. I ought to turn you in or, or shoot you myself." Gold pulled a pistol from a vest pocket, cocked it, pressing the muzzle to his son's forehead. "In fact, I think I'll do that! I'll send you straight to hell, right goddamned now!"

Dobbs turned his gaze from the fingernail project. He'd enjoy this.

The boy gasped, then vomited down his pressed shirt front. He screamed and babbled incoherently, tucking himself into a ball, rocking back and forth like an infant. He'd never seen his father so riled.

This was evidently too much, even for Gold who softened, uncocked the piece, then clobbered the lad across the forehead with the barrel as his son stood to embrace him, to thank him for the stay of execution. Damian crumpled. Dobbs sighed in disappointment, returning to the task at hand.

Turning to the elder son, he spoke as he stormed out. "When he wakes up, tell him to pack and head to Tampico. I'll wire him with further instructions once he's there."

She awoke to the cat trilling and licking her chin, purring as it settled between her breasts. "Jess!" She spoke with faint enthusiasm. The pain in her face and down below taking her breath away.

Billy Livingston smiled. "Well, good morning." He nodded and pointed to the cat. "Captain Welles brought her. Said she jumped in the wagon, think she knew they'd bring her to you, miss." He waved a hand toward the dressing table by the window. "And the captain and Francis brought you all your other cats, your little baubles and brushes and lotions and things too, ma'am."

She smiled, suppressing a grimace as the sutures pained her

so. Billy offered her a dose of laudanum, followed by a glass of water.

"Thank you."

"You're most welcome."

"Who are you?"

"Name's Billy, ma'am."

She felt her face, the long terrible wounds and the silk thread binding them. She put her fingers to her swollen eyes as she noticed Pilar straightening up the room. The old housekeeper nodded.

"Who, who doctored me up?"

"No doctor, child." Pilar tilted her head reverently toward Billy. "Better than a doctor! You got Billy Livingston!" She blessed herself. "Praise to Dios, he was here to help you, child."

"May, may I have a mirror?"

Billy nodded to Pilar who stood, hands clasped in mock prayer. "It is too early to see yet, child. Let the swelling go away, let the bruises fade a little first. Let the stitches come out."

"Please, if'n it's all the same to you, I'd like to see now."

Billy handed her one of Chica's hand mirrors, the one given to her by the old woman when she was a child. The one Arvel had resilvered and regilded as a present for their first Christmas together. Lori gazed into it, suppressing, the best she could, the quivering in her lip. She looked left, then right, then returned it to Billy. She rolled to her side, pulling the covers up past her chin.

In a tiny voice, she spoke into the pillow. "Please, when you're finished, pull them curtains. Turn down them lamps."

Chapter 5

Uncle Bob stood and fidgeted, feeling foolish as Billy read the label on the box of medication he'd gotten for the healer at the apothecary's. "He said it's the latest cure from Europe, Billy. I thought it might help ease the poor child's suffering."

Billy nodded. "Thanks, Bob." He smiled. "One night with Venus, a lifetime with Mercury, think that's the way it goes."

Bob nodded. "Will it help her?"

"No, Bob, it won't. I'm sorry, mate, I would not treat a dog with mercury. Damned quackery."

Bob pulled on his cigarette, blowing smoke at the porch roof. "I well . . . damned silly of me, sorry Billy. Should have known you'd know your business. Should have asked you first. It's only, well, Pilar told me she saw the state of the poor girl, we just thought . . ."

"She's not got the French disease, Bob. Surprisingly, she's clean in that respect."

"Oh."

"She's got a cancer, though. That's what's killin' her. She won't see this Christmas, friend. No potion'll help in that."

They sat and smoked for a while. Billy regarded the old man. It was what he loved most about the Walsh clan. An insignificant whore, a nobody and all the good folks of the ranch worried over her. He thought hard about what to say, how to help his friend cope with the news when Bob interrupted his thoughts.

"She's not in any pain, is she, Billy, I mean from the cancer?"

"Some, Bob, not so much yet. The pain'll come later, as the tumors grow, as it spreads through her body, but I'll take care of that. We've got good things for that." He nodded. "And with the love and care she'll get here, she'll be as comfortable as a soul can hope to be." He stubbed his cigarette butt on the bottom of his boot, tore the paper to pieces and scattered the tobacco to the winds. "I guess in a strange way, her coming here was a blessing. Just wish it hadn't been because of what that savage had done to her."

"Savage. You got that right."

"Any clues?"

"None of great significance, but Dick Welles got an interesting letter. Some dude, silver prospector, rich bastard, wants a meeting. Dick and Dan are going to see him tomorrow."

"About her?"

"Don't know. It was very cryptic, but my gut says yes. By all Dick's detective work, seems a rich dude did this to her. Probably connected. More likely than not."

They were interrupted by the girl's cry. Billy touched his friend's shoulder as he moved to the sick room. He pushed the medicine into Bob's hand. "Go ahead and get your money back, mate." He patted him on the back. "And I thank you for your kindness. I promise, Bob, I'll do the best I can to ease her suffering."

Ranger Private O'Higgins read the note with interest. He smiled at the housekeeper, a rotund widow of a preacher who'd brought her to the West against her will. Now she could imagine no other place she'd rather call home. Francis liked to tease her.

He shook the envelope holding his hand below it to catch anything that might fall out. "Sure there was no money in it, Mrs. Anderson?"

She glared at him. "I beg your pardon!"

"Nothin', ma'am, nothin'." He looked it over again for clues. "And you say it was stuck in the door?"

"That's right."

"And you're sure it's for me?"

"It's got your name on it, Francis. My goodness you can be such a dunce sometimes!"

"Just makin' sure, ma'am." He winked and smiled.

It was a cryptic message, a promise by the one who'd penned it to tell him something important concerning the case of the butchered prostitute if he'd show up at the Birdcage later that afternoon. He checked the clock in the parlor and set his watch to it, knowing certainly that anything as important as a timepiece was above reproach in the Anderson home. He called out to the old woman. "Back later, missus."

She harrumphed, pretending that she did not care.

He liked the Birdcage as it was a lively place. A den of iniquity and, though Francis did not go in for cavorting with whores or gambling or rough talk, he still found the saloon fascinating. They treated him well there, as he'd proven himself twice, beating men much bigger than him both times. He was also polite, could hold his liquor and never had an unkind word for any of them, patron or worker.

The bartender looked the letter over, shrugging. "No, Francis, can't help you." He looked about for anyone who might be the author, then served him a beer, as he knew Francis did not imbibe of the hard stuff while working.

"So, how's the rangering business?"

"Oh, pleasant enough." He raised the glass in mock toast to the barman. "To your health."

A young man sidled up, ordering a beer for himself. He was a big man as he was both tall and muscled with a face that told the story of a doubtless checkered past, well dressed, sporting a small derby as would a man newly arrived to the land.

"Pardon, sir."

Francis looked left and right, as he was not used to be addressed with such formality.

"Me?"

"Yes, heard you said something about Rangers."

"Yeah. I'm a Ranger." He glanced at the star on his vest as a form of proof to his claim. "Arizona Ranger." Francis nodded and extended his hand. "I'm a private in the outfit. O'Higgins, Francis O'Higgins."

The big man grinned. "May I ask you some questions about it?"

"Depends on the questions."

"Oh, nothing bad. My brother and me." He nodded at a near carbon copy at the end of the bar. "We're from Chicago. Been in the region, like to settle, but this damned economy. Not too many jobs. We were wondering if you all were hiring."

Francis shrugged. "Don't know, ain't my place being a private. You can inquire down in Bisbee. Captain Welles. He's your man. He runs the outfit, him and Captain Walsh. They do the hirin'." He looked the man over with a critical eye. "They only hire the best of men, son." He nodded. "Not that I'm sayin' you and your brother ain't, but I can tell you, they'll sniff out a rat quicker than shit goes through a goose, I'll guarantee you that."

"What are the requirements?" The big man nodded to the barman for another round and Francis grinned at the prospect of free beer *and* receiving so much attention. He liked being a celebrity.

He nodded at the fresh glass. "I'm thanking you for that. Well, let's see . . ."

They led him to a table in a corner where it was quiet.

"Well, boys, let me tell you all about it."

★ ★ ★ ★ ★

Dick sat in the opulent parlor, Dan George by his side. They watched Dobbs look tough. Neither was impressed. Dick decided that imparting a little humility was in order and nodded tersely at the henchman as he wound his watch, checking the time. "We'll have a coffee while we wait."

Dobbs sneered but lost his nerve as Dick's gaze bore into his soul. He moved off to the kitchen when Welles stopped him. "Also, tell your boss, we've business elsewhere. We're not in the habit of waiting for anyone. We'll give him another minute."

Dan smiled. He liked when Dick used the hard line. He was a man not to be taken lightly and when he was in his terse mode, appeared even more imposing, threatening, intimidating. The Indian spoke in just above a whisper. "That ought to get a little action."

Dick nodded without taking his eye from the doorway through which the henchman had left them. "See what you can find out about that turd, Dan. No doubt he's been around. I'll bet he's served some time somewhere. So goddamned ugly he will certainly stand out."

"Will do, boss."

They sat, stone-faced as the prospector moved, with great purpose through the doorway and into the room to greet them. He was not used to men not standing when he made an entry. Dick looked past him, through him as Dobbs held the door for an ancient, crooked housekeeper pushing the trolley toward them.

Dobbs bossed her around, tersely telling her where to put the coffee tray. The Rangers interrupted him, standing as they made motions as if tipping their hats.

"Thank you, ma'am." They retook their seats.

The old woman responded as one would to a foreign creature, as she was not used to being thanked for anything or addressed by men in a gentlemanly way.

The lawmen ignored the refreshments, then stared their host down. "Well?"

"Name's Gold."

"We know that. What's your business, Mr. Gold?"

"It, well, Mr. Welles . . ."

Dan George corrected him, "Captain Welles."

"Yes, yes, of course, *Captain* Welles." He pulled cigars from his vest pocket offering one to Dick. He ignored Dan George who plucked the proffered smoke from Gold's hand. He trimmed it with the silver cutter on his watch chain, lighting it with the fancy lighter on the table nearby.

"Must the Indian remain?" He coughed as Dan George blew smoke up his nose. Both lawmen ignored his impudent question.

"That'll be about enough of the bullshit, Mr. Gold. State your business."

"The whore who got cut up."

"You mean the young woman who was murdered?"

Gold waved him off. "Yes, yes, of course." His face turned up into a wide grin. A different strategy was in order. "Look, gentlemen, I'm sorry, but I'll be frank with you, I, well, I've got a good idea who might have been responsible."

"Okay, well, then spill it. Tell us what you know."

"It's well . . ." He nodded to Dobbs who sauntered from the room. Gold followed after him and closed the door. Returning to the lawmen he pulled up a chair and sat across the settee between them. "It's rather complicated, gentlemen, and well, I'd like to just put my cards on the table." He waited for some reaction, some response from Dick who sat, like a dangerous hawk on a wire, waiting to swoop down for the kill. Gold continued. "Captain Welles, I know a thing or two about this Ranger business of yours." He waited and again was disappointed by Welles's stone countenance. "You and Arvel Walsh have one of the best law teams in the country."

Dan George interjected, "*The* best."

"Well, I wouldn't say that, there *are* the Texas Rangers."

Dan blew his answer with his cigar smoke. "Amateurs and children."

Welles was growing impatient. He stood, nodding to his assistant. "Clap him in irons, Ranger George. I've had enough of this nonsense."

Gold stiffened. "Now, now hold on, Captain." He extended his hand, as if to fend them off. "Hear me out."

"Go on."

"What do you know of the Silver Republican Party, Mr. Welles?"

Dan George answered for his boss. "Self-serving kooks."

Gold ignored him. "Let's not delude ourselves, gentlemen, if your Republican candidate isn't elected president, I can guarantee your Governor Hughes won't have a Chinaman's chance of staying on as territorial governor, and that, my friend, will be the end of your Arizona Rangers."

Dan said, "Hughes happens to be a Democrat, so we know he'll be replaced by a Republican, if McKinley wins. Which is most likely."

Gold ignored him again, addressing Welles. "Wishful thinking."

"So what?" Dick suppressed his anger.

"Oh, come, come, Captain. I've been doing a little research. I know that you know well enough that your organization hangs in the balance. Can continue to exist or cease to exist on the whims of the voting public. I know you're worried about it."

"Again, I say, so what?"

"So, I'm in a position of guaranteeing the continued existence of your force, because I can assure you, gentlemen, a

Silver Republican *is* going to be the next president of these United States, and I can further guarantee you, the territory of Arizona will benefit more than any other place in the union from such. I can further still guarantee you that there *will* be a place for your Rangers in the next administration. How does that all sound to you?"

"It sounds like a deal with the devil." Dan George stared at his cigar as he spoke and then at Dick Welles who glared at his assistant in mock derision.

Using a tone the Indian had never heard from his boss, he snapped at his secretary. "Not so fast, Ranger." He turned to Gold. "And in exchange for all this, we're to do a poor job investigating the death of Lori Parker, inconsequential whore."

"Precisely."

Dick stood, towering a little too closely over the dude. He'd like to put a ball through his brain. He was glad Arvel was not with them. He wasn't certain how his partner would handle such a man, but had a good idea. "Who is it, Mr. Gold?"

"Who's what?"

"The man or men you're protecting?"

"That's for me to know, Captain. You can rest assured, what I'm telling you is the way it's going to be."

"Bullshit!" Dan George extinguished the remains of his cigar in one of the fine bone china coffee cups. "Dick, these assholes are the ones with less than a Chinaman's chance at winning the White House. Bunch of shitheads. It's going to be either McKinley or Bryan. Everyone without shit between their ears knows that."

"Perhaps." Gold stared at the Indian. He wasn't used to such articulate savages. "But I've got another ace in the hole. Not only am I connected to the Silver Republicans, whom I'm certain *will* win, but I've got a stake in Bryan as well. So, really, Captain, playing along with me, well, it's logical. If your man

McKinley wins, you win, if the Silver Republicans win, and you play ball with me, you win, and, if the Democrats win, you still win, and . . ." He moved to a table and poured scotches for the two of them.

Dan George once again intercepted the glass intended for Welles. He drank it down in one gulp. Gold ignored him. "And, Captain, I'll make a further deal with you. If the Republicans win, I'll pull out. No sense staying in this country, anyway, if that should happen. I'll be heading down to Mexico. You'll never be bothered by me again."

"And if the others win?"

"I stay, and will be wealthier and better connected than ever. You'll have an ally and benefactor, I can guarantee you that."

"And what of the butchers of this poor girl?"

"*Butcher,* Captain. There was only one, and I guarantee you, he's already gone from the country. He'll never step foot in Arizona again. That I can assure you, sir." He held up his hand. "You have my personal assurance on that."

Dick made himself a drink, then poured another for George. He ignored Gold. "We finished here, Dan?"

"Far as I'm concerned."

"You stay where I can find you, Mr. Gold. We'll be in touch."

"Will do, Captain, will do." He took a drink of whiskey. "Just remember your words, Captain."

"What words?"

"Inconsequential whore. That's what you said. A fitting description. Inconsequential. Reminds me of my interests down in Mexico. The president, Porfirio Díaz, a personal friend of mine, by the way, he calls them *ceros,* zeros, the inconsequential ones. He's a smart man. A wise and practical man. He's putting Mexico on the map, the world map, I mean." He raised his glass as a sort of salute. "Please, Captain Welles, don't ruin everything you've got, everything you've worked for for a cero.

It's not worth it."

Gold watched the lawmen mount up. "Did you hear all that?"

Dobbs spoke to the dirt he carved from under a fingernail. "Yeah."

"What do you make of it?"

"I'd like to gut that Indian."

"Be serious, you ass."

"You're the one without a Chinaman's chance, boss. Those men can't be bought. Walsh and Welles, they're famous for that. Incorruptible bastards. They're unnatural. They believe in all this law-and-order nonsense. That little interview just now proves it to me, beyond a doubt."

"I'm not so certain about that. Walsh is retiring. Welles will be sucking hind tit and he's got nothing besides this Ranger job. He's too old and stupid to do anything else. He'll play." He regarded his henchman fiddling with his fingernails. He wanted to punch him. "You're still certain the girl's alive? If she isn't, we've got to keep our mouths shut. If they had anything solid, they'd be making arrests."

"Oh, I'm certain."

"How?" He was impressed with Dobbs's cunning. No one could deny the miscreant that.

"That cat for one. No reason they'd take a living cat with them. That's not evidence." He looked up. "And the old man of the ranch, Walsh's uncle and partner. He was seen shopping for a young woman, and he was at the apothecary. Bought bandages, salve, mercury pills." His face turned up in a greasy grin. "It all fits."

"So at least we're not looking at murder."

"But there's rape and assault. What Damian did isn't taken lightly, not by these men."

"Can't rape a whore."

"Says you. Remember boss, the court's not your problem.

You can get as many slick lawyers as you want, but that Arvel Walsh, he doesn't do things like normal law dogs. He doesn't like women butchered in his territory, even if they are whores. He'll not let this lie."

"What do you propose?"

"Kill 'em all. We can make it look like Mexicans did it. That marauder from down there, Sombrero del Oro, he and his men have been riding, raping, killing in the region. He could be our scapegoat. We'll go to the Walsh ranch, wipe the whole bunch out, including the whore, of course. Once we get all the information we can out of that kid who was guarding the whorehouse, we'll move forward. Once Walsh is done in, you can do what you want with Welles. He'll be a good pawn in the future. Hell, you might end up governor of this godforsaken shithole of a land."

"You seriously suggest killing that many people? What of the piano movers, I know Damian's lied about them too."

Dobbs tucked the penknife into his vest pocket as he sucked on his bleedy picked-over nails. "You leave it all to me. I know what to do with them and all those mule-ranching bastards."

Chapter 6

"It is a beautiful drawing, Rebecca."

"It's a kitty."

"I see that."

Margarita Maria-Isabel Sanchez-De-La-Barrera-Duran held up the lace to the window as she regarded the child. Only one small pull in the corner. She'd mend it later. She put it over her head, admiring herself in the mirror, as she'd not had such good Spanish lace for a long time. It accentuated her beauty, bringing to its full radiance her pretty copper complexion. "Too good for a prostituta, but if that is what your mother wants . . . ," she muttered in a whisper to her reflection.

"What did you say, Margarita?"

"Nothing, child, nothing. Now, go on and sign it, as I have shown you how."

"Is she very sick, Margarita?"

"She is. Very bad."

"Why?"

"She got hurt."

"How? Did she get kicked by a horse, like Ramón last Christmas?"

"No, child."

"How?"

"Stop asking questions." She held out her hand for Rebecca to follow. "Come now, we will visit her and give her your drawing."

"Margarita?"

"Yes, child?"

"My boots aren't right."

"Come, sit on the bed, let me see."

The little one smiled and patted the pretty Mestizo's head as she worked on making the laces right. The young beauty was accustomed to having nannies, not playing one and the task came to her, at least at first, with difficulty. The entire situation came to her, at least the reality of it, with difficulty. The servant to an Indio and a gringo. What would her friends think of her now?

She patted her little charge on the head and looked into those loving, innocent blue eyes. She was adorable as she'd been blessed with the most beautiful qualities of both parents. Margarita could not suppress her smile. "You would be a heart-breaker in my Mexico, little one."

"Why?"

"Those bonita *ojos azules.* You have eyes the color of cornflowers and your skin that of porcelain."

She patted the child's legs. "Better now?"

"*Sí*, Margarita, muchas gracias."

"De nada."

Margarita went in first and the invalid stirred. The young nanny nodded, suppressing the revolution she felt at both the sight and idea of such a woman as she living under the same roof as the fine people of the Walsh family. A quality she simultaneously loved and hated about them.

"Good morning."

Lori sat up, squinting from the light shining around her visitor. She'd not seen this person before. "H—hello."

"My mistress, your hostess, Señora Walsh has asked me to give this to you." She handed her the veil. "It is from my country, it is called a *mantilla* veil." She nodded. "Please put it on so that it hides your face, as my little Rebecca wants to see you and I do not want her to be frightened."

Lori complied. "Like this?"

"Sí."

Margarita returned with the child. "This is Rebecca Walsh. She wanted to give you a gift, to make you feel well."

"Hello, little girl." Lori looked up. "Is this *your* child?"

"No, I am her nanny. She is the daughter of your host and hostess."

Lori held the picture to the light, peering through the holes in the shroud. "Oh, it's *very nice,* thank you." She reached out to shake Rebecca's hand. "What's yer name?" She blushed. "I'm kinda daft when people say names. Didn't pay attention, darlin', I'm sorry."

"I'm Rebecca."

"Well, Miss Rebecca, I'm thanking you for it. It sure is pretty. I love kitties. And that's yer name down there, ain't it?"

"Isn't it?" Rebecca corrected her in the manner she'd heard Pilar do on many occasions with the hands.

Margarita shook her a little on the shoulder. "Rebecca, shh!"

"No, no, don't! Please don't tell her shush. I talk like a idiot. It's okay." She smiled, nodding to the child. "You tell me when I don't say right, Miss Rebecca. Please tell me when I ain't right."

The cat trilled as she jumped on Lori's lap. Rebecca reached out to pet her. "I like your kitty. What's *her* name?"

"Jessica. But I just call her Jess."

"Do you hurt much, lady?"

She grinned at the absurdity of being called a lady. "No, it don't hurt much. It's much better now, thanks to you fine folks and that nice man who healed me up."

"That's Billy. He's not from around here, you know. He's a, a abroginery."

"Aborigine."

Rebecca smiled at Margarita. "Yes, what Margarita said, he's one of them. He's from Austria."

"Australia."

Rebecca nodded. "He saved my daddy's life one time." Her eyes widened. "Billy drilled a hole in Daddy's head and sewed a gold coin under the skin. Daddy said, thanks to Billy, he'll never be a man without means." She winked. "That means he'll never be without any money. Now he's saved your life. I wonder if he sewed any coins under your skin." She looked curiously, doing her best to see through the holes in the veil.

As if on cue, Billy walked in. "Good mornin', ladies." He looked at the picture. "I see you are the lucky recipient of Miss Rebecca's artwork."

"Yes, sir."

"Come on, Rebecca, leave Billy to his work." Margarita nodded. "Enjoy the veil, miss."

Lori watched them leave and sat still while Billy checked her wounds.

He smiled. "That's a pretty bit of cloth."

"From that young lady." She pulled it back down when he'd finished his examination. It was already a comfort to her. "Who are these people who I'm to be so grateful for, mister?"

"The Walshes, ma'am. Don't tell me you've never heard of the Walshes?"

"I ain't."

"Well, they're fine folks. Arvel, he's a Ranger captain and from back East, a real gentleman, ma'am, and was a hero in the war." He opened a bottle, soaking a gauze with the solution, began dabbing it on the young woman's sutured wounds. "Then there's Chica, the lady of the manor. She's from down Mexico way. Her real name's Maria, but we all, at least those who love her best, call her Chica. Might very well be the prettiest creature who's ever come from that southern land, and then there's Uncle Bob, Arvel's uncle, and, well, I guess Miss Pilar . . ." He winked. "She's the one who you've got to watch. She's the one you don't want to cross, ma'am, she really runs the place." He stepped back and looked as would an artist admiring a particularly deft brushstroke. He nodded as he whispered. "I think Uncle Bob and Miss Pilar are sweet on each other, but don't let 'em know you have an idea." He shook his head. "They'll never admit it."

"And you?"

"Oh, I'm a wolfer, work on government contracts."

"And a doctor."

"Oh, no, ma'am, no doctor. Just learned some things here and there, my old father, back home, he was a healer, taught me some and then I kind of got the itch to learn more and more."

"In Australia?"

"Yes, ma'am."

"Where's that? Back East?"

"Oh, no, ma'am, it's, well, it's all the way on the other side of the world."

"Why'd you come from all that way?"

Billy smiled. "Been askin' myself that for years, miss." He turned his head from side to side. "Tell the truth to you, ma'am, I have no idea."

She watched him work. "You got nice hands."

"Thank you."

"The girls, you know, back at the house, they all said, yer done as a whore if ya ever let a darkie touch ya."

"Oh?"

"I say that's a lotta nonsense."

She pulled herself up in bed and winced. "Sweet Jesus that hurts!"

"You were cut down there."

"I remember, I think, leastways, I think I remember."

"Do you remember who did this, miss?"

"No, no, not that, but I remember, he put something inside me, then he kinda stomped on my belly, down below my belly and then everything went all cloudy in my mind. Don't remember nothing after that."

Billy nodded. "Do you mind if I have a look?"

"Oh, no, go on. Might as well, everybody else has." She laughed. "Can't much shame or pink up the cheeks of a whore."

He examined her and grunted. Pulled his gauze packing and smelled it. "No infection. That's good."

"Yer a brave man smellin' what's come from between a whore's legs, mister."

"Call me Billy." He smiled. "I think you could make an aborigine blush, miss."

"Call me Lori." She shrugged her shoulders up and smiled. "Been a whore so long, nothing seems outta bounds to talk about. Hope you don't think me so shameful as all that."

"I don't think you're shameful at all, Miss Lori. I think you're a fine and brave gal."

"Oh, that's just 'cause I'm good to look at, or, well, leastways used to be." She touched her wounded face through the veil. "Guess not so much now."

"I think you are." He regarded the packing. "I'm not going to put any more gauze up there, Miss Lori. You're healing well and the bleedin' stopped. Just, well, when you urinate . . ."

She cocked her head. "When I what?"

"When you make water, just kind of make certain you keep things dry."

"Urinate." She said the word as if she were chewing on it. "You know some fancy words." She grinned. "I promise. I'll keep dry."

"Good, and when you do, urinate, I mean, wipe yourself

clean with some of the solution in this bottle."

"Guess my whoring days are done."

"Maybe that's not such a bad thing."

She shrugged indifferently. "Only thing I've known since, well, a long, long time." She watched him work and found it odd that he did not lust for her. "They used to say I was the prettiest whore wherever I went. No one could touch me for prettiness."

"I can believe that."

"One time a bunch of Frenchmen put me on a altar down in Louisiana. New Orleans. Had a black mass they called it. They was the most wickedest men I ever saw."

"Really? Did they hurt you?"

"Oh, no! They was sweet as could be. They was really pretty funny. Do you know they said they worshipped the devil?"

"No kidding."

"Yep, they all wore these red robes and real-silly-lookin' masks, like skeleton faces or bird faces, goat faces, all kinds of things and we was in a old church with lots a candles burning and they even had a cross, one with Jesus on it, like the Catholics have, and they had that turned upside down, so's Jesus was standin' on his head. Then they all sang and chanted words I never heard and I was naked and layin' on this stone tablet, all kinda hog-tied, and they all took turns rubbin' me all over with warm oil that smelt really good. They kilt a goat which made me sad for the poor beast and then they poured what they said was his blood all over me, which kinda made my throat all tight and I thought I'd gag and throw up but then I figured out it was really just red wine 'cause the main priest smiled and gave me a drink of it to ease my mind and it tasted good. I was okay after that.

"But Billy, I can tell you, when they was all rubbin' me all over, my God it musta been twenty hands, it felt, well . . ." Lori winked and looked toward the door to make certain of no eavesdroppers. She whispered, "It felt really good, Billy. It made me shake and shudder like I ain't never had layin' with any man, 'cause I can tell you, Billy, there weren't a spot they missed with all that rubbin'."

"No kidding."

"Yep. They give me five hundred dollars in gold coin for all that and they even let me keep the ropes and a nice silk robe all red. Sold the rope for a dollar and the robe for five."

"Speaking of robes." Billy turned to retrieve a package wrapped in brown paper, tied with string. "This is from Uncle Bob."

She held up the nightgown and robe. Lying them aside, she regarded the slippers. "That's mighty fine."

"It is, and I'd like you to put 'em on, Miss Lori, time you got out into the sunlight."

She did and walked, holding onto Billy's arm. They made it to the corral in the yard and watched Chica working a mule.

"That's Chica." He lit a smoke. "Watch her, Miss Lori. Chica's one of the best mule tamers in the land, better to my mind than either Arvel or Uncle Bob." He winked. "Just don't tell anyone I said that."

She was awesome in her vaquero outfit. Her long raven hair peeking from under the sombrero. Her copper skin glistened from the exercise. Round and round the corral she worked the beast and, as if by magic, the young hinny began to comply.

"She's a wonder, Mr. Billy."

"Come on, I'll show you the rest of the ranch." He looked her over with a clinical eye. "That is, if you feel all right."

"I'm good, Billy." She held tightly to his arm. "I'm good."

Alasdair Macdonald, laird of Glen Cowie, regarded his young boss across the big oak desk as the young man worried over

Dick Welles's letter about the dead whore.

The laird would be fifty-seven on his next birthday and had been away from his highland home for going on seven years. He was a big man, not fat, but big, standing over six foot three with sandy-red hair flecked with gray and kind blue eyes. Nordic eyes.

He'd read about Tombstone a long time ago, when the Earps and Clantons had made international news and he had to visit one of the last wild places on earth. It was either Arizona or Africa, and, as he'd spent enough time in the Dark Continent as a youngish man, killing game, he figured the American West was the place to see before it too became civilized and boring.

He'd spent most of his early years managing the family estate, but now that his brother had gone into textiles, and the family fortune was secure, the prospect of spending the rest of his days killing deer or grouse or pulling salmon from his loch bored him beyond sense. Now he was a piano tuner in the employ of a man who could easily be his son, perhaps his grandson, and the reality of his situation was not lost on him. He loved Robert Craster as if he were his own flesh and blood.

Craster looked up from the letter and smiled. "You're up early."

"Lots to do." He grinned as they both knew the Scotsman liked to visit a certain widowed schoolmarm as she walked to her charges of a morning. The woman was an early riser and had, as such, altered the nocturnal habits of the laird, who rarely rose before nine except when on the hunt.

"You'll be back in time?"

"Certainly, lad. Two tunings, be back by lunchtime."

Craster was ambitious and already five men were working for him, covering the territory down as far as Bisbee and north to Flagstaff. In another five years he'd be a wealthy man, as long as his luck and health held out, and there was no reason to believe any of it would not. He was even riding out the bad economy and still turning a good profit. Not shabby for a man who, until just a few years ago, possessed little more than the clothes on his back when he arrived in the West's last frontier.

Craster, like all such enterprising men, was called to the wild Arizona land when he was little more than a child. His first job was hauling freight at the age of fourteen, as he was a big lad and looked at least three years older than his age. He could do more work than men many years his senior, and for this he was sought out. He worked in Texas and New Mexico and even as far as California for a few years, but settled on Arizona. He loved Arizona more than any other place he'd worked, and decided to make it his home.

He was also good with mules, and his mother told him, before she died, that he had a kind heart and animals always knew, and would always obey a man who was kind and just. Robert Craster was such.

Despite the dark business with the Rangers, he was having a good morning. He awoke at three, unable to sleep any longer and decided to start his day. His workman, Sam, would not be around for another three hours, and that was not a bad thing. Macdonald was gone and he'd be alone for a while.

He built a pot of coffee and cooked himself some eggs. He finished his breakfast and thought of the evening planned for him by Ellen. It felt like Christmas. When he was a child, he had always loved Christmas because he would give his mother some little present and that was what made him happier than anything else. He never cared for getting things for himself. Didn't like, really all that much, material things, just what he needed to work and live and get by. But giving things on Christmas was, for him, the highlight of the holiday.

He felt that today would be like Christmas and his gift was himself to Alice, the woman who'd stolen his heart the first time he'd seen her on stage, and for the first time in his life, Robert Craster did not feel the fool for having such thoughts.

He was, indeed, good enough for her. He straightened his back a little as he washed his plate and thought it again. Damn, he was good enough for her. Ellen said that, and Ellen was a smart lady and Alice's best friend in the world and singing partner on stage and if anyone would know, it was she and she said that about him. He was good enough for Alice.

He tried to do some paperwork as the morning progressed but could think of nothing but the woman who'd stolen his heart. He fantasized about being intimate with her. He fantasized about holding her in his arms and kissing her and then doing some other things after they'd married and his heart felt odd in his chest and the feeling of joy ran all through his body and deep into his gut. He could not wait for the evening to come.

Sam arrived and put the newspaper on the desk, as he had done every day since Robert Craster's metamorphosis into a man of the world. He smiled at his boss as Robert Craster had that kind of effect on everyone.

"Go—good mornin', boss."

"It *is* a good morning, Sam. How'd you sleep?"

"L—like a b—baby." He pointed, with his head in the direction of the workshop in the next room. "Get 'er done today." He looked about. "Where, where's the l—laird?"

"We will, Sam." He winked. "Alasdair's gone visiting."

"The, the schoolmarm?"

"Yep, the schoolmarm."

It was another enterprise of Craster's that was evolving into a success. He'd been buying up derelict wagons from the army, refurbishing them, but not selling them. He was, rather, renting them and it was working out well. He had made a deal with the fellow up the street who ran a livery stable, so he would not have to worry over horse or mule stock. He only rented the wagons and the liveryman was now kind of a partner as he rented the beasts of burden, and that suited both of them. The enterprise was thriving in every major city in Arizona.

The region was growing, despite the economy and the mine floods, and folks other than farmers and ranchers needed the conveyances, but not on a permanent enough basis to own.

None of this was lost on Sam, who'd latched on to Craster as soon as the young teamster set up shop. Sam was a jack-of-all-trades and tough as they come. He was nearly sixty, and his long life had taken a toll. Sam had done many things in his time, and every enterprise, while it kept him in grub and clothing, had physically worn him down. But he was a hard-working man and could still do the labor of men many years his junior. Robert Craster found him to be indispensable, and now, with the addition of the laird, they were forming a close-knit business family.

The old fellow had battled a stutter since he was three, and the stigma such a curse brought to its victims. He'd lived with the jibes, endured the assumption that he was not bright, that he was inferior due to his difficulty, and none of it true. He was simply a bright man with a stutter, and after nearly six decades on this earth, Robert Craster, and now the laird, seemed to be the only people to ever have recognized it.

Craster, in particular, was patient with him. He did not lose his composure while Sam fought to articulate his thoughts, never hurried him along or finished his sentences for him. When Sam was trying to convey something especially difficult, Craster would not act any differently than he would with any other man. He'd go about his business or look at Sam in his normal, friendly, casual way, or perhaps busy himself with some inconsequential task, but always listening, waiting patiently and letting Sam take his time. The old fellow took his leave to continue his work on the wagon. He suspected something big was going on with his boss, and knew not to hover over him.

Craster eventually joined him. He hefted the vehicle and Sam smiled, knowing that Craster often did such things, not to show off, but to revel in his own strength. Sam would need a jack to lift the thing an inch; Craster could heft it three feet with one hand.

Craster smiled at the progress.

"This is a g—good one."

He pulled a wheel from the army wagon's axle and propped it in a corner. The mercury reached a hundred and five and the shirtless teamster moved his massive frame about the place with the agility of a boxer. Muscle and sinew rippling through pale skin, long beard plastered to sweaty neck, he worked, always with a little smile on his face, as if every task, no matter how mundane, brought him joy and satisfaction.

"Yep it is, Sam. Sometimes I wonder at how much money the government wastes. I got this one for ten cents on the dollar, and what, we needed to replace just three floorboards and a wheel?"

They worked until just before lunch when the strangers interrupted them. Craster knew the purpose of the visit immediately. Knew that this business with the whore was going to bring him trouble. Now here it was.

He slowly turned his head and looked on the dude as if he'd been expecting him all along. He nodded and then took the measure of the two toughs moving into position, flanking him and Sam. They were big, not as big as him, but big and battle-scarred and tough. He did not know these men, as they were not from around these parts, and Craster surmised that the dude had likely brought them from places in Chicago like Kilgubbin or further east, perhaps New York's Hell's Kitchen, based on the cut of their clothes, and the way they carried themselves.

"How can I help you gents?"

Craster inched toward a crowbar propped in a corner and one of the toughs countered, blocking his path. Sam sensed the danger and tried to retreat to the ten-gauge Robert kept near his desk in the office. The other blocked his way as well. Both henchmen awaited their boss's instructions.

"I'm here to talk about a certain whore." He cast his eyes to Craster's little office, replete with posters and photographs of Alice. He yanked one rudely from its place on the wall by the window overlooking the alley. "You're a fan of the theater?"

Craster grinned. "Sometimes."

"Oh, you mean when it involves these whores?" He looked at a playbill featuring both Ellen and Alice.

"Don't call them that, you ass!" Craster stepped forward and was again blocked by one of the henchmen.

The dude sneered. "Once I get rid of you, I'm going to go look this one up." He pointed at Alice's image. "A shame I won't be able to tell you how she was, but I'm sure she'll be passable."

Craster laughed. "She would not give you the time of day."

"Oh, with whores like that, you'd be surprised. Throw a little money around, and they come running like a bitch in heat. Anyway." He looked at his men and nodded. "I've got enough muscle to hold her down, if need be."

"Sh—shut your m—mouth, yo—you filthy ba—bastard."

"Oh, a stutterer." He looked at Sam and grinned at Craster. "I love a st—stutterer, th—they're s—so f—fun."

Craster had enough, as his temper had taken hold, won out over good sense. He'd kill them all with his bare hands. He turned on his heel, pounding the nearest henchman hard on the nose. The man dropped, his legs buckling as if they'd turned to jelly. The teamster next moved forward, thumping the other one hard when the dude produced a shiny revolver from a pocket, pointing it at Sam's head. "Go ahead, make another move and the stutterer loses his b—brains."

Robert Craster froze, waiting.

Dobbs grinned as he watched his men roll about, holding their painful wounds. "I'm going to make you pay for that, teamster. I'm going to make you pay."

Then, at least for Craster, everything went dark.

Chapter 7

Francis O'Higgins awoke to the smiling, red, bespeckled and unshaven face, peering at him through pince-nez, giving it the appearance of a sunburnt owl.

"You sure know how to take a beating, young man. Thought for a while you were dead."

Francis pulled himself into a sitting position, looked around at the dark cellar that had served as his prison and torture chamber for what must have been days. He'd lost all sense of time. He opened his mouth, assessing the joints and mandible. He winced then pulled at the molar just forward of the wisdom tooth of his left lower jaw. He picked a chunk of skin from between his teeth, held it up to the light for inspection. "Don't remember eating any pork rinds."

"I'll venture that's a hunk of Dobbs's right ring finger."

"Serious?" He smiled, then spat to clear his mouth of any other foreign matter as the thought of human flesh in it made his stomach turn. He looked at the old man. "Who are you? Who the hell's Dobbs?"

"Oh, I'm no one of consequence. Name's Harvey. Hugh Harvey. Bookkeeper for Gold." He looked around the dark basement. "This is my home. Dobbs is Gold's secretary."

"Hell of a secretary." He rubbed his forehead. "How the hell'd I get here?"

"What do you remember?"

"Oh, let's see. I was at the Birdcage, met two fellows from

Chicago. Was tellin' them about rangering, and, then, well, that's about it."

"Yeah, some of Dobbs's men. They drugged you. Brought you here."

Francis held out his hand for Harvey to shake. "Pleased to meet you, Mr. Harvey. When's the beating to recommence?"

"Oh, they're finished with you. Dobbs, Gold, all of them, took off early this morning." Harvey offered him a glass of water. "Hungry?"

Francis drank and nodded. "As a bear."

"I'll get you some grub. My God, lad, you can take a beating."

"Glad to hear it." Francis rubbed his head and neck. "Glad you were about to see it. Can't remember much myself." He squinted at the odd gentleman, then closed his right eye. "Bastards done blinded my left eye. Can't see a damned thing out of it."

Harvey frowned. "Sorry to hear that. Maybe it'll come back."

"Yeah, maybe." He regarded his jailer. "How's it I got Dobbs's finger skin between my teeth?"

Harvey laughed as he moved to his office desk at the end of the room. He cut up a sausage, some cheese and bread, then helped Francis to a chair nearby.

Francis considered the digs. "You got it set up pretty homey down here." He looked at the rolltop and the cushioned office chair, the Persian rug at their feet. Harvey had a diploma on the wall, proof that he was an educated man.

"Old Dobbs, boy oh boy did you piss him off. He called you a mackerel snapper, said you bowed down to the dagos in Rome. Said you'd kiss the Pope's ring and he tried to get you to kiss his." He laughed nervously. "And that's when you told him he looked like a back-washing fairy in a Turkish bath, then you bit his finger down to the bone when he was waving that ring of his in your face. My God, that was something to behold. You clamped down tighter than an alligator on a water moccasin. Took three of them and the truncheon to get you off."

"I kind of remember some of that." Francis ran his tongue over his teeth in search of more skin.

"Have you actually visited a Turkish bath?"

"Nah, I don't even know what that is. I just heard a fellow say that, back in Philadelphia in a saloon one time to get a big man's goat. Boy howdy how it got on that old boy's nerves. He just about wrecked the joint, at least once someone explained all to him." He winked. "You know, he was kinda dense. I guess Dobbs is a bit smarter than that. Always wanted to say it to annoy someone who deserved it." He looked about, trying his best to adjust to the new blindness. "Guess I got my chance with this Dobbs character all right."

"You did at that."

Francis tried to stand and went wobbly. "Jesus, that hurts." He grinned. "Everything hurts." He looked at the contraption in the corner of the room. "What the hell's that thing, anyway, Mr. Harvey?"

"It's an electric generator. They got it off a retired whore in Santa Rosa. She worked in one of those traveling shows. Used to sit on a table and have sparks shoot out of her head. Damnedest thing you've ever seen."

"I remember now. She must have been a tough damned old whore. That thing smarts like I've never known."

"She was grounded, didn't hurt her a whit. You were soaked in water." Harvey shook his head. "Dobbs is evil. Son of a bitch. There's no other way to describe him. Plain evil. Knows his business well, that's for certain."

"And you work for his boss?" It was more an accusation than a question, but Francis already decided that he liked Harvey, though he'd have to admit the old man's intimate knowledge of the torture vexed and annoyed him. Not that Harvey could have intervened, as physically, he was weak and generally a wreck of a human being.

"Yes, well." Harvey looked as if he might cry. He searched the desk, the dungeon-like surroundings as if to offer a kind of apology. "I, well, I'm, guess you could say, *stuck.*"

"You a drunkard?" Francis eyed the empty bottles in the waste can.

"You could say it's got a hold on me."

Francis nodded, patting Harvey on the arm. "I understand. My old pa was a drunkard. He'd sell his soul to the devil if it meant keeping himself in hooch."

"I'll fetch you some hot water, Mr. . . ."

"Aw, none a that. You call me Francis."

"If you'll call me Hugh."

Francis nodded. "Hugh." He rubbed his head and felt the pain on his face, around his eyes. He touched his ears. "Son of a bitch, Hugh, even my hair hurts." He grinned. "How do I look?"

"About like I imagine you feel. You look like you've fallen into a rock pulverizer."

"What did I tell them about the whore, the gal that was cut up so bad in the brothel? I remember, they were right keen on learning all about her."

"Nothing. They worked and worked on you. They're convinced she's still alive, convinced she's at the Walsh ranch, but you gave them nothing, lad. You gave them nothing." Harvey started crying, blubbering into his hands. "You gave them nothing."

"All right, all right, Hugh. The party's over." He patted the old sot's chubby shoulder. "Pull yourself together." He found a bottle and poured for him. "Here, old son, take a drink or two. Calm your nerves."

Harvey did and by the third one he was better. He wiped his eyes with his shirtsleeves, coughed and blew his nose into a dirty handkerchief. "I'm sorry, Francis." He grinned nervously. "I'm just a little overwhelmed."

"Jesus, old son, *you're* overwhelmed!" He laughed. "Go on now, Hugh, go fetch me some water, good and hot and some soap and a towel. I need to get cleaned up." He looked at his dirty and bloodstained shirt and trousers. "Find me some clothes, too. I need to get outta here." He looked him over seriously. "You *will* help me?"

"I will, Francis. I will."

By early evening Francis looked almost human. He felt better with the aid of two whiskies and a slug of laudanum found for him by Harvey in an upstairs bedroom. He was soon dressed in one of Gold's best suits. It looked damned well on him, as the cloth was of a good cut and the two were similar in size.

He also learned that Harvey had been in Gold's employ for going on ten years and his drunkenness had been used against him to good effect. He was Gold's pawn and was kept alone in the basement to do the books and fed a steady diet of cheap whiskey when Gold and Dobbs were feeling charitable. When they were not, he was given beer. When they were in a bad mood, he was given nothing and that was when the very bad times would come to Hugh Harvey.

But they'd underestimated him and that's why they left him alone to guard Francis, as even the worst drunk had his limits, and they pushed him to his, as his heart broke when he'd witnessed the savagery meted out to the young Ranger private. Now that he'd learned what a decent sort Francis was, it made him downright angry.

"Guess I'm ready, Hugh." He looked himself over and was pleased. "How 'bout my traps?"

Hugh did not understand the question.

"My six-shooter and gun belt, where are they, Hugh?"

"Oh, yes, right."

He soon produced them along with Francis's Ranger badge, hat and wallet. The bastards had taken all his money.

"How's this going to look for you, Hugh? I reckon they won't be too happy when they come back and find me vamoosed."

"Hit me."

"What?" Francis grinned at Hugh being brave. The old man stood at attention, as would a scolded child before a schoolmarm wielding her paddle. He removed his pince-nez, placing them on the blotter. He jutted his chin.

"Hit me, *hard,* in the face, Francis. It's less than I deserve for living such a wicked and complacent life, but it will leave a mark. It'll be my alibi."

"No, no, you come with me, Hugh. Hell, no use you sitting around here in the dark. Who knows when someone'll be along to feed and water you? You might shrivel up and die."

"No, I won't, Francis. I'm better use here. I'll be a spy. I'll be *your* spy, Francis. I can send you messages, I can be your eyes and ears on the inside."

"That's all well and good, but I think it's a bad idea. Think you ought to come along just the same."

"Not budging, Francis. Now, go on and hit me."

"Not hitting you, old son. Not by a long ways, you can forget about that!"

With that Hugh turned, grabbed the truncheon lying near the electrical generator and gave himself a good whack across the left brow. He staggered as a torrent of blood ran into his eye.

Francis steadied him, smiling in disbelief at the old sot's actions. "Jesus, Hugh!"

The old man held up a hand. "It's nothing, nothing compared to what you got, my boy. Fair punishment for my complicity in the rude treatment you've received at the hands of these blackhearts."

Francis looked the old fellow over. It seemed to have the opposite effect. Hugh was now more alive than he'd been since their meeting, as if the blow had awakened something in him.

"Don't take the stairs, Francis. Housekeeper, she's one mean bitch. She sees you, she'll raise the alarm. Go out the cellar way." He wrote out an order on an official-looking document. "Take this to the livery stable down on Third and Fremont. They'll rent you a horse. Get out as fast as you can." He opened a metal box. "Here's some petty cash." He counted it out. "About a hundred. Sorry, Francis, it's not more."

Francis took it, placing it in the vest pocket of Gold's suit. "What are they planning, Hugh?"

"Don't know for certain. Gold's running to San Francisco to hide, I guess. He's pretty much written off any prospect of corrupting your boss Welles. Dobbs was going after that piano hauler and tuner. He wants to get rid of any witnesses. He thinks they might know something that'll incriminate Gold's son."

"That's who did it?"

"Yes, he's got two wastrel sons, Damian and Dennis, neither worth the shot and powder to blow them to kingdom come, but Damian's the worst, he's the one." The bookkeeper turned his head from side to side. "What he does to women, it's just shameful."

"Where's the son of a bitch now?"

"Tampico. Gold's got an operation down there." Harvey turned to his rolltop, pulling a document. "Here's a work order with the address on it. They've got a mining office in Tampico, should be able to track the rascal down from there."

"You're a good soldier, Hugh."

Harvey looked as broken as a man can get. "No I'm not, no

I'm not, but I thank you Francis for saying it, just the same. Now, go on my lad. God bless you and Godspeed. You're the bravest man I've ever known."

The laudanum wore off and the horse was nothing like Frank and it all had a peculiar effect on Francis. By dark he was in no mood to ride half the night to the Walsh ranch and now his head was pounding and spinning. A couple of times he thought he might vomit and more than once he lost his balance as he spit over his rental's back. He was cold and it wasn't a cold night.

But more than anything else, for the first time in as long as he could remember, Francis felt afraid. The dark spooked him. Every sound spooked him. He missed his mother. Once or twice he felt his eyes welling up and that only reminded him of his blindness and when Dobbs came into his memory he felt more alone and scared than he'd felt at any time in his life.

What Dobbs had done to him was unconscionable. What Dobbs had done to him was something so foreign to him that he had difficulty believing his own mind, half thought that perhaps the things that he remembered were only a nightmare, conjured up by his fanciful brain.

But his body told him differently. His body, bruised and broken, his blind eye told him differently. What Dobbs had done was real and Francis could not believe that such things could be done by a white man.

Sure he'd read of the stories about the savages and knew what the Indians were capable of, he even met an old-timer in a saloon outside of Houston once who took off his hat and showed him how he'd survived a scalping. The old gent even kept it in a box, the scalp, that is, as he'd been able to recover it some time later when his pards stumbled upon the war party and took their revenge. He offered to show it to anyone who'd want a look. The cost was one nickel. Francis knew about such things, but he still had difficulty comprehending that such brutality had happened to him, and at the hands of a white man. He ran his fingers through his hair. At least Dobbs hadn't scalped him.

As he rode he thought more about Frank. Try as he might, he simply could not remember where he'd left his jug-headed gelding. As if whole patches of his life where unknown to him. Even the few times he'd gotten in his cups, he'd never lost his memory or his horse. That scared him. How could a man be beaten so severely as to lose his memory?

He loved that horse even though he'd owned him for a short time. Got him from a friend, a Mexicano he'd met when he first arrived in Arizona. The vaquero said he *had* to have it, as Francis and the horse shared, more or less, the same name. Francisco shortened by the Anglicized Mexican to Frank to make him more marketable to the gringos, it certainly had to be fate for them to be put together. The ugliest horse he'd ever seen and smarter and gentler and stronger than any beast he'd known or ridden, to include the bag of bones he was on now.

It was the first purchase he'd made when he'd gotten the Ranger pay. That and then a new Winchester '94 in the hot thirty caliber everyone was drooling over and a new six-shooter and leather. He felt his hip and the grip of the gun which he wore high and not cross draw, but straight, like the old-timer with the scalp in the box told him to do. It felt right and the short barrel suited him much better than that old army gun that he'd had since he was seventeen. He *had* to wear that giant thing cross draw. Now he could pull out the new six-shooter and fire pretty fast and hit the target more than not and not by aiming. He liked the caliber better, too. Thirty-two twenty. It didn't jump so in his hand, like the forty-five. He could point and shoot which might someday come in handy. Francis was good at that kind of shooting.

The leather still smelled new and it sometimes creaked when

he moved. He grinned to himself at the memory of some ass at the Birdcage who saw the new leather and thought Francis a greenhorn dude. That boy felt the thud of Francis's left hook that day. No one messed much with him after that. Except Dobbs. Except Dobbs. Dobbs had most certainly messed with him. Messed with him in a big way.

He wiped the sweat from his brow, rubbing his palm dry on the thigh of his new trousers. The fine wool felt good. The whole outfit felt good, as the suit was a good one, custom-made in New York for Gold, at least according to the hand-embroidered label sewn on the inside coat pocket. It might just as well have been made *for* Francis, it fit him that perfectly. He was pleased with that. Glad he could take *something* from the bastard.

He jogged north and made it onto the road to Tucson. The widow Jameson would make it right, and if he was honest with himself, she'd be more of a comfort to him right now than ever could be his old mother, and she more than two thousand miles away anyhow.

In another hour he was calling out to her as he sat ahorse in her front yard. "Hello in the house."

The answer came in a terse challenge. "Who's there?"

"Francis, ma'am. Francis O'Higgins. You remember, ma'am? From back East, the boy from Pennsylvania."

She was a woman of fifty if not perhaps more, tall and bosomy. She wore her hair long and it had turned silver, but not the silver of a granny, as she somehow, almost magically, defied the ravages of time. She was timeless, ageless, stunning in her maturity and femininity. A true curiosity. That was the widow Jameson.

She lived alone and ran what some called a boardinghouse, others a bordello, but that was not a fair assessment of the widow Jameson's spread. She had no whores, no one but a diminutive Chinese named Mei Lin who looked from a distance like a child, though she was not much younger than her mistress. She ran the place, did the cooking and the cleaning and other things as required, particularly when it got especially lonely for the widow.

The interesting thing about the widow Jameson was that she never asked for anything, though tithing was most certainly expected. If cash could not be offered, then chores and yard work, water hauling, wood chopping, would be payment in kind.

In this way, she operated not unlike a church, as the widow had a nearly photographic memory when it came to bible verse and could have given even the most accomplished circuit rider a run for his money in that respect. Curiously, it was during the act of lovemaking that she recited these words of inspiration with the greatest zeal, and with a rhythm, a cadence not unlike the hazzan of the Jewish faith.

At the height of the interlude, and relative to the particular act or part of the anatomy the object of attention, she'd call out to the heavens things like "Thy two breasts are like two young roes that are twins, which feed among the lilies." Or "Thy belly is like an heap of wheat." Or "This thy statue is like to a palm tree, and thy breasts to clusters of grapes." Or "Behold thou art fair, my beloved, yea, pleasant: also our bed is green."

It made the ride, at least for Francis, feel otherworldly somehow. Almost dreamlike, and none of the verses were any he'd heard the preacher recite on a Sunday morning. Certainly no part of the bible he'd ever been taught.

It was why she enjoyed nothing less than complete respect and adoration from everyone who'd known her in this literal as well as figuratively biblical way. The men who benefited from her attentions knew the widow Jameson was special. She picked them that way. She liked young, slightly innocent, moderately dense, or at least, if not dense as in the case of Francis, then naive, good-looking fellows to fill the void created by her lonely state. And because of this, a wink and a nod was all they'd ever offer, each man keeping to himself the memory of the special treatment and congress he'd known. It *was* a special and profound event to be savored, remembered. Something to be shared with no one else.

She had a nice home, built for her by a devoted husband who died of pneumonia one winter more years ago that she'd like to remember. He was a Mormon and she too a devout Christian. She could never give him children and that was why she had the diminutive Chinese for a companion. Over the years she grew to regret not allowing him more than one wife, as was the custom of his faith. At least he would have had some progeny to carry on. But she was a selfish woman that way, unwilling to share him with another. Now, in a strange twist of fate, she shared her love and her body with many. It was her one comfort.

"Francis!" she shouted as she handed the shotgun to the Chinese. Running to him, helping him from his mount when she comprehended his battered state.

"What happened to you, my darling boy?!" She looked for an undamaged place to kiss.

"Oh, just Ranger work, ma'am." He felt proud to say that. Felt proud, like a soldier home from battle. It made the pain feel better, as it was not the pain from a bar fight or from some silly stunt, like trying to break a wild horse for fun, or a roll down a snowy hill as he'd done as a child. He'd been wounded in battle, from battle and it made the pain feel different.

As always, it was bright and cheerful inside, smelled of baking, bread and pie and soup noodles. The widow undressed him as he made his way across the room, first his hat, then his gun belt, and finally Gold's wool coat and vest. She unbuttoned his collar and removed his tie. She sat him to table, motioning for Mei Lin to fetch him something to eat.

"Oh, Francis"—she ran her fingers through his hair—"you

look a fright!"

He grinned and his fear washed away as her pretty hands engulfed the battered knuckles of his right hand. His heart fluttered at the look of worry and compassion in her eyes. "Feel even worse, ma'am, if that's at all possible." He sounded a little babyish when he said that, but he needed babying. He winced and turned away from the pain, nodding to his coat. "Got some of that laudanum, in my pocket there, sure could use some, ma'am."

She fed him and babied him and once the Chinese was retired for the night, led him by the hand to her bedroom. She was gentle with him and made love in a way that made him, at least for a little while, forget all about Dobbs and Gold and Hugh Harvey and even the Ranger captains.

Her chanting was even soothing, not as strange as he remembered as she could be loud and zealous when her body was racked with the fits that such activity brought on. More than a few times in the past, she had even scared him.

Sitting astraddle, she spoke in just above a whisper. "I am a wall, and my breasts are like towers. Thus I have become in his eyes like one bringing contentment." She kissed him. "I am your wall, Francis." She squeezed him in a way he'd never known possible. "I'll protect you."

Afterward, she held him in her arms like a babe, covering him with many blankets as he was as cold as ice. His eyes welled up again and his voice shook as he gazed into pretty widow Jameson's gray twinkling eyes. He stroked a lock of silver from her forehead. "They ought not to have done that to me." He buried his head in her bosom and felt the comfort only a loving woman could provide. "They ought not to have done that to me, ma'am."

"No they oughtn't, but they did, Francis. They did and now, my sweet dear boy, you need to offer up your pain to Jesus, and your loins to me, and together, the Lord and I will make you forget all about it, I promise you." She pulled him to her breasts. "Come let's drink deep of love till morning; let's enjoy ourselves with love."

And for a few precious hours, Francis O'Higgins did.

CHAPTER 8

The Ranger captains sat ahorse and watched the Tombstone fire company put out the last of the dying embers. A young volunteer ran past as Dick intercepted him. "Any dead?"

"No, no, Captain, not that we can tell. Still a lot of debris and such. Won't know for certain until it's all cleared."

Dick wiped his brow. He looked at the laird standing next to him.

"Damned inconvenient timing."

"I saw somethin', might interest you gentlemen." A lanky Negro stood between them. He nodded to Arvel. "Captain, good to see you again."

"And you, John. How's the family?" He turned to his partner. "You remember John Stokes, don't you, Dick?"

"Oh, they's all fine, Cap."

Stokes had been in Tombstone going on five years. Had spent time as a Buffalo soldier with the Tenth and after all the Apaches were finished, decided to stay. He found a devoted friend in Arvel Walsh when he'd arrived with his family to the region.

"What can you tell us, John?"

"I was working this mornin'." He turned and regarded the roof, now half shingled. "And I seen the laird go out and then a little while later a group of men go in. It was strange, Captain, 'cause they had an odd contraption, a fancy circus wagon, all painted red with a cage affixed to the bed. At first I thought it was just some customers, lookin' to have the wagon repaired or somethin', the wheel squeaked something terrible, but I know, they's no travelin' show or my babies would have known about it. They's fond of 'em. I'd a heard sure enough if a travelin' show was in town. That right confused me, Cap."

"What did they look like, John?"

"Well, they was all well-dressed, like city men, maybe Chicago or other big city men. Three of them, two were big as houses, one was just plain. The plain one wored a checkered suit, kinda silly-lookin'. Anyways, they went inside and I didn't think much on it till they was leavin' and when they did, they had that circus wagon with 'em and it was covered, you know, with a tarp, all around, like they was hidin' what was inside it. Don't know, Captain. At the time, you know, it just seemed odd, but I din' see a reason to raise no alarms." John shrugged. "Then about a half hour later, I seen Tommy Hayes runnin' callin' the alarm and that's when I seen all the smoke. Just got caught up in fightin' the fire till now."

"Thank you, John." Dick turned to Dan George dutifully writing everything down. "Take John over to the coffeehouse, Dan, you two go over it again, get as many details down as possible."

Arvel nodded. "So, you're the famous laird of Glen Cowie?"

The laird smiled. "Not certain of the fame, your honor, but I am indeed the laird." He reached out to shake the men by the hands. "I am sorry I wasn't here to help poor Robert."

"Well, at least he's not dead. How many were working in there when the conflagration broke out?"

"Only two, Craster and his helper, Sam."

In short order Dan George was back amongst them, Arvel kicking at the debris of what once was Craster's shop. Dick found some evidence and reported it to the rest, as he'd determined the ignition source and where the fire had been started.

Arvel smiled. "You are turning into a proper detective, Dick."

Welles ignored the intentional jibe. "According to John, they were heading northeast, which should take them out of town."

"Toward my place." Arvel wanted to bolt for home.

Dan George looked his bosses over. "What do you suppose? Kidnapping?"

"Likely worse than kidnapping, Dan. I'm sure they're going to rub these boys out. Get rid of any witnesses to the young woman's assault."

The laird spoke up. "It appears Sam has been caught up as an innocent bystander. He knows nothing. I was with Craster the night the poor woman was savaged."

Dick nodded. "So, we're looking at murder on top of arson, if we don't catch them in time, certain enough."

By late afternoon they'd divided their forces. The laird and Arvel, on the way back home to report to the family, prepare, and summon reinforcements. They'd supply the expedition and a remuda for the men, as they did not know how long the chase would last. Dick and Dan would follow the trail and pick up clues as they went. They'd be hard-pressed not to find witnesses who'd seen a red circus wagon on the main road heading out of Tombstone.

Walsh and his new companion did not get far when they'd heard the call from behind them.

"John!" Arvel grinned at the old soldier's traps. Stokes was ready for action, sporting his army shirt, old and moth-bitten, but otherwise in good trim.

"Thought you might need help, Cap." He nodded to the laird. "Robert Craster's my friend."

"Welcome, John, welcome. We can use a good tracker, a good man." Arvel smiled. "Just don't expect me to deflect any of Dorothy's wrath." He winked, nodding to the laird. "John's wife is not a woman you want angry at you."

They were greeted by Uncle Bob in an uncharacteristically agitated state. "Arvel, lad, I'm glad you're here. Come with me, we've got trouble."

"Not Rebecca or Chica?"

"No, no. They're fine. It's that young Ranger private, O'Higgins, the good-looking boy. He just arrived, in a terrible state, poor fellow. It was Gold's men. Gold's men are planning something to get rid of the evidence to convict his son."

Francis O'Higgins sat and sipped soup as Pilar and Chica fussed over him. His bruises had darkened as he made his way to the Walsh ranch. He looked like hell. Arvel shook him by the hand.

He grinned. "I'm all right, Captain." He turned his head from side to side. "Gave 'em nothing, sir. They were very interested in the whore"—he blushed and nodded to the ladies—"I beg your pardon, I mean, the young woman who got cut up. They're pretty sure she's here, Captain." He looked around the place. "We need to defend it, sir. Need to get that woman outta here. Need to make certain your family's safe."

He began coughing and spit up bloody phlegm. "I'm sorry, Captain, not feeling quite up to snuff, but give me a day, I'll be fit for duty after that."

"You rest, my boy. We think they've kidnapped the piano hauler, the man who was there the night of the attack."

"What they look like?"

Arvel turned to John who scratched his chin as he recalled the events.

"I'll have to think on that. All happened so quick."

"Was one kind of a monkey-faced-lookin' bastard? Scaly red complexion? Muddy-colored hair?"

"Don't know about his face, too far away, but y—yeah, yeah, the rest about describes him. Wore one of them loud checkered suits much younger dudes wear, back East mostly. You know the kind?"

"That's Dobbs." Francis grinned at a particularly amusing memory. "Didn't happen to be sportin' a big bandage on his finger, was he?"

"Don't know. Didn't take note of his hands, I'm sorry."

"Don't matter. It were Dobbs all right. You track him down, you'll get your man, Captain. Maybe we ain't in as much danger as I'm thinkin' if he's tied up with that." He had a thought. "Captain?"

"Yes, my lad?"

"There's a bookkeeper, nice old gent, a drunkard named Hugh Harvey, he works for Gold. I fear for him, Captain. He helped me escape, but he wanted to stay close. I couldn't budge him to come along with me. Thinks he might be a good spy for us, but I fear for him just the same."

"We'll follow it up, Francis." He patted the boy on the arm. "You rest."

"And another thing, Captain. The man who mistreated that poor girl so terribly. His name's Damian Gold. He's hiding in Tampico, sir. He's the rich Gold's son."

Arvel wandered onto the veranda. They sat around the breakfast table and had a proper war council. Bob smoked as he looked out at the corral. "What do you make of it, Uncle?"

"Don't know, son. You're the law dog." He looked at the women. "What do you ladies think?"

"I believe you must kill this Dobbs, my Arvel." She looked at Pilar nodding in agreement. "Dick Welles and Dan George will need you, and Billy Livingston has got the poor girl healing well. You needa go and help your friends. Take John Stokes and this Scottish man. The boy will stay with us until he is properly healed. Billy will cure him." She looked in the direction of the bedroom where they'd put the lad. "Any man who would do that to a boy is evil and must be put to death."

They sat to dinner in the library as it was larger and better suited for feeding so many guests, the laird enjoying himself despite the grave circumstances. He'd heard stories about the Walshes and now he was treated to their hospitality and kindness. At the table sat a Negro, an aborigine, and a Mexicana nanny. Everyone was equal in the eyes of the Walsh clan.

At the conclusion of the meal he stood to await the retirement of the womenfolk, as was the custom of his land. Arvel smiled and beckoned him to take his seat as Chica moved around the table, trimming then handing out good Cubans to everyone. She lit her own first, and moved about with the fancy lighter, a gift from Uncle Bob on her last birthday, attending to each of her guests.

Margarita attempted to take her leave when Chica, with a nod, ordered her to stay. Rebecca was already in bed, there was no reason for the young beauty to leave. Her day's work was done, and Chica had guessed Francis O'Higgins would enjoy the company.

The laird smiled through the cloud of cigar smoke wreathing the table. "Thank you, Mrs. Walsh."

"De nada."

She looked the laird over and decided to learn some things from this one, as he was evidently an educated and friendly man. She enjoyed him admiring her and thought that he might be entertaining. Besides, he had a very queer accent which she found intriguing.

"Mr. Laird . . ."

"Please, madam, call me Alasdair."

She nodded as she blew smoke at the ceiling. "Alasdair, tell me is it true that men in your land wear dresses?"

"Ah, the kilt. Well, yes, madam, in a matter of speaking, more a skirt than a dress."

"Chica, you may call me Chica."

"Chica, yes, it is an old tradition."

Arvel interjected, "From the Celts, I believe."

"Well, yes, some of our Irish cousins would like to lay claim to such, but we, the Scots *and* the Irish have a race from much longer ago than this to thank for, as Miss Chica calls it, the *dress.* The Galicians, long forgotten ancestors of our noble tribe, they wore a kind of skirt or tunic, and really even before that the Romans, in fact, all of our early ancestors, until the advent of riding horseback, wore a kind of skirt."

"Ah, the gringo Romans, the ones who killed our Lord Jesus." She bowed her head. "*Sí,* I have seen this thing." She turned to Arvel. "In the church, on the walls, the stations of the cross, remember, Arvel, the gringo Roman soldier beating Christ, he was wearing a dress and I remember how strange I thought that it looked." She turned to the laird. "Did the gringo Romans mistreat the people of your land as well, Alasdair? They seem to have been a terrible lot."

"Not so badly as the English, but yes, madam, they did." He smiled. "But so long ago that we really harbor no real enmity toward them. The Italians of today are certainly not the Romans of olden times. It is our neighbors to the south who vex us so now. The bloody British, pardon the vulgarity."

"Alasdair, do you ride the horse sidesaddle, like a woman, then?"

The laird smiled. "No, Chica, we wear trews, eh, trousers for riding, but there are not so many horses to ride in my land. It is a poor country. Folks mostly walk to get about, so the kilt remains popular. But you are correct, the kilt is not conducive to riding."

Chica grinned. "It is why I wear man pants when I ride too."

Arvel retrieved a book from his library shelf. He paged through. "Here, Chica, here's a highlander, a man from the laird's country."

"*Ay chingao! Muy varonil,* ah, that is to say, very manly." She winked at the laird.

Alasdair looked over her shoulder and pointed. "That's a claymore he's holding, madam, the sword of our ancient kin. I can assure you, many an Englishman has felt the sting of its blade."

"But you would go to battle in such clothes, señor? He is *muy* prettily dressed." She turned to Arvel. "Is a real word, prettily?"

Arvel smiled. "*Sí. Es perfecto.*" He reached over and kissed her temple.

The laird blushed. "Well, we, ahem, that is to say, madam, we . . ."

Arvel finished the laird's thought for him. "They went into battle naked, Chica. At least, from the waist down." He returned to his library, retrieving another book. "Here's a good depiction, one of my favorite sculptures of all time."

Chica read with interest, "The dying Gaul."

Arvel tapped the page. "Well, he's actually completely naked."

The laird replied. "I'll be. I've always known this sculpture as the dying gladiator." He smiled at Arvel and read the cover of the periodical. "The *American Art Review.* Well, I'll be."

"My late wife was an art enthusiast, laird." He nodded to Uncle Bob who had to look away. The memory of his niece and any talk of her still overwhelmed him. "She was so excited when she read that. She declared I had Gaelic blood running through my veins."

"Walsh." The laird stroked his chin. "Could be, could be. I know a Welshman or two named Walsh. Another fine Gaelic cousin, the Welsh."

"You, the men, they did really fight in battle with nothing on?"

"Yes, señora," the laird blushed again.

"But why?"

"Shock value. A man who will face his foes with naught but a sword and a shield is a man you might not want to face down." He paged through Arvel's encyclopedia, to a battle depiction.

"Pardon the indelicacy, my lady, but back in the day, our ancestors, being so poor, they had no firelocks to fight the better-equipped modern Englishmen. They would charge the British line, drop to the ground at the enemy's first volley, then close the distance before their foes could reload. The big swords and shields would then be used to great effect, and the nudity, well, it would unnerve many of the more proper Englishmen. Many, even to this day, have declared that the Scots are a bit insane."

"I see." She returned her attention to the image of the man, naked and beaten, dying on the ground. She tapped the page with her finger. "The dying Gaul. I see." She looked at Arvel and then the laird. "It change the whole meaning of the sculpture, does it not?"

Uncle Bob recovered and smiled. "How so, sweetheart?" Chica never failed to brighten his mood.

"It, well, this man, he is dying, not because of some silly battle in an arena." She looked about at the men. "I have seen this Coliseum in Rome, where the gladiator men fought. And this is not the same. He did not die in some fight to entertain the Caesar, he died in battle fighting for his home, his family, he fought against the tyranny put upon his people and his land."

The laird stood, raising his glass. "Most eloquently stated, madam." He checked his watch as he suppressed a yawn.

Arvel countered, as he did not want the evening to end. "Who's up for some cards?"

Bob raised his hand. "Only if Chica doesn't play."

"Oh, Uncle Bob. I will be easy with you. I will only win ten hands, then I quit!"

Arvel winked at the laird. "Chica is a cardsharp. We never play for money on the ranch. Just a matter of principle." He nodded. "John, Billy, you in for a hand or two?"

They all did and played until past midnight. The laird serenading them on the piano, and Uncle Bob with his guitar. Despite the evil visited upon them by the Silver Republicans, it had turned out to be a pleasant evening, one that no doubt would stay in the memory of all for a long time.

Arvel wandered about the place until after one. It was a clear night with a bright moon and he could see his whole spread, at least as far as where the little hill dropped off and the road to Tombstone disappeared. There was no sound. He lit a cigarette and held the match to his watch to check the time. Chica must have been asleep or she'd be lurking about, tracking him down. She didn't like when he was wandering so late, as such meant that he had a worried mind.

He smiled at the memory of her conversation after dinner. She was a wonder. She was the life of the party. He wondered how he could have been so lucky to have her in his life.

But he did worry, over the boy more than anything else, as the lad looked terrible and he knew that this Dobbs business would not end well. He took a deep breath and pushed the fury away. He'd try his best not to kill him when they'd finally track him down.

He walked toward the barn and stables then thought better of it. The mules were sleeping and if he'd gone in there they'd hear him or smell him and then they might start moving about and he didn't want that. Everyone seemed nervous as cats, and he guessed for good reason. Mules making a racket would certainly raise the alarm. His people needed sleep.

Instead, he crept back inside to the parlor and had another drink and refilled the decanter with the Dewar's and thought about the poor young woman with her womb destroyed by Gold's son. It made him want to cry and he hadn't felt that way since well before Chica had entered his life. He hated to feel that way and resolved to quit this damned Ranger business just as soon as these devils had been rounded up and either killed outright or brought to justice.

Chica was, like a little ghost, suddenly beside him, raising the hairs on his neck.

"*Je-sus,* Chica, don't sneak up on me like that!"

She pulled him close, revealing to him that she wore nothing under the sheer silk Chinese robe, a gift for Christmas from her uncle Alejandro.

"Do not take Dios's name in vain, Pendejo." She kissed him hard on the mouth. "You taste nice, of fancy whiskey."

"Thank you. Shall I pour you some?" He did without awaiting her reply.

"Why are you not in bed with me? I waited and waited and you did not come in bed and I fell asleep." She took his hand and led him to their room. "You will be gone maybe a long time and there is no reason to not be with me this last night."

They loved a long time and Arvel thought that he might very well send word to Dick to go on without him. Chica seemed to read his mind.

"Pendejo, it is already after three. We might as well get up. I want you on the road before sunrise. Where Dick and Dan are right now is very far, and they will be traveling even farther by the time you catch them up."

"I don't want to go, Chica." He sounded a little silly, almost childish saying that and Chica reprimanded him for it.

"It is not a matter of wanting. You *must.*"

"I wish you were going with me."

"That is no longer possible." Forever the pragmatist, he knew she was right. "If some bad thing happens to you, Dios forbid it"—she blessed herself—"I must remain alive for our little daughter."

"I know, Chica. I know."

"And besides, Señor Welles need you. Dan need you. You are the best when you are all together."

"That new boy, Chica." Arvel swallowed hard at the memory of his condition. "He's been through it, hasn't he?"

"He has, my Arvel, and you owe it to him, too. He was very brave and he did that for us. We owe this debt to him, to bring the bad men to justice."

"I pity him."

She held him in her arms. "Do not pity him. He survived and he proved his worth as a man and a Ranger. He will live proud for the rest of his days because of his bravery. No one will ever take that from him, my Arvel. He has been tested as few are ever tested, and he did well."

"You have a strange way of looking at things, Chica."

"I know, Pendejo. You have told me these thing many times before. I am one in a *millón*."

"You are, my darling."

"And anyway." She got up and put the robe on, stretched and ran her fingers through her raven hair in a way that made Arvel damn ever hearing the word Ranger. She began packing for him as she spoke. "It will give me some time to play as matchmaker for the boy and Margarita."

Arvel laughed out loud. "I don't think that's a very good idea, Chica."

"Why not, you do not think Anglos and Mexicanos should mix?" She winked.

"Yes, that's it Chica, that's *just* it. No Anglos and Mexicanos. It's scandalous. Just the worst thing I've ever heard of." He pulled her onto his lap, kissing everything the open robe revealed.

Exhibiting great restraint, she pulled herself away. "Then why not?"

"Oh, Margarita. She's a proper lady, no doubt. Don't believe she'd find much solace in the boy." He nodded. "Granted, the lad's handsome and well-mannered and brave, but, Chica, he's rough as a cob."

"What is this cob?"

"Mazorca de maiz."

She nodded. "I see. What is this meaning? Rough as the cob?"

"Not refined, not educated, Chica. He's a nice but ignorant and ill-educated young man. Not for the princess, I'm afraid."

"Well, that did never keep us from being together, Pendejo." She grinned. "I am rough as the cob and you are a refined gentleman."

"No, of course not, but well, Margarita, she just doesn't, I don't know."

"You do not like her."

"No, no. It's not that I *dislike* her, Chica. She's, well, a little arrogant. I frankly don't like the way she behaves toward you *or* Pilar. Acts like the Queen of Sheba, looking down her nose at the both of you."

"She is a child, Pendejo, and she has had many bad things happen in her young life." She patted his face. "But you are very sweet to see how she treat me. Just be patient with her. Your wild Chica might just teach her some things. And anyway, it is the way in our land. The fine Spaniards, they do not like wild Indios like me."

"Well I do! The wilder the better, my darling." He kissed her. "And no doubt, if she lets you, you'll teach her some things. Some amazing and wonderful things."

"That telephone is a heck of an invention." Francis sat at table across from the pretty nanny. He felt ashamed of his battered face and every time he looked at her she seemed to avert her eyes. The young Ranger was just dense enough not to understand the full meaning of her actions.

Uncle Bob smiled. "It *is* lad. We got a telegraph in as soon as practicable and now the telephone. What a grand invention. Arvel and John and the men would have been sitting around here for days otherwise."

"Where are they meeting up, sir?"

"Up north, last news they got, the circus wagon went east into the desert from a little hamlet called Myerstown. Not much there anymore but a water stop for the train. At least they had a telephone. Dick and Dan are waiting for them."

"Wish I could have gone along." He coughed, as thinking about the pain under his ribs triggered the response.

Chica reached out and gave him a pat on the hand. "You rest, muchacho. You have earned a good rest and we need the company." She gave Margarita a little nod. "We can all use your good company."

Bob continued. "And besides, Arvel's got another four Rangers on the way. They'll have a formidable crew. Hope they can find them before something happens to that teamster and his man."

My dear wife Dorothy:

I take my pen in hand to write to you and let you know that I am fine. Marty Johannsson is finishing the roof job, so do not worry. The forty dollars in the envelope is payment from the captains for scout work. They hired me as such for as long as this adventure takes. Captain says it is an odd way of doing things, being a paid volunteer, but it all works out in the end. You know how the captain likes to buck the rules. Please don't fret and don't be cross with me. I know I did not give you much notice but could not wait around as there was no time. I want to do something to help Robert Craster. He is a good man and would do the same for me if I was in danger or hurt. The captains have given me a horse to ride so I do not cause Sugar any harm. I will miss him but it is for the best. He is in a nice corral with a bunch of the captain's horses and mules and donkey and Mister Bob and Miss Chica will take care of him. I have two more mounts in the remuda. They are good beasts. I will write every day to you. Tell our babies to be good and that their papa loves them.

Your husband,
John Stokes, Volunteer Scout, Arizona Rangers

Chapter 9

They rode in a cramped cage, an animal cage from a circus, judging by the size and stench of it. It was becoming unbearably hot as they'd not been allowed a hat and they baked in the Arizona sun. Craster looked at Sam and smiled uneasily, the old fellow nodded.

They'd been traveling all night and now it was late morning, heading east on a road that did not seem to enjoy much travel. Craster looked forward and saw only the two toughs. The dude in the loud suit was not with them. He called out.

"You there. We need some water."

The driver stopped. He ignored them as he surveyed the horizon, drinking greedily from a large canteen. He gargled a mouthful and spit it on Sam's head.

Craster, enraged, shook his fist. "I'll break your goddamned neck."

They ignored him. "This is far enough." The other turned and looked them over. He was the one whom Robert Craster had given the broken nose. He did not look well and he glared at the caged teamster, hatred in his bloodshot eyes. "That'll be a good trick with you sitting in there, chum."

"Let me out and I'll take both of you on at the same time. Cowardly bastard."

The man grinned as he climbed up on the cage. Unbuttoning his trousers, he began to empty his bladder on the two incarcerated men. "Here's a drink for you, boys." The other tough looked on, laughing.

"You son of a bitch!" Craster pulled Sam out of the stream and took the brunt of it, across his broad shoulders, resisting the urge to gag.

When the man finished, he nodded to his partner, jumping down onto the wagon's seat.

"This is the end of the line, boys." The broken-nosed tough went on. "Our boss said to unlock you, let you figure your own way back, but he's not here, and . . ." He touched his wounded nose. "We're kind of, well, short memoried when it comes to instructions like that." He nudged his partner. "A little gift to thank you for the broken nose, teamster. Hope it was worth it."

They both pushed on the cage as Craster and Sam looked on in disbelief. The container slid off the wagon's platform and toppled over, rolling, end over end down an embankment, tumbling the men as if they were dice in a chuck-a-luck cage. Both were knocked senseless.

They came to rest and eventually awoke after what seemed a long time, all alone. The sun was horrendous and Craster took a long time to fully awaken and assess their situation.

The henchmen were gone and they were in the desert, a good thirty feet from the dusty road they'd traveled. It was past two in the afternoon, by his best estimation of the sun in the sky. Craster looked in every direction, his view blocked on the western side by the road embankment. He did not know this land, but guessed they were far east of Tombstone. There was nothing but flat desert in every direction. They were in a tight spot.

He nudged Sam and the old fellow came awake. He sat up slowly and held his head. His eye was swollen shut.

"Goddamn, Robert. Feel like I d—drank a whole bottle of that shit they sell to the In—Indians down in that hole outs—side a town."

Craster looked himself over. He could detect no broken bones. He nodded at the old man. "Are you hurt bad, Sam?"

"D—don't think so." He pressed around his injured eye. "Ju—just this."

Craster sat back and gave it all a good think. He looked up at the sun and it would be several hours before the embankment would offer them any shade. He surveyed the cage and it was still sealed tight, the lock as secure as ever. The tumble had done nothing to help free them. He nodded.

"Goddamn it, I wished I'd a bought that wagon and this damned cage when I had the chance last winter, you remember it, Sam?" He didn't wait for a reply. "Bastard wanted too much for it, and anyway, did you hear it? Whoever worked on it last didn't know shit from shoe polish. No gather on the back axle, rattles like a son of a gun." He looked up at the sky. "I was goin' to sell this cage to the blacksmith, he'd cut it up, there's a lot of good steel in this thing. But that boy wanted too much. Who'd want to buy it from me after I sunk all the money into getting that axle right, then painting the wheels, who wants a wagon with circus wheels? Painted up like a Guadalajara whorehouse. Anyway, I don't even know how'd you get that cat piss smell out of it. Have to replace most of the bed boards, I guess." He shrugged. "Sam, we got to roll this cage a couple times more, get us out of the sun."

Sam understood. They worked together and soon had the floorboards serving as a kind of roof. They were at least shaded now.

The big man stood, pressing his shoulders against one of the floorboards. He pushed, trying to straighten his spine. Nothing gave way.

"Son of a bitch, you'd think all that lion piss would have weakened at least *one board,* tight as Dick's hat."

He sat back down and thought about how thirsty he was. He

nodded. "Sorry about all this, Sam."

"Oh, n—no reason to be s—sorry. Glad to see you b—break that b—bastard's nose."

Craster smiled. He laid a good one on him for certain. "Still, maybe if I had not smashed him so good he'd a not left us here to rot. Damned bad temper. It gets me into trouble every time."

"B—boss, that lyin' turd woulda left us h—here, one way or the o—other."

"I guess you're right." He wanted to use his head for a battering ram. Felt the warm steel and thought better of it. "Well, I hope pounding him was worth all this." He tipped his head back and bellowed at the top of his lungs. "Hello!"

He waited and listened. The silence was deafening. Not even the wind blew. They were alone.

"Sam, how long you figure we can go with no water?"

"Oh, n—not long in th—this heat. I ain't d—drank since yesterday, and that w—was coffee. P—pissed it all out." He looked up at the sun and tried to wet his mouth with some spit. Neither man was perspiring. "Couple, c—couple more days. M—maybe. M—maybe not."

"Son of a bitch." He sat down and tried to get comfortable on the bars that once served as roof. "In a tight spot for certain."

"You was s—supposed to meet Miss Alice y—yesterday weren't you?"

Craster sighed. He'd been thinking of her since he awoke from the clobbering he got yesterday. He reached for the back of his head and felt the sore spot, where the sap had met his skull. "I was." He turned to Sam. "Did they wallop you, back at the shop?"

"Y—yeah. I tried to help you when y—you went d—down. Whacked me then. Fell out."

★ ★ ★ ★ ★

Craster watched Sam sleep until late afternoon. They were now in the shade and the desert was already cooling off. By midnight their teeth would be chattering and they'd be lucky to survive much beyond daylight.

He began digging hands full of sand and piling them up to form a berm along the northwest corner of the cage. Soon he had a sizable pile.

This woke Sam and he looked his boss's work over and nodded. "S—sorry for s—slackin', boss."

"Don't give it a thought, Sam. Hope you were dreaming of a big pond of cool water to wallow in."

"I—I'm awful, s—sorry, boss." Sam's face reddened. "I gotta shit. M—mighty sorry."

Craster turned his back. "You go ahead, Sam. Won't be the first time in this cage. Go on in that hole I just dug there, I'll give you your privacy."

Afterward he turned and gave the old fellow a smile. He saw the look in his man's eye and did his best to hide any inkling of concern over their predicament. "Always did hate circuses and traveling shows, Sam. Always felt pity for them beasts, lions, and bears, and such. Now I know why. No creature should live like this."

Sam recovered, swallowing his fear. He looked around them. It would soon be dark.

"Sam, I thought we'd use this here sand as kind of a blanket, we can get tucked in, and no offence, but we might have to get a little cozy. You know, share body warmth."

"O—okay, boss."

By midnight they'd slept for several hours until the moonlight bore into Craster's left eyelid. He awoke to coughing and gagging.

He patted Sam on the back as the old fellow tried to swallow.

"S—sorry, boss. Choked on what little spit I got left. D—didn't mean to wake you up."

Craster looked up at the broad expanse of sky, the stars and moon so bright he could have read by it without the aid of a light had he a book. He tried to change the subject.

"It is a glorious thing, ain't it, Sam?" He pointed to the heavens above. He didn't wait for a reply. "When we get back, and we get cleaned up, I'm going to, after I marry Alice Tomlinson, that is, I'm going to take up huntin' and campin'. I'm going to sleep out under the stars. I'm goin' to take her up to them red rocks, you know 'em, Sam? Up between Phoenix and Flagstaff. Beautiful place. Someone once said it was magic up there, pure magic, like it has some kind of, of well, like the hand of God had touched it. That's what I heard, and I believe it. Sure enough, the hand of God."

He regarded Sam, resting on his back, hands across his chest, as if he were ready for the coffin. The old fellow did not look well, skin pasty pale in the silver moonlight.

"If—if we, we get back."

"Now, I ain't never been a hard boss, Sam, but I'm orderin' you, right here and now, no more talk like that. You hear? Not another word. We're goin' home, and soon. We're goin' home."

"O—okay, boss. Okay."

Craster wasn't deceiving himself or Sam. He knew it in his bones that they'd survive. He put a muscled arm around Sam's shoulder and listened to the old man's breathing as he once again drifted off.

He too was soon asleep and dreamt of Alice. He'd never had dreams of bedding her. They were always dreams where they were together, but fully dressed, in a meadow or riding in a carriage. It was as if his brain and heart would not let him have the ultimate dream, that to have such a dream, to have carnal knowledge of Alice was going too far, and he might not survive it, he loved her that much. No, his mind would keep that notion from his heart until the reality of it. It was the one thing, the final reward that would give him the strength and courage to persevere, survive.

They never talked in the dreams, but she'd hold his hand and smile at him and he'd be happier than he'd been his entire life. He would awaken and be sorry the dream was over, and then be just as excited about the prospect of wooing her for real. He knew, he'd make those dreams a reality.

He slept until morning and had a particularly good dream. He dreamt that he was with Alice at the red rocks and they were resting by a clear stream. They were sitting together, holding hands and swishing their legs back and forth in the cool water. Hers were bare to mid-thigh, pretty knees, flawlessly shaped calves, lovely ankles and feet. Alice reached out with a palm full of water and trickled it over his head.

The dream became too real and Craster awoke to a scruffy dog, leg cocked, emptying his bladder on the teamster's dusty, unkempt hair. It ran down his forehead. He sputtered as he blinked both sleep and urine from his eyes.

"Son of a bitch."

The dog regarded him and yawned. Craster could not help but laugh. Being urinated on seemed to be an ongoing theme these days.

"Where'd you come from, boy?" He reached through the bars and gave the cur a good rub on the ears. He had a thought and called out as best he could, his dry throat not cooperating much. "Hello!"

"Hello." A prospector, about as old as Sam stood between them and the road. It was already hot, and the old fellow looked like an apparition. He pushed a canteen between the bars and Craster took it. Awakening Sam, he handed the container to his old friend.

"That sure is a dandy cage." The prospector talked as if they were resting along the road, awaiting a ride. He admired it as Sam handed the canteen back to Craster who drank freely, using some of the water to wash the urine away.

"Well, mister, if you cut us out of it, you can sure have it as a gift."

"No need for cuttin'." He held up a key as he stepped forward. He opened the door and the two crawled out.

Craster regarded their savior. "If you're a mirage, you're sure a damned convincin' one."

The old timer grinned. "No mirage, mister." He pointed with his head in the direction south, and then nodded at the circus wagon up on the road. "Found this wagon a ways back. Hitched my own beast to it. The key was hangin' on the back a the seat, plain as day. Never thought I'd find the likes a you two, though." He scratched his chin.

"What of the men, two men who were driving it? Did you see them?"

"Oh, sorry to say, if they was your friends, old Gold Hat got 'em."

Sam's knees gave way and crumpled him to the ground. He began to have a sort of fit. Craster grabbed him. "Sam, Sam!"

The prospector took action. He reached under the old man's head and protected it from the rocky ground. "Mister, go on up and get my other canteens. Your pard's got sunstroke. We need to cool him down, and quick or he'll surely die."

They did and used most of the water from two canteens. Sam was soon resting in the wagon, under the shade of a blanket. The prospector was a good nurse, and had Sam's shirt and trousers soaking. He covered his forehead with a wet rag. He nodded to Craster as he grabbed up the reins. "You fan him, mister, keep him cool. We got to get him to my home, soon as we can."

Chapter 10

Francis O'Higgins was feeling better every day and wandered around the corral, nodding a hello to the people on the ranch. They looked upon him with kindness as they'd heard what he'd done to help the whore and what he'd been through to protect her and the Rangers from the Silver Republicans. Even his eyesight was better. Not cured, but now he could see shadows. Maybe Hugh Harvey was right. Maybe it would come back.

The mules fascinated him, as he never did have much use for them. He only knew one mule and that was when he was young. It was owned by an old man, a neighbor who loved the beast. It bit Francis at the tender part on the back of his arm, just below the armpit. Like a surgeon that mule was, and though the assault never broke the skin, it hurt like nothing he'd known, except of course, for Dobbs's treatment, but up until Dobbs, that was the worst pain he'd ever felt.

When he tried to tattle, no one would believe him as there was not more than a red spot and a little welt. His mother declared that a big mule would do far worse to a little boy had he really bitten him, and Francis was convinced the mule knew exactly what he was doing. He never forgot that ornery animal and generally avoided the beasts. Now he was surrounded by a whole ranch full of them.

Gunfire drew his attention and he nodded to one of the hands who seemed unconcerned. "Señorita," is all he said, nodding and pointing in the direction of the sound.

He found her knocking bottles from rocks with a six-shooter. He didn't like the look of disgust on her face as he walked up. He was interrupting important practice. She had too little time to herself these days and little Rebecca's nap would soon be over. Another handsome gringo vying for her affections did not impress her even a little bit.

She turned and glared at him as she dumped the empties from the cylinder of her six-shooter. "Well?"

"Well, what?"

"What do you want, gringo? This is my time off. I need to practice."

"I want to know how to address you."

"What do you mean?"

"Mrs. Walsh said your name's Margaret."

"She did not! My name is not *Margaret.* It is Margarita!"

Francis shrugged with mock indifference. "Margaret, Margarita, all the same to me." He grinned and waited. She did her best to ignore him. He continued when it was evident that she'd not take the bait. "Problem is, I don't know you well enough to call you by your Christian name."

"That is not your business." She reloaded and turned, taking aim as her target shattered before she could align the shot. She'd not give him the satisfaction of ruining her practice. Ignoring him, she concentrated on the next target and it too broke into pieces before she could fire.

"Gringo!" She looked him over as he stood with the pistol in hand. He was impressive, as it was evident, he'd not aimed. "How do you do that?"

"Oh, you just . . ." Francis pulled his hat from his head to wipe his brow, revealing the curly dark locks that women found so interesting. "Ain't telling you till you tell me your name."

"Aren't telling."

"*Not telling,* think that's the more right way to say it."

She turned away again. She'd not play this silly game. She attempted to fire again, and again, the target broke into pieces before she could get the sights properly fixed.

"Ay chingao!" She glared again, and again was impressed by his marksmanship. "I am not telling you my name, gringo." She shooed him away. "And I am running from bottles, so, go away, go and find your own things to shoot at."

"Yer running *out* of bottles, not running *from* bottles, ma'am." He shot another before she could react.

She couldn't stay angry at him. "How do you do that, gringo? Tell me or I'll start using you for the target." She pointed her big six-shooter at Francis's belly.

He held up his hands and smiled, unperturbed. "Not till you tell me your name, ma'am."

He fired his last round and another glass victim fell to his marksmanship.

"You're Miss Margaret *somethin'*." He winked as he emptied his six-shooter, reloading from the loops on his cartridge belt.

"No, I am not." She grabbed a cartridge from a loop nearest his left hip. She laughed as she held it out for inspection. "Little bullets." She winked. "Little bullets for a little man."

Francis enjoyed the teasing. "Never had any complaints."

"My name is not Margaret, gringo. It is Margarita. I am Margarita Maria-Isabel Sanchez-De-La-Barrera-Duran, but you may address me as Señorita Margarita."

"No fooling? That is a lotta names! Thanks for shortening it, and allowing me the liberty of using your first name, but I think my tongue would trip over Señorita Margarita. Sounds like the title of a pretty song. I'll just call you Mags."

"You will not! That is a hideous name!"

"Oh, yes I will, and you'll call me Ranger O'Higgins."

"I will not. I will call you Francis."

"Oh, so you did remember *my* name." He grinned and

enjoyed her embarrassment at having evidently gone through the trouble of remembering.

He watched her load the heavy forty-five. "Ah, ah, Mags, you only load five, not six."

"I load six when I am practicing, Señor Francis." She looked at him dismissively. "I have been shooting guns since before you were playing with the marbles. Do not tell me of guns." She turned to face the enemy, lined up like glass soldiers ready to cut them down. She stopped. "Now, show me how you shoot without aiming."

He smiled, pleased at his new role as mentor. "You just think where to aim. You just think it."

"How?"

"Like this."

He pointed and shot and missed.

She laughed. "I can miss like that too, gringo." She mimicked his actions and the bottle lost its head. She held her hand to her mouth. "I hit it!"

"Beginner's luck."

"I will show you beginner's luck." She fired again and missed. She fired four more times and missed. "It is useless, gringo."

"Don't call me that!"

She was impressed with his show of temper and his ability to control it. She liked a man who was willing to give her guff.

"I don't like that. It's a dirty name and mean and I ain't a dirty kind of man and it doesn't suit a pretty proper lady to say it."

"Francis." She dropped her eyes to the ground. "You are right. I am sorry."

"All right, all right." He touched her elbow, leading her to a discarded door on a pile in a dump that had been the Walsh's shooting range for longer than anyone could remember. Francis propped it upright. "Okay, Mags, we need to train your hand

and your eye to work together." He scratched an X with the tip of one of his diminutive .32s and stood her three feet from the target. "Learned this from a lady circus performer on my way west. She could shoot like you read about." He looked her over and was satisfied with her stance. "Now, hold the gun, comfortable-like in your hand and point like you would your finger at that X." He shrugged. "Then you shoot."

She did and hit the mark.

"Bravo, Mags."

"That is no bravo! It is too close. It is shooting for a child to play with."

"Child's play."

"That is what I said."

"You're an impatient woman."

"Yes, I am." She fired again and hit her bullet hole. Francis nodded.

"Good, now, shoot all your shots and reload."

She did and did well.

"Now, step back a few feet, and aim for your bullet holes."

She enjoyed it. She enjoyed Francis giving her so much attention and in a little while, she was twenty feet from the target and they were both out of cartridges. She suddenly turned nice to him.

As they walked back to the hacienda, Francis asked her, "Why you want to shoot so much?"

"To kill a man."

"What man?"

"What does the O mean in your name, Francis?"

He shrugged. "Beats me. It's just O. O'Higgins. Don't have any idea, Mags. Guess it just means O."

"How many men have you killed, Francis?"

He felt his face redden. He felt as if his manhood, and Margarita's continued interest in him, depended on the answer.

"How many have *you* killed?"

"I am asking the questions."

"And so am I. Who would a pretty young lady want to kill, anyway, Mags?"

She turned on him with a renewed savagery. It shocked him. "That is my business!"

"Settle yourself down, Mags. Jesus, never seen such a touchy woman. What's wrong with ya?"

His candor and kindness broke her shell. She took a deep breath and led him to the shade of the veranda outside her mistress's bedroom. Francis poured water for both of them. He took a seat beside her, a little too close. She didn't move away.

"Porfirio Díaz."

"Who the hell's he, a bandit?"

"He is the *presidente* of my Mexico. And yes, you could say that he is a bandit. He is evil and he is the reason for the death of my family." She looked around her. "He is the reason I am now a nanny to a gringo." She stopped herself. "I, I mean to the Walsh family's child. He has taken everything that I loved. He has done this to many, many people in my country."

"Sounds like a real bastard."

"He is, Francis. He is a bastard, and one day, I will find him and kill him, even if I lose my life in the doing of it."

Chapter 11

They arrived at just after noon in a little hamlet on the edge of the desert, Dick Welles in a foul mood as Arvel and his company rode up. Arvel checked Dan George whose reaction was a shrug. The Indian had no idea what had put his boss in such a funk.

The terse Ranger boss marched about the boardinghouse parlor as he looked over papers, absently shuffling them in his hands. A map was spread out on a table in the middle of the room. He frowned at Arvel and the laird and then at the long case clock in the corner of the room.

Arvel grinned. "Sorry, Dick, we made the best time we could."

"I know, I know, Arvel." He nodded his head in disgust. "Not blaming you. We lost the trail three times and now the last anyone's seen of this wagon was in this godforsaken place"—he pointed with his cigarette as he explained—"heading into the loneliest part of the damned territory."

"Well, let's ride, friend." He considered Dan George in his vest. No one seemed in a hurry to do much of anything.

"Can't, Arvel. Been waiting on you to follow up on a murder scene."

"Gold's men again?"

"Don't know, but the woman who owns this place, she's got a little hovel she rents to a fellow down the road, on the edge of town. She checked on him this morning and he's dead."

They followed, waited as she unlocked the door.

"My God." Arvel winced. "Smells of burning fat."

The walls, ceiling and windows were covered in a brown film, the body lay near the stove, the man had been burned in two.

The laird spoke up. "I have never seen anything like it. Nor smelled any such fat."

Arvel smiled as he watched Dick transform from lawman to forensic investigator. He could not pass up a joke. "Looks like a case of spontaneous human combustion."

"You don't say?"

"Sure, laird, like from the stories, in old England."

"Ah, Dickens!"

"And Jacob Faithful's poor mother." He winked. "Exactly."

The landlady cocked her head like a curious spaniel, but Dick's reaction to Arvel's little joke was not so innocuous or for that matter, charitable.

"If you two are going to make jokes about it"—he pointed with his finger—"do it out there. A man's lying dead at your feet, and I don't find such a thing an appropriate subject for frivolity."

Arvel lost his smile. "All right, Dick, take it easy." He turned to Dan George who smoked pensively. The Indian wouldn't take sides on this one, busying himself instead by sketching the crime scene.

"Come on, laird. The whole affair's given me a bit of an appetite. Wonder if we could get a steak in these parts."

Dick worked on the case for the next hour, nodding, making comments to Dan who scribbled notes. He turned to the old woman.

"He's not been murdered, ma'am." He pointed to a pile of ash where there was once a torso. He pointed again to the many bottles haphazardly discarded around the room. "A heavy drinker was he?"

"Oh, terrible, sir, terrible. Always paid his rent, always behaved like a gentleman, but oh, how he could drink *and* eat.

What's this spontaneous consumption?"

"Combustion," Dan corrected her.

"It's a theory, ma'am, and a false one. A lot of nonsense."

"Oh?"

"Yes, the idea that people like your man here can suddenly erupt in flames, due to the level of alcohol in his system, and, well, other things."

"My God!"

"And it's true, the poor soul's burned up, but not from spontaneous combustion."

"How do you know that, Mr. Welles?"

She was impressive as she was not squeamish. It was evident that she possessed a genuine curiosity regarding her boarder's demise, as she cared about the man, worried over the prospect of his suffering in his last hours.

"You see, ma'am." He stood at the corpse's head. "He was at the stove, cooking those beans, I suppose." He pointed at the pot of coagulated goo. "He was likely quite drunk as evidenced by that half-empty bottle there, and smoking a cigar. He had an event of some kind."

"An event?"

"Yes, ma'am, a fit or a stroke or maybe a heart attack. He fell there, and the cigar landed on his belly, which continued to burn and set his big linsey-woolsey shirt to smoldering."

"Always hated that shirt on him. He could look nice when he dressed himself proper. Had nice suits from the city and clean white high collars and beautiful silk ties."

Dick ignored her comment. "But not so much as to cause a flame. It just smoldered, and, here's the kind of gruesome part." He looked around at the brown film covering everything around them. "The fat from his body served as a source of fuel, like an oil lamp, and he, well, burned up over the course of the past day and night." He looked her over. She held fast. "When's the last you saw him?"

"Two evenings ago."

"Well, that makes sense. No one to check on him. The place was closed up, still as a tomb with no draft."

He nodded at Dan who finished his assessment. "Perfect conditions, right amount of oxygen, an ignition source, and plenty of fuel. He was like a giant candle." Dan looked about. "And all this is the poor devil's remains, vaporized tallow, stuck to everything like the lid of a Dutch oven when you've slow cooked a fatty roast." He sniffed the air. "Though not nearly as appetizing." It wasn't pleasant.

"Well, at least the poor devil didn't suffer." He regarded the face, bearing the expression of one in peaceful slumber. "Likely was dead when he hit the floor, ma'am."

"Well, that's a comfort. Jacob was a good man. A sick man, but a good man. He was a pensioner from back East. Said he worked forty years in a little office in New York City. Got the consumption and came out here to live out his days. But the drink had too great a hold on him, and his last days were spent alone and miserable." She smiled at them. "I tried, gentlemen. I tried, but everything I ever done was for naught. He was too tough, and well, well . . ."

Dan touched her shoulder. "Well, now his troubles are over. He can rest. And I'd say you likely eased his suffering. Sounds as if he had a good friend."

They had some luck as the road heading east was dry, and the circus wagon distinctive in that one wheel not being right made for a distinctive mark and one for easy-enough tracking. John Stokes and a Ranger named Pablo de Santis took up the trail as they were the most accomplished trackers. The rest of the company followed close behind.

The captains, Dan George and the laird rode four abreast as

the path was wide and flat in this part of the desert.

The laird nodded at his mount. "I would never imagine riding a mule, Mr. Walsh. It's a more pleasant way to travel than by horse, especially with the saddles of your land. I am certain the American horse saddle must have been invented by women. I cannot imagine anyone in possession of bullocks considering them a good idea."

Arvel smiled. "One day, everyone will ride mules, laird. You'll never find a smoother gate or an animal of such intelligence." He patted Tammy on the neck. "Or one so sure-footed." He lit a smoke and offered his pack to the men.

"And you *never* want to disagree with your mule, laird. That's one piece of advice I can give you from firsthand experience." He touched the spot where the coin rested under the skin covering the top of his head. "Reminds me of a story, of your country, a soldier fighting in the Crimea, could have easily been a Scotsman."

"Is that so?"

"Yes, he was lost from his battalion and had nothing more than a mule and the clothes on his back and of course, his musket. He was freezing cold and rode back to his comrades, well into the night. At one point, he fell asleep on the back of that mule and was suddenly awakened by the beast stopping short. He kicked that animal's sides, cursed it, got off and pushed its rump, once or twice even quirting it pretty hard on the flank, but everything he did produced nothing more than a bray of protest. That mule would not budge for love, torture or money."

"How do you offer a mule money?"

"Shut up, Dan."

Dan George ignored the reprimand. "What did he do?" As the Indian had heard the story a dozen times, he frankly wanted to get through it. Sometimes, Arvel could be a regular bore bragging on the supernatural attributes of the mule.

"Well, that old boy found a place off the trail to lie down, tied the mule to a tree and they slept until daylight." He took a drink from his canteen and passed it around. "You know, laird, what stopped that mule?"

"I don't."

"I do."

"Shut up, Dan. You are ruining the story."

"Sorry."

Arvel continued. "Well, it was spring at the time and the land where the incident occurred prone to terrible flooding. Exactly where that mule stopped the road was washed out worse than any Arizona arroyo you've ever seen. Had they taken another step, they'd have both broken their necks, the drop more than thirty feet."

"That's *some* flooding." Dan grinned. He always enjoyed pointing out the exaggerations in Arvel's stories.

"But being such a dark and moonless night, the rider could have never known. If he'd been ahorse, he would have certainly been killed."

Dick turned in his saddle, speaking in an offhand manner. "Same thing happened to you, didn't it, Arvel?"

Dan George interjected, holding up a hand. "We don't need to go into that."

Arvel lost his smile, felt his head again which suddenly pained him. "Yes, Dick. I didn't listen to Sally. Nearly lost my life that day, and lost the best girl I'd known in all my time." He tapped Tammy, breaking from the group. He rode up ahead, to check on John Stokes and Pablo de Santis, tracking the wagon.

Dan watched him offer the men a smoke. The Indian turned his attention to Dick, then thought better of making anything of it. The laird broke his concentration.

"Whom, may I ask, is this Sally?"

"Arvel's favorite mule. She was the smartest animal I'd ever seen, laird. Arvel grieves her nearly as much as he does his first wife and little daughter."

"I remember hearing that he was a widower."

"Yes, Arvel was married to Bob's niece. It's why he came to Arizona. Bob, Rebecca, their family, old mule breeders from back to the time of the colonies, they taught Arvel everything about the beasts. He fell in love with Rebecca and mules at the same time. They came out to Arizona to work with Bob on the current operation."

"How did they die?"

"That's the irony of it." Dan lit another cigarette off of the one Arvel had given him. "Arvel's life is the definition of irony, laird. Of all the privation suffered in the wild land, Rebecca and little Katherine died of typhoid fever in one of the poshest hotels in San Francisco." He pointed with his cigarette. "Broke his heart. Broke him until he met Chica. Then he started living again."

"And Sally?"

"Oh, that was back"—he looked at Dick—"right after you two started the Rangers together, isn't that so, Dick?" He didn't wait for his gruff boss to respond. "Arvel traveled down to Mexico to meet a *hacendado,* Alejandro del Toro, to collaborate with him about all the rustling that had been going on back then by that devil Sombrero del Oro, or as we Anglos call him, Gold Hat.

"On his way home, he was ambushed by a gang of Apaches. Arvel bucked Sally's warnings and he pushed her, pushed her right into the path of one of the bastard's bullets. Killed her where she stood. Then they went about beating Arvel half to death until Chica saved his hide."

"His wife?"

"Yep. Before they were married, of course. She was shadowing Arvel from the time he'd left Del Toro's ranch. He's her adopted uncle. Chica and Arvel had been sweet on each other and she was watching over him. She killed the whole damned band of renegades, saving Arvel's life." He took a drink from his boss's canteen and wiped his mouth. "Well, at least she got him to Billy who worked *his* magic. Drilled a hole right through his skull to relieve the pressure on his brain."

"That's a remarkable story."

"It is, and a tragic one." Dan glared at Dick. "I can't imagine why anyone'd want to bring it up, least of all a good friend. Like an old wound twinging when the weather changes, someone comes along and kicks it. Damned rude if you ask me."

He tapped his mount's sides, riding up to join Arvel.

By sundown they had a good camp and everyone settled in after dinner.

Arvel decided that holding court and telling stories of the old days might put Dick in a better frame of mind. One of the Rangers had a guitar and began to play a soft melody. It added a certain drama to the evening's entertainment.

He turned to the laird resting comfortably, using his mule saddle for a backrest. "Too bad we couldn't strap a piano to the back of one of our mules. You're quite an aficionado, laird."

He smiled. "Thank you for the compliment. I wish my old father had shared your enthusiasm."

"Oh?"

"Yes, he told me I'd sound better as a piper."

Arvel turned to Dick who was pensively smoking. "Bagpipes."

Dick huffed. "I know what bagpipes, are. Not *stupid,* Arvel."

"Didn't say you were, friend." He turned to the laird. "Did you study formally?"

"I did, until the age of eighteen, until a woman changed my life."

"Really?"

"Yes, a German by the name of Clara Josephine Wieck."

"An old flame?"

"No, no. You would likely know her by another name. Clara Schumann."

"Ah, yes, the daughter of the great composer, Robert Schumann. I've heard she was one of the most talented performers of our time."

"She was, and I heard her in fifty-six, when she performed in London."

"And this changed your life."

"It did. I'd studied and worked for nearly seven years, day in and day out. Was pretty good, too, until, well, I heard Clara Schumann." He turned his head from side to side. "I knew it at that very moment, I'd never be half as good as she, and I gave up any notion of seriously performing. Just walked away from it."

"And the piano tuning? How'd you end up doing that? That's quite a jump, from concert pianist to such an endeavor."

"Related to my epiphany that fateful day in London, I suppose. I ran from everything, ran away from home, ran away from my studies, though I loved the world of music too much to abandon it outright. Found myself in the company of an old piano tuner and learned all from him. When I first arrived in the West, I happened on a small barge filled with ne'er-do-wells and a drunken pilot who ended up swamping us. Lost everything. It took some time to get my finances sorted and I needed some way of living, at least in the interim. It was then that I learned that piano tuners were in short supply, and once folks came to the realization that not all pianos were supposed to sound like they were being played from the bottom of a well, I became valuable as a tradesman."

"A tradesman?" Arvel smiled. "No offence intended, but I didn't think men of your, how should I say, station in life engaged in *any* kind of work other than, well, being a laird."

"Oh, correct, sir. I cannot deny that, initially, it was a considerable shock to my system and took some getting used to. But, in due course, I learned to work and actually enjoy it."

They sat and smoked. One of the Mexican Rangers had an accordion, and, as it had keys not dissimilar to that of a piano, offered it to the laird to try out.

He worked the thing out and, in a little while was serenading them with a haunting melody. He finished to polite applause.

"Baroque."

"You have a good ear, Mr. Walsh, yes, Jean-Philippe Rameau. Gigue en Rondeau."

Arvel's mood was restored. He looked at the men around the fire and thought a story was in order.

"Any of you boys ever heard of the famous Zooty?"

No one answered.

"He was a dwarf. Couldn't have stood more than yea high." Arvel held his hand a few feet above the ground.

John Stokes spoke up. "You mean San Antonio Tony, Cap?"

"That's him! That's the name he used before Zooty."

"Oh, I knew him all right. He was the most dangerous man I ever met. Whatever happened to him?"

"Killed by a whore."

"I didn't know that."

"He was an educated man. Did you know that?"

"I did not."

"He was from Chicago. From a good family but they were ashamed of him as he was, you know, a dwarf." Arvel pulled out a bottle and passed it around. "He *was* dangerous. Used to go berserk if anyone so much as touched him. Pat his head and he'd use your balls for a punching bag. I'm not kidding.

"Anyway, he once bedded a whore in a rather open bordello down on the Mexico-Texas border a little outside of El Paso.

From what I've been told, you could hear about everything from the bar, and the whore he hired thought she'd be in for an easy ride, you know, him being so small.

"That was the thing about Tony. Everyone was constantly underestimating him. Anyway, when they were getting down to business, old Tony dropped his drawers. The whore, who by the way was French or Creole or something, took one look and exclaimed, *'Zut Alors!'* and from then on, the name stuck, well at least a bastardized version of it. They started calling him Zoot then Zooty. It was the only nickname that didn't piss him off."

"What's it mean?"

"What?"

"The term she used."

"It's a Frenchie term." Arvel shrugged. "Guess it means *'what a big cock,'* I don't know, Dan. Geez, stop ruining the story with a lot of foolish questions. Someone'd think you're a damned lawyer or something with all the cross-examination."

The laird interjected, "It's a term of exclamation, loosely translated, something like *'my goodness.'* "

Arvel nodded. "There you go. Makes sense. Excellent translation, laird, thank you." He raised his cup as a toast. "The counselor for the defense thanks you."

He got some mild laughter from the men, as it was only a middling story; most had figured it out before the punchline. Arvel stood up and stretched, watching Dick as his partner wandered off toward the remuda. He followed behind him.

They nodded at the night wrangler, a lanky young Ranger from California, offering him a smoke. The lad took it and moved on, finding a high spot from which to stand guard over his charges.

Arvel turned to Dick as he lit a fresh cigarette. "All right, Dick, you've got something up your nose, go on and get it out, my friend. Just blow it out."

They'd become more brothers than Ranger partners, and Arvel always knew, with Dick, the longer you'd let him brood, the worse things got, as the problem with Dick was that he was too hard on himself. He could never step back long enough to recognize his own greatness. Arvel knew that he'd have to pry out whatever was bugging him.

"I don't know, Arvel." He looked back at the men around the fire. "I love this so much."

"I know you do, my friend. Why the hell then would it put you in such a filthy temper? You're in your element. Solving crimes, on the trail, chasing after bad men. Hell, this should be Christmas for you."

"No, Arvel. You, you don't understand." He suppressed his rage, gritted his teeth and held up a hand in surrender. "You don't understand one damned bit of it. You've got *everything* in your life. You've got family. You've got money and a beautiful, loving wife. You play at rangering, play with men like me, men who aren't *educated* like you, men who are bumpkins and not up to your high intellect. Men that don't matter." He pointed toward the campfire. "You have your clever intellectual conversations with the laird, and laugh about your books and art and music and Frenchie words. You run on and on about things common men don't understand. Honestly, I'm just sick of it."

"Take it easy, Dick." He worked hard to suppress his own anger. If there was one thing Arvel was not, it was a snob. He took such an accusation seriously. But getting into a fight now with his partner would do neither of them a bit of good, and he knew Dick's true opinion of him. There was something deeper causing so much strife and anxiety in the man's mind. "I'll tell you right now, Dick, I hesitated coming out to meet you. When that young fellow O'Higgins came to the ranch so beaten and broken, all I could think about was my family. How to protect my family, and then Chica said something. You know what she said?"

Dick shrugged.

"She said I *had* to go. And she was right. I *had* to go, *had* to come out here for *you,* Dick, *for you.*" He lit another smoke and took a drag. "Now, I know you're not really that pissed off at me. So, tell me. What's got you so eaten up?"

"Gold."

"Why? He's just another ass criminal we'll bring to justice. He's holed up in San Francisco. Won't do us any harm. Once we catch up to these devils, we'll run down to Tampico and get the son, and then we'll wrap everything up. We'll get Gold in the end, you know that. We always do."

"Not that."

Arvel heard the tough lawman's voice break and could swear Dick was crying. He was glad it was too dark to see clearly.

"Then *what*? Tell me *what*?"

"He tried to bribe me, Arvel. Tried to get me to sell out, sell *you* out, sell the Rangers out."

"Yes, I know all about it. So what?"

"Well, what you don't know is that I nearly took him up on the offer."

Arvel suppressed a laugh, as for Dick, this was no laughing matter. "Come on, Dick. You mean to tell me you've never had your dark night?"

"No! Not like this. Not to this degree of importance. Bet you haven't either."

"Oh, yes I have!"

"Serious?"

"Well, it's not so much a dark night, but a, a rather bad proclivity of mine."

"Speak English."

"A bad habit."

"What?"

"I lust for women."

"So? Who the hell doesn't?"

"So, I think that's a pretty big deal, Dick. I'm married, but I like to look at pretty women. Like to think about, you know, bedding them."

"Do you?"

"Do I what?"

"Bed them?"

"Hell no! Chica'd cut my *cajones* off!"

"That's not why you don't bed them and you know it."

"Precisely my point."

"I'm not following the thread of this conversation, Arvel. Lusting for women and not doing anything about it is not the same as becoming a corrupt lawman."

"Oh, come on, Dick. We all have our dark thoughts. Difference between us and bad men is we don't follow up on them. That's all I'm saying. Look, it's not fair. None of this is fair. It's not fair that good men get pushed around like chess pieces by dirty bastard politicians. Not fair that the existence of the Arizona Rangers should hang in the balance. Not fair that the existence of the best law force in this land, maybe in this whole damned country, relies on the whims of the voting public, most of whom are so *stupid* they should never have the right to vote in the first place. Hell, Dick, I think you ought to be applauded."

"For what?"

"For your intentions. For caring enough. Look, man, you could be elected sheriff in at least three counties that I can think of without even trying, and make five times more money than you make now doing it. You could become a Pinkerton and make a boatload of money doing detective work, which by the way, would not be nearly as dangerous as what we do now.

The world's your oyster, my friend, yet you've stayed with us, with the Rangers and now had the courage, the audacity to think, for a fleeting moment, of breaking the law, not, not for your own gain, but for the preservation of the Rangers. I applaud you, my friend." He patted him on the sinewy shoulder, turning to face him, to shake his hand.

"Now, can we please stop this, because I can't bear to have you angry at me any longer? You're too great a friend to lose, Dick. I mean that."

"You should have been a politician yourself. You've got enough bullshit about you, Arvel." He nodded and had to look away. "Thank you."

"You're welcome. Now, come on back to the fire. Let's get some sleep. Let's get these rascals rounded up and hanging from the rope or at least checked into Yuma for a long, well-deserved prison sentence."

"Arvel?"

"Yes, Dick?"

"I'm sorry for bringing up Sally."

"I know you are, friend. I know you are." He held out his hand to shake. "Now, there's an end to it."

My dear wife Dorothy:

I take my pen in hand to let you know that I am safe. The men and the horses and mules are all right. We have chased the wagon that we hope holds Robert Craster to a little town. A man was found burned up but he was not a victim of the gang that we are following. They say he fell over dead and his cigar caught him alight. Captain Welles figured that out on account that the man died all alone and no one was about to tell anyone of how he died. It was not very pretty to see. I did not much like it. It put me off my victuals of one night but I am better now. The horses are fine and the weather agreeable. We spend pleasant days on the trail and all the men are okay and I am sure you are not surprised to hear this because the captains are the kind of men who pick the right types. No one is mean to each other. They remind me of the boys from my army days with the Tenth. I forgot to write to tell you about the agreeable time at the Walsh ranch the night before we lit out. Miss Chica played us at cards and beat every man jack one of us. It was right funny. She only plays with beans these days as Captain Walsh won't let her take anyone's money. He says she is retired from the business of cards. Little Rebecca is very fine. Sweet as ever, growing too fast and smart as a whip. She has a pretty Mexican nanny named Miss Margarita who treats her nice. Miss Pilar and Mister Bob are good too. Tell our babies I love them.

Your husband,
John Stokes, Volunteer Scout, Arizona Rangers

Chapter 12

It was a wild ride and Craster was impressed with the prospector's ability to make the circus wagon move, despite the bad wheel, at such a brisk pace. In an hour they were at the base of some rocks along a deep slit, a canyon in the middle of nowhere. This was the man's home.

In a little while he had Sam resting in a comfortable bed, made up of quilts on the floor by the fire ring, deep in his cave dwelling. He worked quickly, pulling off the old man's boots, then trousers and shirt. Sam was no longer convulsing, but he did not look well, skin red, face swollen, lips cracked. He breathed like a man fighting a death rattle.

The prospector held his palm to Sam's forehead and turned his head from side to side. "Wish we had some ice."

Craster responded. "Will he die?"

"I hope not." He pulled a basin hanging from a hook on one of the cave's walls and filled it with water. Handing the teamster a wash rag, he said, "Keep dousing him." Craster complied.

They both took to placing and replacing wet rags on Sam's forehead, under his arms, and at the crook of his legs. "Gotta get his temperature down, mister, or he'll end up either dead or addled."

He nodded to Craster. "Keep feedin' him as much water as you can, mister."

He leaned in close to Sam. "Mister, you gotta drink, hear me? You gotta drink."

Sam did not respond.

But by evening Sam was sitting up, taking soup. He could not speak or follow directions well yet and had a vacant look about him. The prospector was not encouraged. He shrugged at Craster. "Time'll tell."

Craster now had the opportunity to look the place over. It was fascinating, as it was apparent that the old fellow had been living there a long time. It had many of the comforts of home, to include a real feather bed, table, chairs, several oil lamps, a Persian rug, and an iron cookstove. He had a fire ring in the center and the ceiling was blackened by years of use. It drew well, and the place was clean. Warm and dry and not smoky. It was a regular home. The old fellow watched as Craster admired it. He was a house-proud hermit.

"Been here goin' on twenty years."

"You don't say." He had a thought, as if considering the hermit's digs reminded him of the dangers involved in living in such a place. "What of this Gold Hat gang? Commancheros?"

"Oh." He sat down and poured more soup into Sam's bowl, then nodded for the old fellow to continue to eat it. Sam, like a well-behaved toddler, complied. "Gold Hat. He's a Mexican. Terrible bandit, been running amok, mostly down south of the border for years." He found a bottle and uncorked it, then poured for the two of them. "Cheers." He took a sip and continued. "Thought when they rounded up old Geronimo things would be peaceful 'round here, but Gold Hat'll keep you puckerin'."

Craster was curious about the fate of his tormentors. "What of the fellows, the ones with the circus wagon?"

"Oh." His face paled. "Those boys were not your friends, I take it."

"The opposite."

"Well, then I don't mind tellin' you. Old Gold Hat's got a

trick. He ties his victims together, when he's got more than one, and when they're men. You know, chest to chest. Ties 'em together, then puts a couple of sticks a dynamite between 'em." He shivered. "It does not render a pretty sight, mister; I can assure you of that."

"Jesus."

"Amen to that."

Craster stood and no longer felt wobbly. He stretched, arching his back. "That animal cage was kinda crampy."

"You wouldn't . . . by the way, I'm an ignoramus for not saying this before, name's Pike, Stanley Pike." He extended his hand. "Go by Stan."

"Robert Craster." Craster shook him by the hand. "This here's Sam."

"Pleased to know you both. How'd you boys end up in a cage, anyway?"

Craster rubbed his chin. "Guess that looked a bit peculiar. We were kidnapped. Seems this bunch is tied to a rascal who murdered a whore in Tombstone, and the night she bought it . . ." He shook his head in disgust. "She was cut up something terrible. I was there delivering a piano that night. I run a freight hauling operation out of there. I guess they were trying to get rid of me, thought maybe I knew something, which I don't. They woulda pulled it off, if it weren't for you."

"That's a hell of a story." He twisted a cigarette. "Cut up a whore, you say?"

"Yes, I heard it was gruesome. Poor thing."

"One thing I never miss out here, Mr. Craster. Human beings are the cruelest animals." He poured again. "You wouldn't happen to be a whist player, I guess, Mr. Craster?"

"Oh, passable. A lady friend's been teachin' me how. I'm a little thick about it, so you'll have to go slow and put up with some mistakes. You don't mind that, I'll play."

Soon they were playing and Craster was pleased to see it have such a positive effect on the old fellow. He decided to pry.

"Don't you ever get lonely out here, Mr. Pike?"

"Oh, well, no. Only problem is cards, can't play nothin' but Patience all by myself, but other than that, it ain't so bad." He looked Craster in the eye and went ahead, answering the question that would be on any man's mind. "Had a little Apache squaw for a few years." He spoke at his cards. "Little bitch used to bite me when I got her aggravated about something."

Craster smiled. "What became of her?"

"Don't know. She went off one day, to hunt, never come back. My God how she could hunt. Never used anything but a stick or a rock, tried to give her my twenty-two, but she'd have none of it. She could throw a stick or a rock better than most men can shoot a gun." He shrugged. "Went away one day and never come back." He looked at Craster. "Skinny little thing." He winked. "But just the same, she was rather companionable in the sack." He watched Craster's face redden. "Sorry, that was indelicate."

Craster turned his head from side to side. "No reason to apologize."

"Used to have a pair a big old buckteeth, like a beaver or a rat." He screwed his face up, baring his own dentition as a way of making his point.

"Used to be fond of armadillo. You know, you can get leprosy from an armadillo?" He shrugged. "I never knew that. Stopped messin' with the damned things after I heard that. Taste like shit anyways, least the way she used to cook it. Matter of fact, when it comes down to it, she was generally a pretty shitty cook. Used to fry everything, and I mean everything, in old fat. Shit tasted rancid more often than not." He stared at his cards for a while. "Looked high and low for that scrawny little thing. Never could find her."

He had a thought, conjured up by his remembrance of the woman with the protruding incisors. "You ever hear of a wild Mexicana, runs around dressed like a man, pair of silver six-shooters on either hip?"

"I have. I always thought she was a rumor, made up by a newspaper dandy from back East."

"Oh, no, sir. She's real all right." He gave Craster a look somewhere between longing and reverence. "I met her."

"Do tell."

He nodded at his cards. "Yes, sir, down in Mexico, just acrosst the border. I wandered down there prospecting a few years ago, and I was just pokin' along and she was there, standin' in a stream and guess what she was doing?" He didn't wait for an answer. "She was washing out a severed head!" He grinned at Craster's expression.

"Go to hell!"

"She's the most beautiful woman I've ever seen." He looked off in the distance, conjuring her up in his mind's eye.

"I've heard that. Heard her beauty was astounding." Craster smiled at the smitten old fellow. "What was she doin' with a head?"

He shrugged. "The head belonged to a bad man. He was a bad man, harmed a child, and the beauty, they called her the beautiful devil, you know, she gives bad men hell." He took a deep breath to settle his voice down. "She give me that head."

"Do tell!" Craster cocked his head sideways. "What did you want with a head?"

The prospector became a little embarrassed. "To tell you the truth, Mr. Craster, I just wanted to get it away from her. She was a tortured soul. Seemed so alone and lost. I got to say, that head, it was an unholy damned thing and I just wanted to get it away from her, like a curse it was and I just wanted to get her shed of it."

"What did you do with it?"

"That's an interesting question. At first I was going to bury it. You know how hot it gets down that way and, despite all the washing it was starting to stink pretty bad, but, funny thing was, I didn't. I kept that head for a while. Packed it with rock salt, that slowed things down for a while. Then I, after a while, ran across this fellow with a traveling show. Sold it to him. What he wanted with a head, I'll never know, but he paid me twenty dollars for it. Seemed quite pleased with it."

"Do tell." Craster looked over at Sam who was sleeping. He was not so red. He nodded back at his host. "I sure thank you for savin' Sam, mister. For savin' us both. Do you suppose he'll get his mind back?"

"Don't know." He nodded. "He can listen well enough, can follow commands. He's also swallowing good, and keepin' everything down. I think he's got a little better than a fifty-fifty chance, Mr. Craster, he's got that."

Craster slept sixteen hours straight. He awoke late the next morning, the dog pressed against his backside. Sam was still asleep. He got up and relieved himself and worked on building a pot of coffee. He thought about Alice and how the dude said he'd rape her and that made his gut flip-flop.

Well, he'd have to do that without his henchmen helping, that was for certain, as now they were not much more than a pile of guts in the desert. He felt better at that thought. The dude was trying to anger him. The dude wouldn't be able to rape Alice. He couldn't, and Craster could not think any more on it. It was too much for his brain to process, so he stopped. He put it out of his mind altogether.

As he downed a cup of coffee, he read a note from the prospector.

> Mr. Craster, help yourself. There's a .22 or even bigger artillery if you get the hankering to do some hunting. Good rabbit and chicken hunting around, also pig and deer if you're real quiet. Be back soon, couple or a few days. Don't go anywhere the dog won't go and you'll be fine.
>
> —Pike

He didn't much like it, but figured he'd be stuck there anyway, until Sam could travel. There was no way Craster was going anywhere without Sam and it was certain that the old fellow was too sick to handle a wagon ride back to civilization. He looked his friend over causing Sam to awaken. The old fellow sat up and rubbed, first his eyes then the back of his neck. He looked at Craster and the teamster was pleased to see a light in those old tired eyes.

He nodded. "M—mornin'."

"Good morning. Well, we didn't cure your stutter, Sam." He smiled. It was good to hear the old fellow talk sensibly.

"G—got the worst headache."

Craster poured him coffee and ladled out some more soup. He watched Sam look around.

"A fellow named Pike; he's a hermit, a prospector, saved our hides, Sam. This is where he lives."

"I re—remember. Where's he now?"

"Good." He beamed. "Sure am glad you're not addled Sam. Thought we lost you a time or two yesterday." Craster shrugged. "Don't know where he went. Left a note, said he'd be back."

Sam lay back on his bed and began to doze again. Craster decided to do some exploring. He opened the strongbox where the prospector kept his shooting irons. He had a pretty good arsenal, the .22, a couple of six-shooters, a double-barrel, a Winchester and an old Remington rolling block, like what they used to kill buffalo. He looked at the scruffy hound and nodded as he loaded the rifle. "Lead on, Macduff, lead on."

It was a fascinating place, as it was kind of the opposite of a mountain, consisting of a long trench dug wide by years of erosion, and Pike lived in one of the cave dwellings that had been scooped out along the cavernous sides.

It was ideal for hiding from intruders, as no one on the mesa above could observe his activity. Even the smoke was broken up so much during its upward travel through the rocks above Pike's home that it seeped out of the ground over a large expanse, and went undetected.

The dog was not much of a guide. He mostly ensured that Craster would not get a shot at anything, rabbit, chicken or otherwise, and spent his time wandering from rock to rock, relieving himself along the way. Craster followed.

He found various projects, completed by Pike over the years to keep his active mind occupied. At one point he came upon a pile of rocks, arranged to look like a miniature church, replete with arched window frames. There, of course, was no glass, and no roof, as wood of any significant size was non-existent in this part of the desert. But there was no mistaking; it was a miniature cathedral.

He continued on and here and there, Pike had made little representations of rock dwellings, like what one would see up in the north, in places like Walnut Canyon outside of Flagstaff, or still further north, where the Hopi lived. Now and again he came across signs, meticulously crafted with whimsical messages, like "Broke Nose Pass." Another pointed at a little hillock named "Witch's Teat," and it did look like an old woman's saggy bosom. He had some that gave silly directions, like "North Pole, that away."

Everything was well preserved, as, if nothing else, the desert was a good place to prevent things from rotting or falling into decay.

The dog tired of waiting for Craster to look each item over, and wandered off, leaving the teamster to explore by himself. Off to the right, he found a narrow slot, a slash in the cavern wall, not much wider than Craster's torso. He observed, overhead, that Pike had mounted a sign, which read "Hell." Off to the left he discovered another sign pointing to a narrow stairwell leading up to ground level. It read "Heaven."

He followed that path first and was treated to a magnificent view as, from this vantage point, one could see the entire range west. It went on for miles. Pike had even built up a kind of stone settee, and Craster availed himself of it. He sat back and enjoyed the view for a while and then looked up at the sky and thought how splendid the stars must look from here at full dark. He decided right then that he'd one day share this spot with Alice. Perhaps they'd make love right there, under the stars, at the foot of the stone settee. That thought made him happy.

He wandered back to the Hell sign and peeked in. It was too intriguing for Craster to resist and soon he was wandering through the dark place. Light came through in little slits, and he needed no torch. He took another half dozen steps and the place began to buzz.

He was surrounded by rattlers, which would unnerve the average man, but Craster had no fear of snakes as he had played with them as a child, at least the garters and the rat snakes, but no snake, even the poisonous variety, gave him much bother. He shot the closest one, a fat boy, bigger around than Craster's forearm, as he didn't want to eat so much of Pike's victuals, and thought he and Sam would dine on it that night.

The others became still, and began to calm down. Craster continued further in. The place was fascinating.

He wandered down a path and had to jump onto a flat area, about three feet down. Further yet he could make out an old blanket or perhaps a pile of clothing of some type piled up in the middle of the trail. Now he was too intrigued to go back as he liked old things and was curious to find out if these were perhaps the remains of ancient people of Stone Age times. The rattlers were not here, as it was cooler, and they more interested in the area closer to the entrance, where the sun warmed the rocks.

He came upon the mummified form of Pike's lover, facedown in the repose of the dead. He turned her onto her back. The buckteeth were a dead giveaway. This was the rock-throwing Apache squaw, certain enough.

Craster recreated the tragedy in his mind. She'd apparently wandered in there, perhaps following up on some wounded game and tripped, hitting her head on a rock ledge near where she lay. She likely died instantly, as evidenced by the orientation of her body.

Pike must not have ever gone in there after her death, as he was likely not fond of rattlers, thus the sign designating it as Hell. Had the dog been a better guide, Craster would have never discovered the poor woman's fate, either. He was kind of glad he had. It would bring some closure for Pike, as it was evident to Craster, her disappearance bothered the old gent.

She weighed almost nothing, as she was tiny in life and now little more than dried skin and bones. Craster bundled her up in the blanket she'd worn the day she'd passed on, and carried her out into the sunlight. He laid her down on the ground and remembered the rattler he'd shot.

The dog showed up and Craster wagged a finger in its face. "Don't you piss on her! I'm going back to get that rattler, don't you dare molest her."

The dog sat and licked its lips, then gave a little whine. He waited for Craster to return. It seemed the animal remembered her and did as he was told. He awaited Craster's next command. It was all very somber, even for a dog.

He decided to bury her right away and did so in the backyard of the little church Pike had constructed further up the trail. She looked pretty terrible and Craster could not see any reason to keep her above ground any longer. It would not be good for Pike to see her this way. He marked the spot with a cross, though he, of course, wasn't certain if the woman had taken on the faith of the white man. It didn't much matter, Craster knew, it could all be changed later anyway.

He stood back and looked at the dog watching his progress. "There now, a nice Christian burial." He nodded again and wagged his finger at the dog. "Don't you piss on that, either." The animal whined once more.

He thought a lot about Alice Tomlinson as he worked. He wondered how she was. He wondered what she was thinking about him, what they all were thinking about him. He did not know that his business had been burned to the ground, or that the Arizona Rangers were hot on his trail trying to save him and Sam from the kidnappers.

He was certain Alice, or at least Ellen, was worried about him, however. By now, Ellen had likely told Alice about their scheme, the now seemingly ridiculous idea to turn Robert Craster into a gentleman, and they were both probably curious as to why he'd not kept his date with his mentor and the woman he'd found so irresistible.

But there was not much he could do with the prospector gone, or without a conveyance, or anyone to guide him on his way. Fact was, he didn't have a very good idea where he was, and Sam wasn't in the least ready for travel anyway.

He wandered a little more and came upon the circus wagon, as Pike left it, preferring his own sturdy rig. He thought of the two toughs, how they'd mistreated him and Sam and wondered at what kind of lousy bastards they must have been to leave two men to die in the desert the way they had. Craster wouldn't have done that to a dog. He wouldn't have done that to his worst enemy. He wouldn't have done it to either of the miscreants, or even, for that matter the obnoxious dude in the checkered suit, wherever he was, even though he had threatened to molest Alice.

He thought about what they must have felt when Gold Hat blew them to smithereens. He wondered if it hurt much. He felt a little pity for them, as Robert Craster was that kind of a man. Even the worst low-down bastard didn't deserve a death like that to Craster's mind. He was that kind of man.

He soon had the rattler skinned and cleaned and cut up for frying. He found some potatoes and onions and cut them up and eventually had a pretty nice skillet of victuals frying. This woke Sam and he sat up. The old fellow looked around and decided to make an attempt at standing. He wandered over to a chamber pot and urinated.

"F—first time I had a piss in three days, boss."

"Good man, Sam. Means you're gettin' better."

They ate and said nothing for a while. Craster didn't tell Sam about the squaw as Sam had no knowledge of the woman. He had been asleep and sick when Pike had talked about her.

The dog dropped down and rested his head on Sam's leg. "H—hello, boy." Sam liked dogs, and they him.

They found some of Pike's tobacco and Craster twisted them a couple of cigarettes. They smoked in silence for a while.

"How's the headache?"

"G—gone."

Chapter 13

"How do you like Arizona, laird?"

"It is beautiful country, Mr. Walsh."

Arvel pointed southeast as they rode, along with Dan George, bringing up the rear of the company. "Before you leave, you've got to venture that way, to the Painted Desert. There are fossilized trees around there. Amazing things to see. Huge and they look just like trees, though made of stone. Incredible."

"I have heard of this petrified forest."

The laird took a long drink from his canteen. "This place feels very familiar. It brings me in mind of the Kalahari."

"I've always wanted to visit Africa. What did you do there?"

"Just adventuring. Did some hunting, angling. It is, like Arizona, a beautiful though unforgiving land."

"Did you ever kill an elephant?"

"I did not. I did not have a rifle powerful enough. Mostly focused on the smaller hooved creatures, though I did shoot a rhino and one Cape buffalo and several kudu. Amazing creatures, kudu, and excellent to eat."

Dan spoke up. "I'd guess a rhino would be about as difficult to take as an elephant."

"You are correct, Mr. George. And I would never have attempted it, had the monster not been provoked enough to charge us."

Arvel smiled. "Can't imagine beasts like that. Only thing we've got in this country are big bears, though the last grizzly I heard of was, my goodness, some ten years ago. Think they've all been killed off in this locale. You heard of any, Dan?"

"No, Arvel. Have never heard of one since I've lived here and certainly don't mind a bit if I never see one. From the stories I've been told, it is not a creature you want wandering into your camp in the wee hours."

"Elephants always fascinated me. I had an old friend." He turned and gave Dan a smile.

The Indian rolled his eyes. "Oh, Jesus, not another story."

Arvel held up his hand. "All true, all true." He turned in his saddle to the laird. "I had a friend from my school days, laird. Became a scientist and wanted to study the wild beasts of Africa, you know, with the whole Darwin thing. He was convinced he'd find *something,* the missing link, the cradle of civilization . . ."

"I thought that was in Mesopotamia."

"Yes, well, Dan, I didn't say he was necessarily a smart scientist." Arvel handed out cigarettes. "Anyway, my friend became interested in elephants. Particularly in a phenomenon that was recurring in a certain part of central Africa at the time of his travels."

"Oh?" The laird lit his cigarette and looked genuinely interested.

"Yes, well, these particular elephants, they kept coming up with this strange affliction. A tarry substance had started forming between their toes. It stunk to high heavens and everyone, especially the white hunters of *your land,* laird, were particularly concerned, you know with ivory fetching such high prices. They were worried that the elephant population was in jeopardy of extinction or at least decline enough to render the enterprise no longer viable."

"What did your friend discover, Arvel?" Dan asked, forever the devoted straight man.

"Well, Dan, laird. He found out it was not some sort of

disease or fungus or affliction at all. What that stinking mass of tarry material was, was actually, believe it or not, slow natives." He grinned. "Slow natives. Get it?"

"You're a funny man, Arvel. A funny, funny man."

"Uh-oh." Arvel squinted up ahead. "Looks like our fearless leader's onto another clue." He nodded. "You men act serious now. Don't want to vex Captain Welles. He's not a man who enjoys a lot of frivolity."

Dan agreed. "Or *any* for that matter."

It was the animal cage and the tracks left by the recent occupants. Dick moved about the site with care. He looked off south. "Appears the wagon continued on." He wandered a bit. "Then came back." He paced about some more. "Then went that way, with a heavier load than when it traveled north."

Dick conferred with John Stokes and Pablo de Santis. The men nodded in agreement.

John commented. "I agree, Cap. Looks like heavier load on the wagon going south, then lighter coming north, then heavier yet goin' east."

Pablo nodded.

Dick gave the orders: "John, Pablo, you two follow those tracks south. Don't know what you'll find but I'd like to. Take your remuda horses with you and enough grub and water. Don't know how long you'll be gone from us. Once you find the end, double back and then follow our tracks going that way." He pointed in the direction of the wagon's travel. "You'll catch us up then."

John gave him a salute. He nodded to Pablo as the others fetched them their spare mounts.

Arvel called after them. "You boys be careful."

By late afternoon they were into a steady cadence, their little band resolved to find the circus wagon and end this nonsense once and for all. They were on high alert now that they were so far east, as it had been reported that Sombrero del Oro's gang or at least parts of it had been marauding this far north.

Dick sent out scouts, both to the left and right to ensure they'd not stumble onto anyone or anything unawares. He stopped and Arvel pulled up.

"Got that twinge, don't you, Dick?" He smiled at the laird. "Dick can feel trouble like an old-timer feels rheumatism when the weather's about to turn ugly."

"Don't need a twinge, Arvel, look at this Mex sign." He pointed at his horse's feet.

He was right, of course, and it took no expert to figure it out. Corn husk butts abounded and the remains of the native food, thrown into the fire ring still warm from a recent encampment. Empty Mexican beer bottles littered the little hillock.

They dismounted and dug about. Arvel held up a handful of empty cartridge cases. "Forty-three Spanish."

One of the men called out.

"Two horses barefoot Captain, another six shod." He pointed. "Headed thataway."

Arvel smiled. "Looks like they're tracking *our* boys and we're tracking them."

Dick mounted up. "Well, let's give them a warm welcome from behind."

They lay on their bellies and peeked through field glasses. "Lazy bastards. All they seem to do is camp and eat."

Dan interjected, "And drink."

Dick nodded. "Ever known an ambitious bandit?"

"Thank God I've not, friend."

Arvel stood and squinted at the sun making its way toward the horizon. "In another half hour, that sun'll be about right to blot me out." He nodded. "You get half the boys in place on each side. We'll have a regular shooting gallery set up. I'll ride in on them and see if they'll surrender peacefully."

"Don't like it, Arvel."

"Oh, *now* you're not worried over shooting them before we offer them a chance to surrender?"

"No, just don't like you riding out there by yourself."

Arvel smiled. "Maybe you could wait till dark, call out to them. Do your Buffalo Bill impersonation. I'm sure that'll have 'em come out running, hands held high."

"Very funny."

Arvel held up a hand. "My rule, Dick. You know my rule and anyway, your skinny ass needs to stay safe, get our boys back in one piece. I won't risk another man to do it. It's my job. My prerogative. Age before beauty, you know."

"I'm older than you, Arvel."

"And I'm prettier."

Dan George kept the laird close, explaining all as the drama unfolded a hundred yards away.

"They're bandits all right. Too stupid to post a guard, laird. Generally, they spend most of their time drunk or sleeping a good one off." He saw Arvel picking his way toward them. At thirty yards he called out, the setting sun blotting him out, offering no kind of target, just as he'd planned. He held his Henry high, his signature white handkerchief tied to the muzzle, proclaiming his intent.

He called out. *"Buenos tardes, muchachos."*

But the sun did double duty, obscuring the symbol of truce as well. Three rifles fired on Arvel simultaneously. Dick cursed as he assaulted the gang on foot, his favorite mount Rosco hidden in an arroyo, too far away.

Arvel was quicker yet, and Tammy made a good charge. Rider and mount now among them, it was unsafe for the Rangers to pour fire into the clump of bandits, for fear of hitting their boss. The Henry barked flame again and again as Arvel rode among the confused mob. Men fell all around mule and rider. Mexicans screamed expletives of anger, terror and pain, then mercifully, everything went silent.

The laird was the first to comment as the Rangers closed in.

"You killed them all, Mr. Walsh! You killed them all single-handedly. Every blessed one!"

Arvel worked the magazine spring of his old rifle, charging it with fresh cartridges. "That boy there's not dead." He pointed as Tammy wandered in a tight circle, doing her best to avoid dead Mexicans. "Pulled the shot a little on that one, boys." He lit a smoke. "Must be getting old."

He was right and one bandit lay with the side of his jaw torn away. With each labored breath an ominous gurgling sound. A Ranger knelt beside him, but it was for naught. The lad was done for. He'd be of no use to them. Dick finished him off with a bullet to the brain. He looked at Arvel and shrugged.

"I know, I know! Know just what you're going to say Dick and I'm sorry. Really I'm sorry."

"Don't be, Arvel. You gave them a chance. Fair enough. Just wish we had one to interrogate. But then again, with bastards like these, not much we'd likely get out of them."

They settled down for the evening and made good use of the Mexicans' fire. They checked the bandits' traps and found a few items of value. Some unopened bottles of beer and a couple of jugs of mescal. The victuals were uneatable, though they did have a freshly shot deer which was butchered by a couple of the men and put in the skillet for frying.

As Arvel ate he nodded to Dan George, motioning for him to attend to the laird, off on his own, fidgeting and pacing in circles.

The Indian offered the Scotsman a beer and a fresh smoke, the laird taking them with trembling hands.

"Forgive my behavior, Mr. George. I've seen little of such. It's rather overwhelming."

Dan grinned. "You get used to it. Especially traveling with Arvel."

"I've never seen a man act with such little regard for his own well-being. Mr. Walsh is a phenomenon."

"That's one way to describe him."

"He, Mr. George, used his guns with the precision of a surgeon." The laird ran a trembling hand through his head of thick hair. "I swear, I've never seen anything like it."

"Gun, laird. He only used his rifle. The Henry."

"My God, you're right."

Dan decided to walk the laird for a while, as it was evident, like a horse after exertion, he needed to burn off some adrenaline, cool and calm down. They wandered in the desert, away from the campfire and the Ranger company. He lit another cigarette for the laird who smoked it with enthusiasm.

"Arvel Walsh is the most remarkable man you'll ever know. He is kind, gentle, intelligent, and the best and most loyal friend you'll have. He's also among the most ruthless killers who've ever trodden this godforsaken earth. And I mean through the ages, laird. He is Genghis Khan, Hannibal, Julius Caesar and Alexander the Great. He's a samurai warrior, a Mahdist. He's King Leonidas and his three hundred Spartans, all rolled into one. God bless him."

"The dying Gaul."

"Yes, the dying Gaul." Dan smiled. "He showed you that picture. He's right proud of that. And yes, you're correct. That's him. That's Arvel Walsh. The dying Gaul."

"Thank you for the walk and the smoke and the talk. I'm a bit ashamed of myself."

"No reason to be." Dan George touched the Scot's elbow. "Let's wander a little more."

They made it to a rise and could see the entire valley all around them, the moon showing silver on everything. The laird took a seat on a flat rock as Dan George watched two riders approach in the distance. Placing a hand on the Scotsman's shoulder as a warning, he pointed. "Don't be alarmed, laird. It's John Stokes and Pablo de Santis, riding up."

The Ranger scouts drank beer and smoked but did not imbibe of the venison. Neither was much interested in eating, as they'd lost their appetite.

Arvel smiled. "You boys look like you've seen a ghost."

John looked up. "Might as well had done, Cap. Never even seen the Apaches do what we seen done to them men back there." He nodded to his partner. Pablo looked as though he might vomit again.

Dick handed them another bottle of beer. "How many did you find?"

"Two, Cap. I mean, as far as we could figure. It was, my God, like nothin' I ever seen. But we did find two heads."

Pablo added, "The rest was just muddled pieces." He belched, trying to calm his stomach. Arvel offered him a cigar and some peppermints.

"What about that bastard Dobbs?"

John responded. "I don't think he were one of 'em, Cap. No checkered suit, or at least, pieces of one. I think these was the men that I seen that day. Remember . . ." He nodded to Dan George. "They was three, so I think this was the two. Dobbs weren't among them."

Dick Welles stood, brushing the seat of his trousers. "He's likely in Tampico, along with the rest of the bastards." He pointed to two men as he consulted his watch. "You boys take the first guard." He nodded to another pair. "You lads the second. We'll take up the trail as soon as we can see. Once we get to the end and find out what's happened, put this puzzle together, we'll head down to old Mexico." He turned to his partner. "That ought to suit you well enough, Arvel. You can admire some of the local gals without Chica getting wind of it."

Arvel stretched, speaking through a yawn. "Sounds like a dandy idea, Dick. A dandy idea."

Neither man could sleep and the laird found himself on a ridgeline, sitting next to the Negro. He offered John Stokes a cup of coffee.

"Someone told me you're one of the famous buffalo soldiers."

"Yes, sir." He looked down at the chevrons on his sleeve. "At least was."

"Your feats are legendary in our country, Mr. Stokes."

"Oh, that's mostly just made up. Dime-novel stuff."

"We call them penny dreadfuls."

Stokes cocked his head. "I never heard 'em called that."

"Chiefly British." The laird reclined, weaving his fingers together to form a pillow against the hard Arizona ground. "Those stories in the novels were what inspired me to travel out here."

"Hope you wasn't disappointed."

"Not a bit." He watched the Negro scan the horizon. Always vigilant, always aware of what was going on around him. In this way, he was not unlike the natives of Africa, the Bushmen who guided him on Safari. "So you are no fan of those who mythologized the West?"

"Don't know about that, Cap. All's I know is, one time I read one of them novels, had a big picture of soldiers like me, shooting Indians, you know, on the cover. Nothin' I read was anything like I ever did or seen." He laughed. "And that idear that the Indians thought so much of us, you know, bein' dark and shaggy-headed, callin' us buffalo soldiers out of respect, well, I'll tell you now, Cap, ain't never met an Indian in all that time was too charitable. Most just wanted to shoot me dead."

The laird admired the stars. "You've got to admit one thing, though, Mr. Stokes. It is an amazing place, this Arizona land."

John Stokes considered the gentleman. He liked him. Felt sorry for him as he could see it, hear it in the laird's voice that the earlier battle had affected him. It would be a long time before he'd fully recover from that. "That Captain Walsh is something, ain't he?"

The laird perked up. "Oh, you heard about it?"

"Oh, yes." He laughed. "Seeing the captain get his blood up is always something worth talkin' about."

"How long have you known Mr. Walsh?"

"Oh, goin' on, well, I'd have to think on that. I guess five years. He was always charitable to us, really to any folks who's poor or, you know"—he held up his arm—"dark or foreign or different. The captain is kind that way. He knows what it's like."

"What it's like?"

"Yes. What it's like to be different."

The laird laughed. "Until now, Mr. Stokes, I would have not understood one bit of that, Mr. Walsh being a wealthy white gentleman. He's the picture, the very definition, at least on first glance, of what it is to *not* be different." He nodded his head in enthusiasm. "But now I understand completely."

"I'm glad you see it, mister. And, well, sir, I'll tell you, Arvel Walsh is the guardian of the different. God bless him, that's what he is. Negroes, Indians, Papists, Mexicans, half-breeds, whores, Jews, anybody else you can think of who's different. He's the guardian of the different. Wish there was more like 'im in the world. If there was, it would sure make it an easier thing, and easier place to get through. I'm certain, there'd be less misery and unhappiness."

My dear wife Dorothy:

I take my pen in hand to write and let you know that I am fine. I went with Pablo de Santis on the trail away from our party on account Captain Welles says Pablo and me are the best trackers. We had to follow up a trail that went in a direction other than the captains wanted to go. I like Pablo. He is a nice Mexican. He is really from New Mexico, but we all call him a Mexican. He had family that died at the hands of Apaches and he is right pleased to hear my stories about fighting them when I was a corporal in the Tenth. We found two of the bad men in the desert. Gold Hat's gang did some things too bad to write down. I did not like seeing that very much. It made Pablo throw up. Made me have some bad dreams gone on a couple of nights. I am better now. The horses and mules are all good. Please kiss our babies for me and tell them their papa is all right.

Your husband,
John Stokes, Volunteer Scout, Arizona Rangers

CHAPTER 14

Lori awoke to a new visitor in her room. Francis smiled as he stroked the cat on his lap. Scooping the animal up, he stood, nodding as he placed the animal on the invalid's bed. "Good morning, ma'am. Billy Livingston told me to sit here, hope it's not bothersome to you. He said you needed to get up. Has plans for you."

"Who are you?" She grabbed the shroud, donning it.

"I'm Francis, ma'am, Arizona Ranger."

"You're the man that took that terrible beating for me."

"Oh." He rubbed his chin. "It weren't all that." The cat trilled for her mistress. "That's the nicest little cat I ever met, ma'am. She's a sweetheart." He watched the animal rub against Lori's leg. "Never had much use for cats, but that one's changed my thinking about 'em."

"Her name's Jess." She fiddled with the lace covering her head as the handsome man reminded her of the terrible disfigurement, her destroyed face. She wanted to crawl under the covers and hide. Francis sensed it.

"Well, you rest, ma'am." He looked about the room. "You're safe now, certain enough, and Billy says you'll be healed up and moving about in a little while." He nodded. "Have, have a nice day."

Margarita startled him as he made his way to the parlor. "Ah, the *prostituta,* she is open for business again?"

Francis smiled. "Don't think so, Mags." He looked back in

the direction of Lori's room. "She looks pretty beat up. Still pretty sick." He winked. "But I'll let you know soon as she's fit, since it seems important to you." He enjoyed the anger flash in her pretty brown eyes, as it was evident, the Mexicana was not accustomed to being teased.

She folded her arms in disgust. "I am not interested in what she does."

"Oh, I see."

"You see what?"

"You're only interested in what *I* do." He leaned forward, giving her a peck on the forehead before she could react or protest. "That's awful sweet of you, Mags."

She glared as she wiped the kiss away. "How dare you!"

He kissed her again as she raised a hand to slap him. She hesitated, then pulled him into her arms, offering her lips this time. He obliged her.

He looked her in the eyes. "Well, it's a lot more fun when you cooperate, ain't it?"

"Isn't it?" She led him by the hand to her room, closing the door, locking it behind them. She kissed him again. "Tell me you like the prostituta now, Francis. Tell me you want her. Want her for a lover."

"I don't, Mags." He ran his fingers through her raven hair. "You are the prettiest girl I've ever known."

She pushed him away, turning her back to him. "I am no *girl.*"

"You're no grown woman, either. How old are you, anyway?"

"I am nearly twenty."

"You look a lot younger."

"Says you!"

Francis smiled. "Most gals find it a compliment when someone thinks they look younger than they are." He placed his hands on her shoulders, pulling her close, pressing her back against his body. He kissed her neck, and her knees buckled. He had her under his control now and it made him happy.

"Well, when's the big day?"

She recovered. Repositioning his hands around her waist, she pressed them against her womb.

"My God, child." He adjusted his hands, as if to form a belt with them around her waist. "I can just about touch my fingers together, you're so danged tiny."

"Do not say Dios's name in vain. And do not believe I am weak just because I am small." She had trouble breathing. She was trembling to the point of distraction. "What big day, Francis?"

"When we get married."

She turned to face him, ready to be angry at his impudence. He wasn't smiling. He wasn't teasing. His countenance was disarming. He was genuine.

"What do you mean?"

"I've kissed ya. You don't seem like the kissin' type, unless it's serious. So, we kissed, might just as well get the marriage over and done." He gazed at her breasts, her pretty neck as she threw her head back, enjoying his worship of her body. He stroked the cleft between her collarbones. "If we want to do more, we got to be married."

"How are you so sure that is how I am, Francis?"

"Oh, I'm sure, Mags. And anyways, whether it's how you are or not doesn't much matter." He poked himself in the chest with an index finger and straightened his back. "It's how *I* am." He framed her face with his palms. "You are so doggone beautiful, Mags. It makes my heart hurt to look at ya."

"And so you propose marriage to the first pretty woman who kisses you."

"No." He pressed his lips to her forehead. "I propose marriage to the first pretty woman I fall in love with."

"And you are this way with me? After knowing me for so little time?"

"Don't need time, Mags. I fell in love with you the first moment I saw you. The very first moment." He kissed her neck, and her knees buckled again. He helped her to the bed. "I'm going to leave now, Mags." He looked about the room, to the locked door. "Because if I stay . . ." He turned his head from side to side. "There might be a scandal." He kissed her again on the mouth with a tenderness, a love, a passion that melted her body. She reclined, pulling him onto her body. The bed, like a safety net. She felt as if she were falling a mile.

"Love me, Francis." With trembling fingers she worked the collar buttons of her dress. "Love me. Love me now."

He smiled. "Not now, Mags. It's daytime, too risky." He kissed her again, took a deep breath and blew it out. He rubbed his head. "You've made me dizzy, girl. You've made me so dizzy, feel like I could fall right out."

She stretched, arching her back in a way that tested his decision to leave her bed. "You have made me feel all dreamy, Francis."

"Well, you go on and dream, Mags." He kissed her again.

He got up and unlocked the door, opening it a crack to check for any activity. "You take a little rest, Mags, and remember, we got a date with the preacher."

He felt and looked invincible. Uncle Bob met his gaze as he passed the corral. He smiled at the young man.

"Good morning, lad."

"It is the best morning of my whole life, Uncle Bob. It's a glorious morning."

"What's got you in such a mood?"

He suppressed the urge to tell him. Suppressed the urge to shout to the world that he was in love with Mags and she him.

"Oh, lots of things, sir, lots of things."

A rider approached and they watched as the man rode poorly, slumped over the horn, he appeared unconscious. Francis recognized him and more importantly, his horse, immediately. He broke from Uncle Bob and was on them as Hugh Harvey fell from his mount, the pince-nez tumbling, becoming coated in the red Arizona dust. Francis sat him up as Bob ran for help.

"What the hell you doin', Hugh, riding with no hat?" He picked up the bookkeeper's glasses. "Jesus man, the sun'll boil your pickled brains." Despite Hugh's condition, Francis couldn't help but be pleased. He patted his gelding. "Where the hell'd you find Frank?" He looked at his horse and smiled. "How you doin', old buddy?"

The animal snorted. Evidently pleased to be reunited with his master.

Hugh smiled and nodded at Bob as two of the hands scooped him up, carrying him inside to the parlor. Francis fed him water, followed by a quick shot of Arvel's decanted spirits. He handed Hugh his spectacles.

"Ah, that's good stuff, good stuff." He cleaned his lenses, placing the spectacles back on the bridge of his nose. He focused on his surroundings. He squinted at Uncle Bob as the rancher worried over him.

"This is Uncle Bob. You're on his ranch, Hugh."

"Pleased to meet you, sir." He held out his hand.

Bob shook it as the clerk winced.

"Hugh, you look like you're a step away from the grave, old son. What did they do to you?"

"Oh, the usual. Didn't shock me, Francis, but . . ." He held up his hands, the fingers swollen and bruised. "They broke all the bones in my fingers, Francis. Beat my knuckles with a mallet." He began to cry. "I fear I'll never write again."

"Son of a bitch Dobbs." Francis fed him another shot.

Uncle Bob exclaimed, "I thought he was on the trail, kidnapping the teamster."

Hugh Harvey turned his head from side to side. "No, sir, he's in Tombstone, or at least, he was. His men took that teamster, but Dobbs came back." He sat up straight, grabbing Francis by the collar. "He's sure the whore's here, Francis. He's sure she's alive, on account Captain Welles and you took her cat. He's planning to ride, hire some Mexicans to ride here and kill her, kill you all if he has to."

Francis turned to Uncle Bob. "Jesus, Mary and Joseph." He looked back at Hugh. "*You* told 'em didn't you? God damn you, Hugh, you told them!"

"I didn't, Francis, I didn't! I, I they, they never asked me anything, Francis." He cried into his mangled hands. His voice cracked. "They just beat on me, broke my fingers on account I let you escape. I swear, Francis. I swear to God almighty, I swear. Never gave them anything. It was that cat gave you away. That cat."

Bob interjected, "Okay, Mr. Harvey." He patted the bookkeeper on the shoulder. "When are they planning to carry out this assassination, this attack on our ranch?"

"Don't know for certain. Likely soon, likely in the next couple of days. They kidnapped the teamster in order to pull your Ranger captains off the ranch. They're planning to kill them in the desert. Then Dobbs would find it easier to come in here to wipe you all out. No witnesses. Damian Gold can't be convicted if there are no witnesses, that's the plan, sir, that's the plan. He said he'd have no trouble coming in here with just you and a few ranch hands to defend the place. They're forming a gang of the worst cutthroats right now."

Bob smiled, focusing his attention on Chica who'd made it into the room. She sidled up behind him. He nodded encouragement to his new guest.

"God help them if they think that, Mr. Harvey." He pressed

Chica's hand to his shoulder, could feel the very energy radiating from her body. "God help the fools for thinking that."

They held another little war council to include Chica, Uncle Bob, Pilar, Billy Livingston, Francis and finally Margarita, who sat, stone-faced, arms folded. She wouldn't look at her new love, which drove Francis to distraction. Hugh Harvey was left alone to rest as the trauma required an inordinate dose of spirits. He was sleeping off a good drunk.

Uncle Bob deferred to Chica as she was the most seasoned warrior amongst them.

"There is no use trying to call for help. My Arvel and Dick Welles are too far away. Even if we knew where to find them to tell them, they could not get back here in time. We should not contact any other Rangers, either. This might alert the bad men that we are expecting them. It will be our advantage if we know their hand without them knowing ours."

"Agreed."

"Pilar, you will tell the women to take the children away from the ranch. We will give them money. They shall travel north to Tucson."

"And Rebecca?"

"No, my baby will stay with me. With us. You will take care of her, Pilar. You will hide her in the cellar."

"Sí."

Margarita watched her mistress who seemed to know what was in the young woman's mind. She nodded at the nanny. "Margarita, you and Francis will go with Billy and the sick girl to Rebecca Place. You will hide there. You will kill anyone who tries to hurt the girl."

She turned her attention to Uncle Bob. "We will defend the ranch. Call our men together and warn them. Tell them they will have a fight."

Margarita stood. "Señora, I do not want to go with the prostituta, I want to stay with you and Rebecca." She looked at Francis, the young Ranger staring blankly at his hands, appearing much as would one who'd had the wind kicked out of him.

"No, child. You will go. You have learned well. You can ride and shoot nearly as good as me. You will be a good guard and good help to Francis and Billy Livingston." She touched her cheek. "Do not be afraid, little one. It is not likely that these men will even go to Rebecca Place. It is too far and they will never suspect to find anyone there. This is the best part of our plan."

"I am *not* afraid." She flashed an angry look at Francis. "I do not want to go with *them*. I do not want to go to a place that will not see fighting. I want to stay where I am useful. I am *not* afraid, señora. Please do not make me leave you and leave little Rebecca."

She didn't wait for her reprieve, as she could tell by her mistress's expression that her pleas were for naught. She stormed from the room in disgust.

Chica shrugged. "No matter." She patted Francis on the shoulder. "Tomorrow you all will ride and she with you. She will be better then."

They worked late into the evening and by eleven, had a proper little apartment set up for Pilar and Rebecca in a place Uncle Bob had created in the early days when Apaches were still a threat.

He checked on the progress as he held Rebecca in his arms. She was sleepy.

"How is my little one?" Chica kissed her forehead as she ran her fingers through Rebecca's long raven hair.

"I'm tired, Mamma."

"I see you are tired. Did you see the nice little camp we have made for you and Auntie Pilar?"

"Why must we stay here, Mamma? I like my own room. I like

when Margarita puts me in my own room to go to bed."

"Oh, it is just for a little while, *cielito.* Do not worry. Mamma and Pilar will be here always, but for now Margarita must help the sick lady." She held her in her arms, kissing her again. "And you will not have to come down here until maybe later. Maybe not at all. It is just a, a . . ." She looked at Bob. *"¿Cómo se dice precaución?"*

Bob nodded. "Pretty much the same, Chica, precaution."

"Just a precaution."

Rebecca rubbed her eye then gazed at her mother with a dreamy look. "What's that?"

"It mean, just in case, darling, just in case."

"Of what?"

Bob interjected, "A big storm, love. There might be one. We don't know, but a big storm might come and we want you to be safe. The cellar is the safest place on the ranch."

"What of the mules and the horses and the donkeys, Uncle? Will they come down too?" She looked about. "There isn't much room. What of the ranch people and you and Mamma?"

"No, darling." Chica held her close. "You are so smart, just like your papa. The mules and others will be fine. We'll close up the stables and they will be safe. Uncle Bob and the others will be safe. I promise."

Francis couldn't sleep and after he'd gotten his kit in order and the guns from Chica squared away, he roamed about the place, hoping to bump into Margarita. He wandered to the veranda where Billy was smoking a cigarette and joined him.

"Miss Lori going to be all right traveling to this place, Billy?"

"Oh, sure. She's up to it."

"Good, good." He looked around the corner of the veranda, doing his best to not appear that he was spying on his love.

"You two have a quarrel?"

Francis grinned at the glowing tip of his cigarette. He nodded. "Good, glad I'm not the only one to take note of her foul mood. What do ya suppose is eating her, Billy?"

"Don't know, mate. What did you say to her?"

"That I was planning to marry her."

"No kidding." Billy grinned. "You work fast. How'd she take it?"

"Fine, fine. She was happy when I left her this morning. Then Hugh Harvey comes along, we have this big war council, she's told to go with me and she gets all funny."

Billy nodded in the direction of her bedroom. "Go on, go straighten it out."

"Seriously?"

"Yes, Francis. We got a storm brewing, we can't have you two sulkin' around, at each other's throats. Things are too important for such childishness. Go on, mate, make it right."

"Thanks, Billy."

He did and approached her room. A light under the door suggested she was still awake. He tapped and waited, heard rustling, Margarita moving in bed. She called out. "Who is it?"

"Me, Mags."

"Go away, Francis. I do not want to talk to you."

"Jesus, woman. What the hell you mean?" He knocked again. "Open the damned door."

"Go away."

"Goddamn it, woman, open the door *now* or I'm kickin' it in."

She peered between the door and jamb. "Do not say Dios's name in vain."

"Oh, bullshit!" He pushed past her. "What's going on?"

"I am sorry, Francis. I cannot, can never see you again."

"Why the hell not? We're going to get married."

"No, we are not." She wandered to the bed, sat and offered him to sit down beside her. She looked him in the eye. "You are a nice boy, Francis. You will make someone a fine husband someday, but, but this is not how it is to be for me. For us."

"Why the hell not?" He grabbed her hand and held it. He'd never felt anything so delicate and soft.

"I am not, this is not the life I am supposed to lead, Francis. I am a woman of station, a woman of property. I should marry a man of the same. I am not to be the nanny to a half-breed or the wife of a Ranger private. I am, it, it is *not* my destiny."

"Well, I think it is."

"What do you know of any of it?"

"Mags . . ."

She cut him off. "Do *not* call me that ugly common name. Do not address me at all if you cannot address me properly."

"All right, your highness."

She wanted to hate him but couldn't. "Do not be crass."

"All right, Margarita." He stood up, pacing back and forth.

"Way I see it, you don't have a pot to piss in or a window to throw it out. That cancels out that you are a *woman of property.* You got nothing, girl, and you might just as well learn to live with that. Old Portofino dumb ass or whatever the hell his name is has taken that life. It's done, girl, it's done, and I'll tell you another thing. There's no going back to ole Mexico for you and, pretty as you are, I'm also declaring that you ain't going to be pullin' any big-shot American tycoon to marry you."

He stopped pacing to check her reaction. She sat, stone-faced, staring at the floor. He went on.

"I'm your best prospect, so you might as well come to grips with that." He immediately regretted saying it. Could see the pain he'd inflicted. Could see the hurt in the attitude of her body.

She did not take the insult lightly. As if finally awakening, she turned on him. "No you are not!" She tried hard not to cry but could not help it. The tears came when she thought of her family, her hacienda and her wonderful life. "I will go and kill the bastard Díaz. I will do this thing, and I will restore my life. I *will* and it will not be with you, gringo!" She pointed to the door. "Now, get out!"

He stood. "I'm not taking no for an answer, Mags. Now, I'll make a deal with you. We get through this thing. We bring old Gold and Dobbs to justice or send them to hell. The captains got the government to put up reward money, and we'll have some comin' to us once everything's settled." He held out his hand. "I promise you, Mags. We get through this, I'll give you that money. I'll travel down to old Mexico and turn Mr. Portobello shithead's skull into an ashtray if that's what'll make you happy." He nodded. "Then you can decide if I'm good enough for ya." He reached over and kissed her hard on the mouth. "Until then, you're stuck with me. We're going up to this Rebecca's Place and we'll be likely campin' out together for a long time, so you might just as well make the best of it." He reached over and kissed her again. "Good night, your highness. Good night."

He finally drifted off two hours before he'd have to rise again. He dreamed of Dobbs and the little dungeon where Hugh Harvey lived. In his dream he was tied to a chair and he watched as Dobbs pulled out a cross peen hammer from a bag of torture devices. He was going to crush his knuckles just as he'd done to the bookkeeper. He waited for the pain and it never came. He looked down at his hands tied to the arms of the chair and they were no longer his. They were Margarita's beautiful hands, soft and delicate and then he was high up in a corner, levitating over the scene and his beautiful darling was trussed up and Dobbs was going to break those lovely fingers.

Margarita! His Mags ready to suffer the terrible treatment and he, paralyzed, unable to move, unable to help her, do for her, be for her, just frozen like a statue in a garden.

He forced himself awake and sat at the edge of the bed for a long time, trying to catch his breath, trying to make sense of how his mind could come up with such a scene. He grabbed the blanket from his bed. He'd sleep in front of his darling's door until these devils were either planted or at least safely locked away in Yuma prison.

Chapter 15

Craster could not deny that he was having a bit of fun, living rough in the hermit's cave. He was sorry to be away, though, and knew everyone who cared about him was likely worried, and that his men, his teamsters, the ones up north in Tucson and Phoenix and Flagstaff were likely holding their own without him, but the situation was far from ideal and any pleasure he'd derived turned quickly to a feeling of utter guilt and despair.

Sam was better, and could have traveled by now, but the prospector had left them, as they had the circus cart, but no way of pulling it. They also still had no earthly idea where they were, nor more importantly, how to get back to Tombstone.

The teamster resolved to pass the time doing some hunting when shots, off from the southeast, got their attention. They both climbed up on one of the lookout rocks and saw their man riding his wagon with the same enthusiasm he'd had the day he'd spirited Sam back from the cage and certain death.

Eight men followed, some firing Winchesters and others six-shooters. Sam was the first into action. He scurried back to the hermit's cave, flung open the strongbox and began pulling out weapons, handing a Winchester to Craster. He tossed him a box of ammo. He grabbed the Remington and a leather belt full of cartridges. He ran back to the lookout spot as he stuffed a six-shooter in his waistband.

Craster was a good shot and soon had the Winchester barking flame. He dropped the lead bandit and this slowed the others significantly. He turned to grin at Sam and found that his friend was no longer by his side. He discovered where he'd gone when the report of the old Remington, up high on the bank overhead, gave him away. Sam was working the rolling block like a veteran and dropped another three. The rest seemed too stupid to give up the game and kept coming.

Pike made it the rest of the way on foot, abandoning the wagon. Plopping down next to Craster, he trained his rifle on the mesa. He'd been shot in the backside, but was otherwise in good shape. The three men poured a deadly fire into the hoard and soon the bandits peeled off in every direction. Continuing the fight was senseless and this seemed to finally sink in.

"What the hell happened, Mr. Pike?"

"Glad you boys can shoot." He turned and looked up at Sam above them. "Howdy."

"H—howdy."

"Glad to see your man's doing all right."

"Where the hell you been, Pike?" Craster was a little annoyed at him for both his long absence, and dropping bandits into their laps.

"Sorry, had to visit some traps, then one thing led to another." He looked over the horizon for more trouble. "You boys sure whittled 'em down. Thank you." The remaining bandits were nowhere in sight.

He looked about, assessing their situation. The reality of what he'd done to Sam and Craster hit him. "I *am* sorry, Mr. Craster. Was boneheaded of me to leave you two so long. Been on my own so long, kind of forgotten about I was holdin' you boys up. Time's gotten to have little meaning to me, and to tell the truth, I thought Sam up there'd need a few more days to recuperate. He's a tough son of a gun, ain't he?"

Craster couldn't stay angry at him. He nodded and smiled. "What of this bunch, when'd you pick them up?"

"Part a Gold Hat's gang. Back at a watering hole, yesterday, well, last evening, anyway. That's when they started tracking me. I rode on through the night. I can navigate this land with my eyes closed, and that kept them at bay for a while. Then a while ago, they tried to sneak up on me, but I'm too quick for that nonsense. Killed two of them then, and rest've been tryin' to run me down ever since. Bastards, leastways one of 'em, shot me in the ass."

Craster looked the wound over. "Just in the fleshy part, looks like. In one cheek and out the other."

"Good."

Craster looked back at their fortress. It was a pretty good place to hide, but not much for defending an attack, as they were below ground.

Sam called out to them. "F—four left."

Pike tried to stand, and the pain caught up to him. He winced, working hard to swallow it. Craster helped him back into the cave. He called out to his man. "Keep an eye out, Sam. Pike's hit."

"Bad?"

"Not so, I think. Just in the ass."

"O—okay, boss."

He settled the prospector down and Pike nodded to a corner. "I got some corn liquor over there, do me a favor, Mr. Craster, pour some of it on my ass."

He did.

"Hate like hell to waste that." He cringed as it burned his wounds. "It's pretty good stuff. Kind of mild when you mix it with a bottle of Dr Pepper. Ever had that? From Waco. It's pretty good, Mr. Craster, if you like things on the sweet side."

Craster looked Pike's backside wounds over. "When'd you get shot, Mr. Pike?"

"Oh, just around sunset last night." He looked behind him,

but could not get a good view of the holes produced by the slug. "Ain't infected, is it?"

Craster shrugged. "Time'll tell." He lied, as he'd lied to Sam when they were in the cage. He settled the wounded Pike and grabbed some canteens and grub. "You going to be all right for a while?"

Pike took a long drink of water. He ignored the food. He wasn't hungry. "Think so, Mr. Craster." He nodded. "Go on up and have a look about."

He topped off his Winchester. He'd take up a position with Sam and wait to see whether or not the bandits had had enough.

But when he got up to the spot, Sam was gone. He settled in, as it offered a good vantage point. He saw smoke and surmised the bandits were setting up camp, likely deciding how they'd attack. They were, no doubt, in for a tough time.

The dog joined him and lay down, pressing itself against his body. It was trembling, and Craster gave him a reassuring pat on the head. "What sort a frontier dog are you, scared over a little gunplay?" The animal whined. "You're a loyal bastard, ain't you? Your master's layin' back in yonder cave, shot in the ass, and up here you sit with me. You're a worthless damned devil, ain't you?" The creature dropped its ears, and Craster was a little sorry for making such mean comments. "Come on, it's back to the cave for us. I got to get more firepower. We gotta find Sam."

Craster was relieved to see Pike sleeping, lying on his side, as it was evident, he'd not sleep on his back for a long time. He rummaged around the strongbox and found a six-shooter, loaded it and stuck it in his waistband. He grabbed another handful of cartridges and two bandoliers. These he threw over each shoulder.

He began to walk out, dog following close behind. "No." He pointed. "You stay with Pike, you damned Judas. Stay here and keep your master company."

Pike stirred. "What's going on?"

"Sam's gone. Don't know what the old boy's up to, but I gotta find out, Mr. Pike."

At that, the report of the Remington could be heard, a couple of hundred yards off. Then another, then two more, then quiet.

"Son of a bitch, what do you suppose happened?"

Pike shrugged. Craster rushed in the direction of the firing.

Craster found Sam picking through the dead men's traps. He'd shot them all, through the head while they sat about working on a jug at their campfire.

He nodded at Craster. "B—boss."

He was shaking, still on the battle high. Craster twisted cigarettes for both of them.

"Jesus, Sam. Never took you for a sharpshooter, my God!"

"Th—they was fixin' to a—attack us in the n—night."

They worked together, going about the business of collecting the booty. In all, they had nine horses and tack, to include the ones that originally hauled the circus wagon, sixteen six-shooters, five shotguns, five Winchesters and four old Spanish rolling blocks. There was also more than four hundred dollars in paper money, some American dollars, some Mexican pesos, and fifteen hundred in gold, the spoils of a recent holdup, no doubt.

Craster shot one of the horses, causing Sam to jump.

"Sorry, friend. The poor beast was gut shot, guess from our firing earlier. Had to put it down."

Sam stared blankly at one of the dead Mexicans. Craster touched him on the shoulder. "All right, Sam?"

"Th—that one there. Can't b—be more than fifteen y—years old."

"He was old enough to carry a six-shooter, Sam. Old enough to shoot Pike in the ass. Old enough to try and rub us out."

"W—wish we could bury them." He shrugged. "J—just too many. J—just to plague—ed hot."

Craster looked off at the horizon. It would be dark soon and they had a lot of work yet to do. "Tell you what, Sam. I saw a bit of a trough over there, nice divot on the edge of that hillock. Let's drag 'em all over to it. We'll cover 'em with some big rocks. That away, no critters will molest them. What do you say to that?"

Sam nodded. Immediately got to work, starting with the boy. He waved Craster off. "I, I g—got him, boss. Don't w—weigh hardly nothin'."

They led the herd back, untacking then corralling them in a little box canyon Pike had fenced off over the years, evidently another project to keep him occupied.

Craster called out as they entered the cave, unable to contain his enthusiasm. "The hero returns!"

Pike awoke from his fitful slumber.

"Thanks to Sam, no need to worry over those bastards any longer, Mr. Pike."

Pike nodded, shifting to move away from the throbbing. His backside was paining him something terrible now. He watched them go in and out again and again with the treasure once belonging to the dead bandits.

Sam plopped down in his chair and stared into the fire. He could not stop the tremor. It was exhausting him.

Craster fed them and after a long while, Sam began to talk.

"U—used to shoot b—buffalo." He nodded. "L—lots a f—fellows liked the Sh—sharps, but I al—always just had a Re—Remington. Couldn't afford nothing better." He nodded at Pike's rifle as Craster ran a cleaning rod down the bore. "Th—they used to tease me, on account, they l—liked them f—fancy Sharps rifles. S—said I had a Me—Mexican army rifle." He shrugged. "Hell, big shaggy d—didn't know any difference."

He tried to twist a cigarette and dropped tobacco all over his lap. Pike leaned over and grabbed the paper and pouch out of his hands, finishing the job for him. Sam smoked and continued reminiscing.

"M—made good money for a while, b—but soon, everybody was in on it. Th—they say, government d—did it, g—got so many of us to h—hunt 'em, to starve out the I—Indians. Don't know 'bout that, but it was kind a sad in, in the end. Once saw a picture of two fellows s—standin' on top a mountain of buffalo skulls. Ain't much proud of my p—part in all that."

He got up. "Th—think I'll t—turn in, g—gents. Mighty tired. M—mighty tired."

Robert Craster could not sleep and decided to wander to the stone bench labeled Heaven by his host. The stars, as he expected, were magnificent, and he and the dog sat together for a long while admiring them. He thought about Alice again and was pleased with the prospect of heading back to Tombstone in the morning. He was concerned about Pike and wanted to get the old fellow to a doctor, or at least to civilization, as soon as possible. He knew they could fit a proper bed on the prospector's wagon and he'd drive that while Sam would handle the circus wagon loaded with all their traps. The horses that once belonged to the bandits would follow along well enough, and if not, and if they lost a few, well, that was no great loss.

Pike mentioned that they were not more than forty miles from Tombstone, and if they rode with diligence they should make two miles an hour. They'd hit the hamlet of Carlsberg as it was around the halfway point, by the end of the first day. They could rest there and maybe sell the Mexican horses. They should be able to get Pike some medical attention there as well.

It was Sunday and he thought that, at least by Wednesday, he'd be back, he'd get cleaned up and Sam and Pike settled, then he'd go and see Miss Alice. He'd already decided to propose to her and forget all this nonsense of becoming a refined gentleman. It pleased him to think about that.

He dozed as he was more tired than he thought. Battle had a way of doing that to a man. He slept well until the dog started kicking in his dreams, nearly digging a hole in the teamster's thigh. He wandered back to the cave and found Pike babbling. He looked the man over and he was not well. His legs had swelled in the night and were an unhealthy dark red. He handed Pike a cup of coffee as the prospector had awakened. He drank and regained his faculties.

"Son of a bitch, Mr. Craster, can't feel my feet at all." He turned his head from side to side. "I hate to say this, but I think those Mexican bastards have killed me." He took another drink. "It's the dirt and wood from the seat, picked up by the bullet passing through that did it. You can't have that shit in a wound and expect to survive." He spoke clinically, almost as if he were assessing a stranger's condition, as Pike was that kind of man. "Too late for the liquor." He nodded. "Mortified." He looked at Craster. "Smell it? I can smell it. Mortified."

"Oh, none of that." Craster lied. Gangrene would be next to set in, if it hadn't already. They both knew it and he did not hold out much hope for the prospector. He made him comfortable and began packing.

Sam was awake and saw what was happening. He fetched the horses and hitched them in the dark. The sooner they were on the road the better.

"Mr. Pike." Craster touched him on the shoulder, as the old fellow had once again drifted off. "We're goin' to make a dash for civilization. What's the most likely spot we can get you some help?"

"Just head west. Head west toward Tombstone. I'll lead the way."

"Mr. Pike, I forgot to mention this to you, with all the ruckus, with the bandits and you being shot, but I found your little buck-toothed Apache."

Pike was drifting. "You don't say."

"Yep. In hell."

"Oh, Jesus." He opened his eyes and looked at Craster. "The dog didn't let you go down in there. Lousy with rattlers it is."

"He did. And I found her. She didn't suffer, Mr. Pike. Appears she wandered in there for some reason, maybe followin' up on a wounded critter and hit her head and fell down dead. I buried her behind the church."

Pike reached out and patted Craster on the shoulder. He nodded. "I thank you for that; I thank you, Mr. Craster." He fell silent for a while and Craster continued working.

When they were packed, it was nearly daylight. They were ready to move. Craster tried to wake Pike and eventually he came to. He nodded and winced in pain. His feet had swollen double and they were turning black. He shook his head.

"Nothing doing, boys. Can't move from this spot." He pointed with his head. "Follow my trail due south, from where I was running from those bastards. You'll go a couple a miles and then you'll hit a road. Go right, it will head you northwest. Stay on it and you'll make it to Tombstone." He felt around his chest and reached into his shirt, pulling out a small compass he'd kept around his neck on a rawhide lanyard. "Take this." He grabbed Craster by the hand. "I'm sure glad I got to know you boys, and thanks for finding my girl. Always knew she'd never walk out on me. Maybe I'll see her again."

He fell back on his bed and rested. The death rattle was clear enough now. It was only a matter of time and Craster nodded to Sam. They'd stay with Pike until he was gone. He rummaged around and found the old fellow a bottle of pop. He opened it and mixed it with the rest of the corn liquor, nodding to Sam.

"At least it might ease his sufferin' a little, my friend."

The old man looked on.

But it was no longer needed. Pike was dead.

Chapter 16

Everything was settled and confidence high. They knew the villain's plans and would be ready for him. Chica and Uncle Bob put the word out and everyone within thirty miles of the mule ranch was on alert. They had spies everywhere and it would be well-nigh impossible for anyone to so much as place a toe on their spread without their knowledge.

Chica, mounted astraddle Alanza, watched the men prepare. She distributed cigars as Billy loaded the last crate of supplies and victuals into the wagon.

Margarita made one last plea to remain behind. She'd not acknowledge Francis and this put him in an especially dour mood. It was as if they were strangers and this more annoyed than confounded him. "Señora, may I *please* stay with you and take care of little Rebecca?"

Chica ignored her, waiting for Francis to finish rigging his jug-headed horse to the back of the wagon. Chica leaned close, pulling his hat from his head, she placed a scapular around the Ranger's neck. She kissed him, patting him like a loyal canine. "You take care of them, Francis." She looked each one in the eye in turn. "You take care of each other."

Lori smiled uneasily as it was evident, she was incapable of even taking care of herself. She looked and felt a terrible burden. She could only nod and smile through the mantilla veil, suppressing the urge to cry.

Chica completed her send-off with Billy, sitting behind the

mules in the driver's seat of the wagon. She kissed him, handing another three of the sacramentals to the healer. "Dios protect you, my Billy. I will come for you when the danger is done."

He took them and nodded, not certain what to do when Margarita relieved him of the symbols. She placed one around Billy's neck, the third she handed to Lori who followed the Mexicana's lead, placing it around her own.

Margarita addressed them. "The *escapulario,* it is to remind us of God and to remind us of our commitment to Him."

The nanny held her new gift tightly in her fist. She nodded to Chica. "Muchas gracias, señora."

Chica squeezed the prostitute on the shoulder. She nodded, offering a blessing with smoky breath. "Adiós."

Francis eyed Frank plodding along behind them. His gelding appeared happy to be traveling without the weight of a rider. The beast reminded him of Hugh Harvey and he wondered how the old fellow had ever recovered him. He turned his attention to Margarita who sat, like a statue, staring off at nothing. He could not, at that moment, decide if he loved or hated her, and couldn't help but push her a little, speaking a bit too loudly, first at the other passenger. "How you doin' back there, Miss Lori?" He nodded, and then at the nanny. "How about you, your highness?"

Lori smiled uneasily, snatching a glance at her companion who did not alter her posture. "We're both fine, Francis, thank you."

He turned to Billy. "What's this Rebecca's Place, Billy, one of your line cabins?"

"No, Francis. We're heading to the prettiest little camp you'll ever know. Rebecca's Place is named after Arvel's first wife."

"Did you know her, the late Mrs. Walsh?"

"No, I met Arvel long after his first wife had passed on. Met him in the desert. He spent the night at my camp and then a couple of days later, Chica brought him to me, half dead, brain swellin' after some Apaches tried to rub him out." Billy nodded gravely. "Poor fellow was a mess."

"She's a remarkable lady, Miss Chica, ain't she?" He said it loudly enough to hopefully invoke Margarita's ire. "A loving companion, even if she isn't a highfalutin lady like Mr. Walsh's first wife probably had been." He pulled his hat from his head, wiping his brow. "I mean, with all them books she had, the late Mrs. Walsh must have been a sophisticated lady." He turned again as he lit one of Chica's cigars, blowing smoke over his shoulder in hopes of further annoying Margarita. "What's your opinion on such things, Billy?"

The healer was too crafty to fall into such a trap. He shrugged. "Not my area, Francis. Could not offer you anything of intelligence on the subject, one way or the other, I'm sorry."

"Well, my opinion is, love conquers all. That's what I think, Billy. Don't matter if the two in love are young or old, rich or poor, educated or not." He turned and glared at Margarita. "That's why I think they make a loving couple. You could say, a marriage made in heaven, sure enough, despite all the many differences."

The place was especially beautiful, lush as rainfall and snow had been plentiful over the winter, and the mountain springs feeding the little pool ran with abundance. It even smelled nice there. Clean and fresh and of life.

"You folks take care. This place is a Garden of Eden, replete with snakes. Rattlers like it here, so watch where you walk." He tipped his head to Francis. "You and Miss Margarita'll take the cave." He pointed up the hill a little ways to the restored structure, a home to an Indian family going on a thousand years past. "It's dry in there. You'll find all the comforts of home. I'll put Miss Lori in the cabin."

Francis grinned at the nanny's expression. The prostituta

treated to a proper building while she lived like a savage.

She glared at Francis. "You will *not* stay in there with me. So do not even consider it. You may camp outside." She waved her finger at the bags in the back of the wagon. "Put them inside."

"You carry your own bags, your highness. Ain't a porter on some fancy ship line sailin' off to Havana." He helped Lori down from the wagon and prepared to escort her inside. He smiled as she hid the expression of pain. "How you feelin', sweetheart? You need me to carry you or can you make it by yourself?"

She blushed. "I been better, Francis." She held tightly to his arm. "If'n it's all the same to you, I wouldn't mind if you carried me."

He half smiled, half glared at Margarita. "My pleasure, darlin'." He scooped her up in his arms. "My goodness, Miss Lori, you weigh almost naught. You go on and take hold around my neck, rest your head on my shoulder."

Billy settled her in for a long lie down and by evening resolved to check on her.

"Good evenin', Miss Lori. How'd you sleep?"

"Like a baby, Billy." She stretched, arching her back in a way that, even though the bedspread covered everything, took his breath away.

"I had a good dream." She looked the room over. "This place, you know, the look of it, and the smell of it, reminded me of something and I had a good dream, well, at least, kind of."

Billy smiled as he worked at the foot of her bed, putting things in order. "Tell me."

"When I was a babe, I mean, when I was a little girl, the old woman who took me in, she had a cabin like this, up in Michigan."

"I didn't know you were from Michigan."

"Yes, I think it's why I like sunny places, Billy." She sat up in bed, arranging the covers over her lap. "It weren't a good dream, really, Billy, but I can't rightly explain it. It made me all fluttery for the rememberin' of it." She looked him in the eye. "Have you ever felt so sad that you felt good, Billy?"

She didn't wait for an answer. "The old woman who took me in. I don't even know why, but she did. She was *old,* Billy, and she lived alone. Barely had enough to get by herself, but she, after my pa did what he did to me, she took me in and we were happy sometimes." She fiddled with the pull on her mantilla veil. "She used to take in sewing. That old woman could sew."

"How long were you with her?"

"Oh, not long. It's all kinda cloudy, you know, in my mind. I was pretty young. Can't remember much. Couldn't have been much older than little Rebecca. One winter it was real bad and she used to hold me tight in bed and she was warm. Even though she was scrawny, she was warm. We'd get under about five quilts and she'd hold me and whisper psalms in my ear." Lori smiled. "Her breath stunk. But I didn't care because she was good to me. Anyways, she, bein' so old, she died, right in bed next to me and I didn't know it for a whole day until I woke up and felt her, stiff and cold."

She looked up at Billy. "I laid there with her for another day 'cause it was so cold and I didn't know what to do and then somethin' started bangin' on the door. Bang, bang, bang, it was scary. I thought it was the grim reaper, come to take her and me away. She used to talk about the grim reaper. Said he'd come knockin' on the door for her. She laughed about it and I never did like that too much on account she showed me a picture of it one time. It was a skeleton with one of those grain scythes. Never could figure out what she thought was so funny about that."

She took pills from Billy and a drink of water to swallow them down. "But you know what that bangin' was, Billy? It was a nanny goat the old woman kept. The poor thing was almost as cold as the old woman and hungry and I guess just scared, you know, because no one had come out to it, to the little shed, because of the snow. So, I found it some cereal and fed it and I pulled all them blankets off the bed and put 'em on the floor and that goat got right in that bed with me and she was just like a dog." She looked up and smiled. "Ain't that the strangest thing to remember, Billy? After that, well, when the storm broke, the landlord came checkin' on us and that's when I got put in the orphanage."

She watched Billy work about the neat little cabin. Everything was in order, well maintained, clean, even elegant in its charm. The cat trilled as it rubbed under her mistress's neck. "You must think little of me."

Billy looked up from his work and smiled, realizing she was addressing him and not the cat. "Why would you say that?"

"I don't know. I shouldn't think such a thing with you fussing so over me, but I just feel like I don't belong amongst you good folks."

"I wish you wouldn't feel that way." He wouldn't take his eyes from his work. "I think very much of you."

"How's it you're all so kind?"

Billy shrugged.

"Don't shrug, Billy. I'm a whore. I've known what proper folks think of whores, and yet, you folks don't act that way. I don't understand it."

"I think what you've lived is the last slavery. The last slavery in the whole of the world, what's been done to you, Miss Lori. I don't think little of folks, you know, the Negroes, who were born slaves, so why would I think little of you?"

"What do you mean?"

"Well, you know what slavery is, don't you?"

"Oh, sure, back before the war, when the darkies were like

livestock owned like animals, and President Lincoln set 'em all free." She knitted her brow. "I don't know how that's got to do with me, Billy. No one ever owned me."

"I'd argue differently."

"How?"

"Well, how much money do you have?"

Lori shrugged. "Not much."

"Why not?"

She shrugged again.

"You been at this a long time?"

"Yes."

"I bet since you were a child."

She shrugged up her shoulders. "Thirteen."

"Yet you've got no money."

"Lots of folks work all their life and don't have money."

"Lots of folks *do* work all their life and *do* have lots of money, especially folks without children to raise or a household to maintain. I know an old Chinese gal, took in washing. She washed for twenty years, ended up with enough to buy a boardinghouse. Lives well now. Nice way to spend her dotage."

"Don't understand what you're getting at, Billy."

"Why don't you have any money, Miss Lori?"

"It just, well, everything always cost a lot. You know, the folks who run the houses, you know, it all just cost a lot and then the clothes, the other things, room and board, it all adds up, Billy. I give 'em the money and my cut never amounted to much. And that got spent up." She grinned. "One time I tried keepin' a little, you know, tucked a bit away until the fellow runnin' the place caught me. Beat me pretty bad. I never held out after that." She smiled. "Not worth it."

"Well, that's why I call it the last slavery. And it's not just the fact that you never received your pay. You were, people like you, you're reduced to the realm of objects, like the Negroes. You're not human beings, you're things."

It made her heart all fluttery to hear Billy say that. "Things?"

"Sure. You've been reduced to a commodity. And on top of that, you've had the best years of your life stolen from you. When all the other young girls were being girls, and later young women, flirting with their beaus, planning a future and a family, you were being used up. The flower of your youth plucked and used up and ultimately destroyed. Turned into a thing that was soiled, corrupted, bad in the eyes of society." Billy looked her in the eye. "How many retired whores do you know, Miss Lori, I mean, who aren't worn out, addled, or turned themselves into madams, so that they can continue the cycle on and on? How many?"

She shrugged.

"Well, that's why I call it the last slavery. Damned sorry it happened to you. Damned sorry it happens to anyone, but I guess that's the way of the world. There'll always be folks like you and there'll always be the predators and weak and pathetic men, the johns, who keep it going. Keep feeding it. It's just the way of the world."

"Billy?"

"Yes, Miss Lori."

"There's something more wrong with me than just being cut up, ain't there?"

"Why do you ask that?"

"Well, I've been poorly a while, goin' on a year. I used to bleed a lot, down there you know, and not just when I had my time. I used to, well, after doin' it, it used to hurt a lot and, well, I've been sick. Sick for a long time. And I heard you and Miss Pilar talkin'. I know you were talkin' of me, know you were saying things you didn't want me to hear and I didn't, but, Billy, I ain't stupid, and I ain't a little child, so tell me what's wrong."

He sat on the edge of her bed, twisted a cigarette and offered it to her, which she refused. He lit it and thought for a while. He spoke to the ash growing at the end of his smoke.

"You've got a cancer, Miss Lori. A cancer down there, and well, it's spread in your body. I can feel it when I press on your belly, can hear it when I listen to you with my stethoscope. It's all over your body."

"I see." She fiddled with her veil, spreading it out on her lap. "So, no matter how well you doctor me up, Billy, I'm gonna die soon anyway, ain't I?"

"Hard to say when, but, yes, Miss Lori, you're going to die soon, sooner than you should, I'm sorry to say. Probably in a year or maybe less."

They dined outside, near the pool as it was a glorious evening. Billy was in a good mood, despite breaking the news to Lori. It was a load off his mind and Lori knew it anyway. Talking about it seemed to make the terrible reality less burdensome.

The aborigine finished Pilar's stew. "That is *the best* hotpot I've ever eaten."

"Never heard it called that." Francis picked his teeth, more in a way to annoy Margarita than for any other reason. "Always known it as stew."

Billy laughed at a memory. "My old father called it that. From his country. He was Dutch, you know. Grew up in England, but was born in Holland. He could make the best hotpot from a bit of kangaroo, potatoes, carrots, and yams."

"He the one taught you all that doctoring?"

"Yes, Francis. He went to Australia to make his fortune. Never did, except, well, I guess he got one fortune. He found my mother. She made him happy. And he her." He looked at the quarreling lovers. "I've never seen two people more pleased with each other as were my ma and pa."

"Hotpot." Francis looked at Margarita out of the corner of

his eye. "Sounds like poor people food."

"Oh, well, my old father, he never was a man of means. He was happy but poor. He always said, 'A day late and a dollar short.' That was the story of his life. Always just missing the golden opportunity."

"My old mother made potato soup." Francis smiled at Margarita who was doing her best to not look interested. "My pa, he died in a mine and my ma, she could feed a whole passel of people with a few potatoes and a cup of flour. It was some good eating. She was happy too. Happy and poor, just like *your* father." He glared at Margarita. "I'd take happy and poor over rich and miserable any day. Wouldn't you?"

By dark Francis had a fire going. They sat at the edge of the little pool, soaking their legs in the cold water. Francis moved a little closer to his love, and Margarita too exposed to move away, sat, stiff and immobile as a garden ornament. She was, in a way, once again his captive.

"You know"—the young Ranger pointed at the stars—"that there is my favorite thing about this country, folks. The stars. Sometimes when I'm sleeping rough, I can't help but stay awake all night just watching them. You wait and watch long enough, you see shooting stars. That's a real treat."

Lori considered the expansive sky. "I never paid any mind to 'em. You're right, Francis. It's beautiful." She yawned into the back of her hand. "Wish I could stay up longer to watch 'em, folks, but I'm too tired."

Billy got up to escort her and she held up her hand. "I'm okay, Billy. You go on have a sit for a while. You enjoy your night."

He couldn't be dissuaded, though, and the young couple found themselves alone. Margarita looked about self-consciously. She wanted to stay, yet knew encouraging Francis was unkind. She watched him snuff out his cigarette, strip to his underwear and prepare to go for a swim.

"What are you doing?"

He eased himself into the pool. "Just wadin'. It feels good. Feels good to be cold. My God this water's like ice!" He waded further out. "Then after, you know, when you're all cold and shaking, you get right close to the fire and warm up. Feels good. Ya ought to try it."

He suddenly lost his balance, foundered in the frigid water and called out as he went down. "Margarita, help! Can't swim!" His head went under and came up, bobbing like a cork. He just as quickly went under again. Margarita sprang forward and was immediately in, fully clothed and frantic. He grabbed her up in his arms as he stood upright in the waist-deep water.

She pounded him hard on the shoulder. "You devil!"

He laughed. "Sorry, Mags." He pulled her to his chest, kissing her on the mouth. "Come on Mags, come on, please just stop this."

She broke away and sulked as she waded to the bank, crawling out with difficulty, the soaking skirt and petticoat weighing her down. "Look at my dress! It is ruined!"

"It's only water, you'll dry." He splashed her playfully, soaking her back.

"You are not easy to hate, Francis."

"That's a strange compliment, but I'll take what I can get."

He followed her to the fire, pulling her into his arms again. "I love you, Mags, I love you."

Her eyes fluttered and she was under his spell again. This time he'd make it stick. This time he'd make her commit. He'd *have* to make her commit. "How 'bout if we get outta these wet things, go up and rest in that old cave for a while?"

She smiled. "And perhaps do some other things?" She looked around, searching the dark between them and the Indian dwelling. "I'm afraid of snakes, Francis."

He picked her up, carrying her in his arms. "I'll protect you, darling."

They loved a long time and it was more glorious than he'd imagined. Better than with the widow Jameson, as this congress was with love. Mutual and complete love. Francis was not certain he'd survive it.

Afterward, they rested in each other's arms. She kissed him on the forehead. "You are a good lover, Francis." It was her turn to tease him a little. "Was that your first time?"

He cocked his head to the challenge. "Did I behave like it was, Mags?"

"No." She decided to pry. "Who was she?"

"Who was who?"

"Your first one?"

"It's a secret, Mags."

"Tell me. We should have no secrets between us, Francis. No secrets from now on."

"The widow Jameson."

"Who is she?"

"She's an old woman, lives out on a spread all by herself, well, with a Chinese, but not with anyone else. She was my first."

"An old woman?" She wrinkled her nose.

"Oh, she ain't like an old grandma. I mean, well, she's oldish, but she's beautiful, Mags. Not beautiful like you, but she's beautiful all right. And sweet. She's sweet and kind. She's, well, she's the kind of old woman you don't mind seeing in the flesh, if you get my meaning."

Margarita looked him in the eye, appearing a little wounded. "It sounds as if you love her."

"In a way I guess I do, Mags. Not in the way I love you, but in a way, nonetheless." He ran his fingers through her hair. "She says bible verses during the act."

"Really?"

"Yep."

"What kind?"

"Oh, nothin' I can remember, but I can tell you, Mags, they're real bible verses, just not the kind you'll hear the preacher quote on a Sunday meeting, that's certain."

"Was I *your first,* Mags?"

"What would you say if I said no, Francis?"

He smiled and swallowed hard to quell the pain in his gut. Shrugged. "Who?"

"My husband, Francis."

"Oh." He had a thought. "But you are called señorita."

She began to cry and he held her to his chest. "I was married, Francis, to a wonderful man and had a little son. Porfirio Díaz killed them when he murdered my family." She searched his eyes. "Señora Walsh said I should be a señorita. She said I was too young to be a widow. She thought it would be better for me in el norte."

"I'm sorry, Margarita, I'm so, so sorry." He petted her.

"Oh, Francis. Hold me. Please hold me."

"Now, calm down. Calm yourself, darling. I've got you. I won't let you go."

They slept until a little after three, awoke and made love again. Francis could not help himself. "Does this mean you'll start being nice to me, again?"

She rubbed her eyes with her palms. "Can we just live one day at a time, Francis? I cannot calm my mind long enough to know what I want anymore." She cried again. "I am so sad all the time. I am sad to have nothing and I'm sad because of the good people of the Walsh family"—she turned and kissed him—"and because of you, because of your kindness . . . , it should make me less sad, but it only makes me feel worse. I love and hate all of you so much."

"Why?"

She sat up, found a nightgown and put it on. She paced about until he beckoned her to sit down. He held her hands, kept her from fidgeting.

"I do not know how to make sense of it, do not know how to explain it, Francis. When I am happy, it makes me sad and guilty because I am not remembering them, not grieving for them, and you make me forget my hatred for the bastard."

"I think I understand, Mags." He lit a cigarette and blew smoke at the cave ceiling. "But, Mags, tell me something, your husband, your little son, your ma and pa, would they like you to be unhappy?"

"No, Francis."

"Would they like you to be eaten up trying to avenge them?" He shrugged. "Which, by the way, is, I think, the stupidest idea I ever heard of, and trust me, Mags, I've seen and been in on some real hare-brained ideas in my time."

"Why is it stupid?"

"How long has this old boy been in power? I mean, did all this just happen, or has he been at it a while?"

"No, it did not just happen, Francis. Many years, many years he has tortured my Mexico, since I was a child."

Francis shrugged. "So, there's your answer. All these years he's been allowed to run roughshod over your country, your people, and now a twenty-year-old widow with nothing to her name is going to waltz in to his office and put a bullet through his brain?"

"It could happen."

"Yeah, and winged pigs could fly out of my backside!"

He was pleased to make her smile a little.

"No it couldn't! Don't you think a bastard like that's created a lot more enemies than just you over time? Don't you think a man like that knows how to protect himself? Jesus, Mags, he's probably surrounded by guards." He had a thought. "And on top of that, I don't want you to go killin' anybody."

"Why not?"

"You once asked me if I've ever killed a man. Well, I have." His color faded and he ran his trembling fingers through his hair. "On my way west, found myself on a riverboat, you know, working for my passage as a stoker. We were down in the boilers, and there was this one fellow. He was big as a mountain and stupid as they come. He picked on me, you know, me being kind of smallish and from back East, and well, you might not know this, Mags, but I can be kinda smart-alecky, especially with bullies. Anyway, this fellow lost his temper with my teasing and he wanted to thump me, and one thing led to another, and then there was more than fists and I shoved a blade into his liver. Killed him dead."

Tears ran down Francis's face as he looked into those beautiful brown eyes. "When we were fightin', Mags, I was all fury. I was like a wild animal and then, when he was dying, all I could see was the fear in his dying eyes. I don't ever want to see that again." He rubbed his cheeks dry with the palms of his hands. He pulled her onto his lap and breathed in the scent of her hair. "Certainly don't want you to see it. Don't want you to know that, Mags. It's an ugly, ugly thing to know that, have that hangin' over you for all your life, even if the man you kill deserves it. Don't want that for you, Margarita. Don't want you to ever know any of that."

She let him hold her, let him comfort her.

"I have nothing, Francis."

"Yes, you do. You have the memory of a loving husband and baby and your folks. You have the Walshes, and if you let me in, you have me." He smiled. "You've got the prospect of a future, Mags. You've got your brains and your education and a good heart and your youth. You've got me and I know I'm no genius, not refined or educated, but that's not all there is.

"I'm ambitious, Mags, I'll do what you want, be what you want, we could start our own operation, we could do anything! The whole world is wide open to us, and I swear, I'll be a good husband. I'll run a ranch, get a job, work in a factory, do whatever you want, just as long as you let me in your life. I swear, Mags, I swear."

"You make it sound so easy."

"Well, it *is* easy, if your first goal in life is to be happy. Hell, being happy is more important than anything else."

"It does not pay bills."

"Depends on the bills. You think being rich again is going to make you happy, Mags? Hell, I knew this one rich family, from my hometown. They ran a tanning factory. Richest people in the whole county. All stunk like rotting flesh. They even had a box in the church, you know, with their name on it. Big brass plate with their name engraved fancy like. Hell, they didn't need to put their name on it. No one ever wanted to sit in that box. Most folks didn't even want to sit downwind of them. Damn stench of stinkin' hides leeched right into the wood of those church pews. Plain disgusting. And dull! They were the dullest people I've ever known. *And* miserable. They were the most unhappy people I ever met.

"No, I wouldn't trade being them for all the wealth they had. Not by a long ways I wouldn't." He held up a hand. "Not that I'd shy away from money, Mags. But, maybe if we get the happy part figured out first, the wealth might come after. Might come and then you can live like your proper station in life. Teach me to talk smart, educate me, dress me like a gentlemen. Hell you can do with me what you want. Ain't stupid, Mags, just rough! Like a diamond you pluck from the ground, just need polishing, Mags. I swear, I just need polishing." He kissed her on the forehead. "I am like wet clay in your hands. You mold me into whatever you want."

He was up early as he had dreamed again of Dobbs and could not lie in the cave any longer. Billy joined him as Francis put a pot of coffee on the fire.

"How'd you sleep, mate?" Billy eyed the camp and saw no sleeping bag. He patted Francis on the shoulder. "You two patched things up I see."

"We did, Billy, we did." Francis felt a little happy talking about it.

The ladies slept late and they had a good morning doing nothing. Billy found some fishing tackle in the cabin and they pulled some fat trout from the floor of the deep pool. They worked together on cleaning them for supper.

"I'm damned disappointed in old Hugh Harvey, Billy."

The aborigine shrugged. Billy had given up a long time ago expecting much from his fellow man. Hugh Harvey had been brave just coming out to warn them. It was too much to expect him to stay around. He wasn't surprised he'd disappeared. "Where do you suppose he went?"

"Beats the hell outta me, Billy. Probably the nearest saloon, crawl into a bottle, damn his weakness."

"Well, you never know. He might surprise us all. You never know about men like that."

"Well, if he's anything like my pa, he won't surprise me at all."

Francis stood, knocking the dust from the seat of his trousers. "Well, might just as well do some hunting. I've hauled water, hauled firewood, caught every snake and scorpion, even one Gila monster within three hundred yards and took 'em to a new home, on account Mags doesn't like creepy crawlies. Now I've caught trout. I'm about bored to distraction, Billy." He looked off in the direction of the Walsh ranch. "I hate being out here when I know the folks back at the spread might need help fightin'."

"Wouldn't mind some deer for Lori, Francis. The child needs red meat." He nodded. "Go on, do some hunting, mate. I'll watch over them."

CHAPTER 17

Craster dug a grave next to the Apache. He left Sam in the cave to collect the rest of the prospector's effects. When he'd finished, he wandered back, dog in tow. It looked like the animal had already found a new master.

"How's it goin', Sam?"

"Oh, al—alright, boss." Sam wiped his cheeks dry. The heatstroke and the bandit attack, and now this business with Pike had overwhelmed him. He recovered and held out some papers he'd found in Pike's old clothes trunk. "He, he had a si—sister, boss. Last letter, just this pa—past August."

Craster walked up on his man, patting him on the shoulder. "Good find, friend, we'll collect his traps and sell what's of value, send what we make off it to his sister."

"A—and the booty from the bandits, boss. I—if'n you don't object. L—like her to have it, don—don't want that blood money. Don't want no—nothin' to do with it."

"Well, that's fine, Sam. We'll sell it all and send it to Pike's sister. We'll give it all to her except the gold, we'll turn that into the law, sure someone's missing it somewhere. If there's any reward, well, we'll send that on to her as well."

He looked about. It was sad to see that the homey place would soon be abandoned. "We'll leave the stove. To tell the truth, my back's about worn out, Sam, from crouchin' in that cage so long. Doubt we'd get too much for it anyways. But we can take the rest."

Sam looked at Craster a little less despondently now. He motioned to his boss. "I—I f—found a nice blanket to wrap him in, boss. Y—you want to ca—carry him out, I'm ready."

"Okay, Sam."

They did and Craster read over the prospector. He looked up at Sam and then the dog and then at the Apache's grave. "I'm glad we were able to place 'em side by side, Sam. Hope, well, maybe they're together now."

They no sooner patted the grave mound flat when a call from a distance got their attention.

Arvel rode up first. "Robert Craster and company, I presume." He looked the fresh grave over. "Who'd you plant?"

They watched the company move in. "You must be the Rangers."

"We are, lad, we are."

"This was Stanley Pike. He saved us from that animal cage." He nodded behind him. "This is his digs. We've been staying here while Sam recuperated from the sun."

"What happened to him?"

"Bandits. Shot him in the ass. Got blood poison, couldn't make it."

"I'm mighty sorry to hear that."

They shared a meal around Pike's fire ring as the Rangers interrogated the survivors. Dick Welles spoke as Dan George wrote all down.

"So, there was just two who'd taken you into the desert."

"Yes, sir, and according to Pike they're dead. Blown up."

Arvel interjected, "Yeah." He nodded at John Stokes and Pablo de Santis. "We know about that. What of the dude, the one with the loud checkered suit?"

"Oh, haven't seen him since he come into the office, Captain. They whacked us on the head and threw us in that cage, but that's the last I seen of him. Just those two brutes who took us for the one-way trip to kingdom come. Looks like they got it the other way around."

Dick nodded. "Got to be in Tampico with Damian Gold. Only place that makes sense, Arvel."

Walsh looked around at his surroundings. "This is a dandy home."

"It was." Craster felt the regret welling up in the pit of his gut. "Should have seen it before we moved all into the wagons. It was right homey, wasn't it, Sam?"

"I—it sure w—was, boss."

"Captain, we're planning on selling what was of value, send the money to Pike's sister. Seems the only family he had left." He pointed to the cave entrance. "We also got some things from the Mexicans we killed. All the same to you, we were going to sell that too for Pike's sister, all except the gold. Imagine there's word out that it's missing. We'll turn that in to you gents, any reward, you can forward it on."

Arvel shrugged, looking at Dick for approval. "Don't see any harm, as long as anything stolen can't be traced back the rightful owners."

"No, sir, they did have money, mostly in pesos, some American, and their traps and horses, you all look it over. Don't want any part of profiting from another man's loss."

Sam stood up uneasily.

Arvel worried over his condition. "You boys going to be all right riding out on your own? We can send some men to escort you. Who knows how many of Gold Hat's men are still lurking about, though, between us, I'd say we pared them down considerably."

"No, Captain. You keep your force intact. We'll be all right, won't we, Sam? Need to be getting back, lost enough time from my business." He checked Sam's reaction. "Both of us need to get back to work as soon as practicable."

"Sorry to say, Mr. Craster. The blackhearts burned you out."

"Oh."

"Yes, but we're heading down to Tampico."

"Isn't that a little dicey? American lawmen going down to Mexico? Don't mean to tell you your business, Mr. Walsh, but is that even legal?"

Dick smiled. "Arvel doesn't worry over such trifles, Mr. Craster."

Arvel replied. "We'll see what we can do to make it right." He winked. "This bastard Gold, I mean our Gold, not Sombrero del Oro, well, the son of a bitch has lots of cash. We might very well get you enough to rebuild and then some. Least we could do to ease your suffering."

Chapter 18

"How you doing, old girl?" She'd finished praying and worked the big sack of a nightgown over her head. It brought a thrill to his heart whenever she'd do that.

They loved and rested afterward.

"When will they be here, Roberto?"

"Daylight." He looked at the clock on the wall. "Another eight hours, I guess."

"We have good friends."

"That we do, darling. Those bastards can't go to the jakes without someone knowing about it."

"Tomorrow, when there is fighting, please, Roberto, stay close to the cellar. Stay close so that I can hear you shoot." She pressed her eyelids to keep from crying.

"I will, old girl. You don't worry, they'll never get to you and little Rebecca. I promise."

"Where is Maria?"

"Preparing. She'll fight ahorse. She'll ambush them out on the rise. She'll kill as many as she can with her fancy rifle, then ride amongst them." He laughed. "Probably won't be any left for us, time she's through whittling them down." He sat up and found his cigarettes. Thought better of lighting up. "I kind of feel sorry for the poor bastards."

"Go to her, Roberto. Go and be with her. I worry over her. You know I love her?"

"I know you do, old girl. We all love Chica, no doubt." He kissed her on the forehead. "And Chica loves you, old girl."

He waited for her to finish her Act of Contrition at a little alter she'd set up a while back next to the stable office for the men. She smiled at him as she finished preparing.

He handed her a basket. "Pilar made you something to eat while you wait."

She looked through it and smiled. She'd not eat. She smoked only cigars before battle. "Do you remember the first time we met, Uncle Bob? Pilar made me and Arvel such a basket to take up to Rebecca Place."

"I remember."

"It was chicken. Arvel thought it might have been poisoned. He wanted to know if I planned to kill Pilar because she called me a whore."

She hung the bandoliers on her tiny shoulders, then fastened the gun belt. She pulled her knife, checking the edge for sharpness.

She kissed Bob on the cheek. "You take care of them, Uncle Bob." Chica suppressed an urge to cry. "Take care of my little one. Make certain she does not go too soon to God."

He watched her mount Alanza and gave the mare a loving pat on the neck. "You girls give 'em hell." He suddenly looked fierce, hateful, speaking between clenched teeth. "Kill 'em all, Chica. Kill every goddamned one of 'em. Just kill 'em all."

The news finally came, and, though, inevitable, it still weighed heavily on Francis's mind. Dobbs had done something to him. And, though it was irrational, the young man could not help but become literally scared out of his wits whenever the bastard came to mind. The experience reminded him of a story once told to him by an old-timer, Pep Young, a war veteran who'd become Francis's friend after his father had died in the mine.

Pep was in the worst of it, fighting for the north with the Eleventh. He'd survived Second Bull Run, Antietam, Chancellorsville, and Gettysburg. The old fellow found, in Francis, a kind and understanding soul, and subsequently, he was not afraid to share with the lad, that, by the fourth battle, he was terrified. Had even once bolted and turned tail. Francis remembered when Pep held up the stump where his right arm used to be and said losing it was the best thing to ever happen in his life. It got him off the line. It was something, an admission a lesser man would want to take to his grave, but he told Francis. It seemed to do him good. A catharsis of sorts, and Francis never wavered in his loyalty and high opinion of his friend.

Now Francis thought he understood how the old soldier must have felt. The thought of Dobbs terrified him and this was silly, downright ridiculous, as Francis was younger, stronger, tougher, a better shot, and a better fighter in general than was Dobbs. The reality was that Dobbs had gotten the upper hand. But it didn't matter. He worried over how he'd behave, how he'd perform if Dobbs rode into the camp. He didn't know what he'd do at the moment of truth and it worried him.

The cabin being the most conspicuous structure, they resolved to hide out in the cave dwelling. It was a good plan, as the structure was a fortress, and it would be unlikely for anyone not familiar with the place to take notice of it. Perhaps they could survive by hiding.

Francis would keep vigil outside, high on a ledge that afforded concealment and a commanding view of the road from the ranch. He pulled on his bandoliers, grabbed his Winchester and hat. He kissed Margarita on the temple with a reassuring smile.

"You stay in here. Anyone comes in who's not me, you shoot.

And if it is me, I'll say a code. *Yankee Doodle.* If I don't say that, you shoot to kill, and I mean me too, 'cause it'll mean I've got company."

Margarita wandered out into the night. Lying down beside him.

"Can't sleep?" He pulled her close, covering her tiny shoulders with his arm.

"The prostituta is snoring."

"She's gotta name, Mags."

"I'm sorry." She pressed herself against him. "Let's not fight, Francis. Please, let's not fight."

She turned onto her back and stared at the stars. He joined her.

"Give me your hand, Mags."

He held it and kissed her palm. "You got the prettiest, softest hands I've ever felt."

"Thank you." She looked him in the eye. "You are trembling, Francis."

"Oh, it's nothin'."

She worried over him. "It's not cold tonight. Are you not well?"

"Maybe something I ate, Mags." He lied. He couldn't get the image of Dobbs out of his mind. Her attention brightened his mood. "You act like you're a little worried over me."

"I am."

"Do you love me, Mags?"

"I do, Francis." She fell back onto the blanket next to him. "Tell me about our future, Francis."

"Oh, okay." He played with her fingers as he gazed into the heavens. "First, once we get this reward money, we're going to start our own place." He turned and looked at her. "If that's what you want, at least. What do you folks call it down there in your home country, a hacienda, right?"

"Yes, Francis, the house and plantation, or ranch if that is what we will have is called the hacienda, and you would be known as the hacendado." She hugged him. "And yes, that is what I want."

"Well, we're going to have a hacienda, and a grand one, in the Mexican style, if that's what you want. We're going to raise cattle and sheep."

"That is what my family had, Francis."

"I know."

"How?"

"Don't worry how I know, I just know."

"You've been talking to the Walshes about me."

"I have." He looked to check her expression. "That don't vex you, does it?"

"No, Francis." She pressed her head to his chest. "It does not bother me."

"Well, then, once we get established, we'll take the money we make and we're going to invest it, like proper rich people do."

"In what?"

"Oh, all sorts of things. I been talkin' to Uncle Bob. He says Captain Walsh has connections, he and his mother back East in Maryland. They're proper rich folks and they know all about investing in stocks and bonds and the railroad and now what they call communications. You know, the telephone and electricity. It's soon to be a whole new century, Mags, and lots of new things on the horizon. Pretty soon there'll be no reason to even own oil lamps. The whole doggone world'll be lit up with electric lights."

She was pleased. Dreaming about these things with Francis made her happy. He would be good enough for her and, for the first time in her life, Margarita had a new thought. The thought that she could be good enough for another. She could be, would be, good enough for Francis.

He turned to see movement and pulled Margarita close. "Look there, Mags, can you see her?"

A young vixen had returned to her den with a rabbit nearly as large as the diminutive mother. "She's called a kit fox, least that's what Billy Livingston told me. I been watchin' her since we got here. Beautiful. ain't she?"

"We call them *zorra del desierto,* Francis."

"Really, Mags? That's a lot prettier sounding than kit fox, I'd say." He kissed her. "But then again, words always sound prettier coming from you, Mags. Especially the Mexican ones."

"The Indians are very respectful of the kit fox, Francis. She is intelligent and she is never harmed or eaten. She is the good fox, not like the gray fox who is a fool, a trickster who should never be trusted." She watched the babies appear and help the mother break the rabbit down. "This little one is to be revered." She kissed Francis on the cheek. "Perhaps seeing her, having her nearby, with us, is a good omen."

"Hope so, Mags." He turned and kissed her on the mouth. "I sure hope so."

Chica watched the night pass and could see the entire valley between them and Tombstone. She thought about everything that had happened since that fateful night. That night, not unlike this night, when she rode up to the mule ranch in the dark, watched Arvel asleep in his bed and ultimately had the courage to seduce him. It was the greatest, most pivotal moment of her life.

She thought about her darling baby, now lying comfortably, safely in the cellar. Pilar would have sung her to sleep. Her womb tightened and her breasts ached, not unlike when she'd been nursing and her little one would cry. This is how she felt now, at the thought of her baby. Her second baby. Rosario was her first. She thought back to that time in her life, so long ago when she was young and a little happy sometimes. The old man who taught her cards and what a good man was and how to not hate and the old woman who taught her compassion and patience.

She remembered Crisanto, her first lover and the first one to come completely under her spell. She'd teased him, told him she'd marry him if he captured the most beautiful wild horse of the land. It killed him to try and she regretted that. But how was she to know? She didn't and never would play such a trick if she'd known it would turn out in such a way. Never thought the boy would seriously try something so bold and reckless.

She thought about the old priest who was good to her and wondered how he was. Hoped he was well. She remembered the old priest's lover, the ancient nun they'd visited in Mexico City and how heartbroken he was because she'd chosen the church over him. The nun was she and the priest was poor Crisanto. At least Crisanto was not burdened by a lifetime of longing, a lifetime of suffering for the unrequited love. She'd given him the best gift she could, nearly at the moment of his death, and she'd have given him a child, had she not been too young. She wondered at all the sadness in the world and worked on her cigar.

But now she was not sad, thanks to her Arvel and her family. Thanks to her baby and all the good people of the land who made her feel loved. The thought of the bad gang coming to hurt them infuriated her and she had trouble calming herself. She did not like to be angry in battle. It betrayed her mind and reflexes. Fighting with fury was not a good thing and she swallowed hard, pushing the anger away. She'd be logical in battle. There would be no hate or malice or cruelty or joy. She'd act like a surgeon cutting out a festering cancer.

She lit another cigar from her stub, looked up at Alanza dozing in the moonlight. She remembered the day Uncle Alejandro gave her such a wonderful gift. She thought about all the good people, her neighbors, now spies, all of one purpose, to protect the people of the Walsh ranch. She took another deep breath, remembering what she was told. More than thirty of the worst devils anyone could conjure in the bad places of the land. Many would be men from the evil Sombrero del Oro's gang, and she knew well enough what kind of malice they were capable of serving up.

Thirty bad men and she would make the first assault. She checked the fancy rifle she'd stolen from the American colonel. Colonel Gibbs, the man she'd run through the worst of the Sonoran desert. He'd given her a gold watch as tribute. She looked through the scope, carefully opened the bolt to check that it was loaded properly. She thought of the laird.

Shock. That's what he called it. The wild Scottish men. Now she was the shock and they'd never know what hit them once she started firing. She played out the attack in her mind as if rehearsing a play. Two hundred yards away the road narrowed, framed by steep hills. It would force them to bunch up. She'd kill at least three there. She could fire and work the bolt and not have to move the rifle much as the targets would be close together. That would leave twenty-seven.

They'd realize they were under attack, likely bolt forward, to get past the narrow part, closing the distance between she and them. Then they'd spread out, offer fewer targets. If they weren't cowards, they'd ride to her smoke, at least if it were daylight enough. She'd kill a couple more then. Twenty-five.

She suddenly had an epiphany and smiled at Alanza, awaking her horse with her new idea.

"I know just what to do, my Alanza." She laughed a smoky laugh. "I know exactly what to do."

★ ★ ★ ★ ★

The lead bandit dropped and they knew they were under attack. More shots and three more lay dead. Dobbs shouted orders as the gang broke from the confines of the narrow road. They could not locate the shooter as it was still too dark.

Suddenly she was amongst them. A Mexican beauty bareback and naked, the bandoliers doing little to obscure her womanly charms. It had the desired effect as bandits sat ahorse, dumbfounded. They did not know whether to lust for her or kill her and, with jaws agape, froze into inactivity like lambs to slaughter. But they soon learned to fear her as she rode, like lightning, in a great arc around them, her Winchester barking flame as man after man was cut down.

Two broke south and she watched them for a moment as she traded the empty Winchester for her Schofields. She'd have to run them down and kill them. She'd take no prisoners and could not risk letting them flee or flank her as she continued her attack toward home.

A bullet passed her ear with a buzz and she turned long enough to see Adulio Sanchez riding next to the city man with the plaid suit. The very man they'd been warned about. They were riding full out toward her ranch.

She called after them. "I should have killed you when I had the chance, Adulio. I will get you yet, bastard."

She'd dropped ten of them before they'd gotten free of her, but delayed following up the rest long enough to finish the two fleeing Mexicans. She rode up close, so close she could see the whiskers on their cheeks. They fired wildly and she let them, awaiting patiently the empty click, click, click of hammers on spent primers. Both of the bandits' six-shooters were now empty.

She was between them, casually galloping along as if they were riding a Sunday race, each man doing his best to quirt his horse into full gallop, but all for naught. She was better mounted, light on her Alanza who could not be bested. She smiled and this unnerved them further.

She called out. "I think you are in a lot of trouble, muchachos." Arms extended, like Jesus on the cross, she fired both pistols simultaneously. They crumpled. Chica wheeled for home.

She laughed out loud at the memory of the astonished men. Nudity in battle was most certainly a novelty in the Arizona land. It worked better than she could have hoped. As she loaded her six-shooters, she squeezed Alanza between her thighs. She bent down, kissing her mane. "You did well, darling. Thank you."

She lit another cigar as she watched the battered gang move toward her home. Her Winchester now loaded, she followed, hoping to kill a few more before they would arrive.

Uncle Bob stood dumbfounded as she rode up on him. Dead men littered the ground. The Walsh ranch hands dispatching them in little more than a minute. It was a slaughter.

He averted his eyes. "Is there a reason you're wearing naught more than your birthday suit, Chica?"

She ignored him. "Where is Adulio Sanchez?" She searched the ground around them. "And the man with the checkered suit?"

"Who?"

"Adulio, you remember, he worked for us last winter. We run him off, Uncle Bob. I should have killed him then, but Arvel would not let me. He let him go. He was with the city man in the checkered suit just now. They are not here among the dead! They must be still alive."

"No, child, no. Come on down now, they're all dead, Chica, they're all dead. Come now, come inside."

She kicked Alanza hard. "No, they are not, Uncle Bob, Adulio knows of Rebecca Place!"

"Chica wait! Just a moment. Wait!"

She stopped. "What is it, Uncle Bob?"

"Just hold on!" He ran to the house, was gone momentarily and emerged with one of her cotton dresses, a straw sombrero and her old worn army boots. "Put these on, girl! You'll get sunburn, sure as hell."

She rode hard north, dressing as she galloped her girl.

Francis watched the riders make their way to the cabin. They paid no mind to the cave, as he predicted. He had them cold as he worked his way silently along the ridgeline. He'd let them dismount and then he'd take them.

He called out to Dobbs as Sanchez stepped from his stirrup. "How's the finger, partner?"

Dobbs smiled. "Why don't you come down here and find out?"

He pointed his Winchester at the Mexican's head. "You go on and step from your mount, son, then drop your gun belt." He nodded to Dobbs. "Thanks all the same, but I'll stay right here where I can put a bullet between your beady damned eyes if you make it necessary."

Francis was pleased. Facing Dobbs was not as intimidating as his wandering mind made it seem. "You, go on and put your hands up high, you monkey-faced bastard."

Dobbs complied as he turned his mouth up into a greasy smile, nodding in the direction behind Francis. "One thing I'll say. You've got some pretty damned whores in this territory."

Francis turned to his lover. "Go on back to camp, Mags. I got this. Go on, wait for me with Billy Livingston."

"No you do not, Francis." She pointed her Winchester at the men. "Kill them! Kill them both!"

Sanchez raised his arms skyward, screaming in terror, "No, señorita, lo siento mucho, no. *Por favor,* no!"

"It's for the law to handle, Mags. I got 'em, no need to kill anybody. Now go on."

"I will not, Francis." She cocked the Winchester, planting the stock in her tiny shoulder. "They must die. They will try tricks and they will kill you, kill us if they can. It is better to shoot them dead now, Francis. Shoot them dead now." She took up the slack on the trigger as she found her mark.

"No, Mags, no!" He turned toward her, giving the men enough time. Three guns fired simultaneously, Sanchez crumpled, a ball to the chest. Margarita was down. Francis felt the searing pain burn his guts as if he'd fallen into the center of smithy's forge.

He jerked the trigger, once at Dobbs, delivering a slug to the head and again at Sanchez who'd by now regained his saddle. The Mexican bolted over a rise and was gone, holding his bleeding thigh.

He carried her to the Indian dwelling, screaming "Yankee Doodle" all the way. Margarita smiled then licked her lips to clear the blood. "I'm sorry, Francis. I'm sorry. Please forgive me, please, my love, please."

"Shush, Mags!" He cried out. "Billy! Billy! Help us, for Christ's sake, help us!"

The aborigine took her from Francis and laid her down. Francis brushed the tears from her cheeks, holding desperately to her breast, covering the terrible wound with the palm of his hand.

Billy surveyed the wounds and knew it was only a matter of time, minutes perhaps, and there was not a thing he could do about it. He helped Francis as the poor fellow was a dead man walking and didn't know it. It was clear enough to Billy, he'd been liver shot. He nodded. "Go, Francis. Lie down with her. Hold her, mate." He pressed a hand to the lad's forehead. "Both of you, hold on to each other and rest a while."

He looked at Lori, worry and despair consuming her. She

knew as well. Her eyes darted to the cave entrance, giving Billy a questioning shrug.

"Are any still out there, Francis?"

The lad pulled himself from his lover's grasp. "I, I don't know, Billy. One ran off, leaking a good bit a blood. Dobbs is dead. I shot him in the gourd sure enough. I think that's all there was."

The Ranger returned his attention to Margarita who offered a weak smile.

"Hold me, Francis. I'm so cold. Please hold me. Please hold me, my love."

"I'll hold you, Mags. Not goin' anywhere, sweetheart. Not goin' anywhere, darling."

Her eyes moved to Lori. She smiled. "May I have a drink of water, señorita? I'm so thirsty."

She checked with Billy. He nodded. Lori ladled a cupful. "Sure, sure. Got some nice fresh water from the spring. Still cool."

She left them alone together, following Billy into the stark sunlight of a beautiful Arizona morning. He loaded the double and nodded. "You wait here, Miss Lori. I'll be back." He pulled his six-shooter, handing it over. "You know how to use this?"

"I do, Billy." She cradled it, as if the weight was too much to endure.

"All right, Miss Lori." He winked. "Stay put. I'll be right back."

She did and listened to the lovers say their last good-byes. It broke her heart. Why was there so much sadness and cruelty in the world? Why did it have to be them?

"Francis?"

"Yes, Margarita?"

"I love you."

"I know you do, Margarita. I know you do." He smiled and

did his best not to cry. He brushed the hair from her forehead, running his fingers through her raven locks. He now had difficulty seeing her, as he was losing sight in his good eye. "You are the most beautiful thing I've ever known, Margarita. You're the most beautiful thing I've ever known."

"I wish I could have had your baby."

"Maybe you still can."

She winced and tried to move away from the pain. "Maybe in heaven." With shaking hands she pulled the bloody scapular from around her neck, pressing it to Francis's breast. "Maybe in heaven, my love." She squeezed him tight, drawing him as close as the pain would allow. "Oh, Dios, I am so very cold. Hold me, my Francis, hold me."

Dobbs peered into the mirror in the little cabin at the crease across his forehead and not even the sight of brain matter could melt his icy cold countenance. Had Francis's shot been a little truer, he'd certainly be on his way to hell. He turned to face the aborigine pointing the double at his abdomen. Dobbs was impressive as he seemed unconcerned over his predicament.

"What do we do now?"

Billy lit a smoke as he motioned with the muzzle of the shotgun for the blackheart to move outside. Dobbs complied.

"Now what?"

"Shut your mouth."

"Don't forget your place, nigger."

"I said, shut your mouth." He blew smoke skyward. "Speak again and I'll knock every one of your goddamned teeth out with the butt of this shotgun." He pointed to the corral and again Dobbs complied.

He spoke over his shoulder as he walked. "You think you're going to take me in, nigger, you're out of your mind."

"I don't think I'm taking you in, mate. I'm just gettin' you close enough to a wagon so's I don't have to drag your filthy worthless carcass any further than required."

Dobbs stopped, turned to face his captor. He'd not make it easy for Billy Livingston.

The aborigine pulled the trigger on the left barrel and Dobbs's knee came apart, dropping him with a thud onto the hard desert ground. He screamed in agony.

"That's for Margarita, mate. Hurts, doesn't it?"

He finished his cigarette as Dobbs writhed about. The tough went for his six-shooter, and Billy kicked him hard in the hand. "The next one's for Francis, and'll be in the guts. And, just to set things right. I'm not a nigger, I'm an aborigine, *and* half Dutch."

Billy wheeled at the sound of horse hooves.

"Do not worry, Billy. It is just I."

"Chica! Glad to see you're all right."

"So this is the bastard called Dobbs."

"What's left of him."

"Good shooting, Billy"—she stuck a fresh cigar in his mouth—"though I cannot see how you could miss at such a distance with a shotgun. How are the others?"

"Francis and Margarita are dead by now, Chica." He pointed at the cave. "Miss Lori's fine."

"I am sorry, Billy. They should have been married. They should have been together for life. That was my plan, to keep them out here, safe and . . ." She wheeled. "It would have all worked if not for the devil Sanchez."

"Chica, there's one left, a Mexican. Francis shot him but he rode off." He nodded to the tracks heading south.

"I know who that is, Billy. Dios help him when I catch him up."

She didn't have far to travel and when she came upon him, Sanchez was doing his best to stay out of the sun, his horse lying beside him with one of Francis's thirty-thirty bullets in its gut. The Mexican looked up at her through weary eyes.

"Ola, Señora Walsh."

"Ola, Adulio." She dismounted and lit a cigar, lit another and pushed it into the bandit's mouth.

"Muchas gracias, señora." He looked at the glowing tip as he blew smoke. "Muy bien."

"De nada."

He smoked and winced when he tried to move. He waited.

"Are you hit bad?"

"*Sí*. Two times, the girl shot me in the lung and the boy in the thigh."

She sat across from him, Indian style. "Why did you do this stupid thing?"

Adulio shrugged. "Why does anyone do anything that is stupid and evil, mistress?"

"But, Adulio, you know me, you know my family. How could you think that you could possibly come to our home and kill us? Not with one hundred men could you do this thing, and you had no more than thirty."

Adulio shrugged. "The money was too good to pass up."

"How did you know the prostituta was at Rebecca Place?"

"Oh, just a good guess. Or maybe not such a guess. Do you remember, señora, when I first started working for you? You had me come with you to this place to clear away the snakes, in preparation for a camp out with your little girl, before I angered you and you fired me. You said that it was the best place to hide and to take a stand." Adulio shrugged. "I just thought it would be where you would hide the girl. The gringo Dobbs knew she was here because of el gato. He knew that Dick Welles would not be bothered with a cat unless the girl was alive." He had a thought. "Where is the gringo Dobbs now? I saw him fall, but he is a wily one."

"He is dead, Adulio. With his guts scattered over the desert."

"Good." Adulio spit a great wad of bloody phlegm. "He was a rotten bastard. I really did hate him."

"But you loved his money."

"I guess so, señora, I guess so."

Chica took a long drag on her cigar. "A lot of good the devil's gold will do you now." She stood, dusting her dress clean of sand. "Do you want a bullet or the blade?"

"I'd prefer neither, mistress." He smiled bashfully and winked. "Maybe you could, perhaps take me to a doctor?"

"Maybe I could perhaps leave you here to rot in the sun with the scorpions and snakes." She stood, folding her arms, impatiently shifting her weight from one foot to the other. "What shall it be, Adulio? The bullet or the blade? Do not make me angry, or I may start cutting things that will not kill you right away."

"Oh, the bullet, señora. The bullet, muchas gracias." He had another thought. "Señora?"

"Yes, Adulio?"

"It was never personal. Know this. It was never personal."

She cocked her piece, pointing at the bandit's forehead. "With me, it is always personal, dear Adulio. Know this. With me, it is *always* personal. I guarantee you that."

Chapter 19

It was Dick's idea to make a beeline from the hermit's camp to the nearest good port on the Gulf. They'd take a steamer from there to Tampico and settle everything once and for all with the black-hearted Gold family.

They arrived in Port Isabel by late afternoon, locating themselves at a well-ordered establishment backing up to the ocean basin. A nice breeze cooled the place. The saloon was patronized, it seemed, exclusively by old men.

Everyone, especially Arvel, was in a jovial mood, despite his inability to contact Chica and Uncle Bob. Neither Mr. Bell's invention nor the telegraph would cooperate. He'd have to wait, likely until their arrival in Mexico to check in and let them know their progress.

He liked Texas, more so when he was playing at rangering as so many of the citizens of the less-traveled places, such as the one they were in now, did not much care for men of authority. The proprietor did not disappoint, and soon Arvel was annoying the gruff barkeep with his ubiquitous Cheshire cat smile.

He'd put Ranger badges on every one of them, even the laird who was so pleased he had to borrow a Winchester from one of the men and have his photograph taken to memorialize the event. He was more proud of that star than any family crest or emblem bestowed upon all of the ancestors from home.

Arvel grinned at the barman as he looked the place over. It was decorated in boxing motif, as the proprietor was an enthusiast of the sport. Every bit of wall space was covered in photographs and posters. Gloves of varying weights and sizes hung from ceiling hooks.

"Boxing enthusiast, are you?"

The barman, stone-faced, responded. "How did you guess?"

Dick interjected, "He's a detective."

The bartender either ignored or did not understand the irony. He looked askance at the entourage, muttering under his breath.

Arvel deemed him a nitwit and decided to have some fun. "What's that?"

He nodded. "Nothin'."

"Oh, it was *something.*" He peered down at his lapel as it was the object of the man's derisive gaze. "Oh, I see. You're admiring our stars."

"More Ranger nonsense. Ain't it enough we have the bastard Texas Rangers pokin' their noses in our business, what we need with a bunch of the same from Arizona?" He huffed. "Wait till Bryan wins, you boys'll be hocking those tin stars then, once your Republican bosses are run outta Arizona. That'll be a day for celebration, no doubt."

Arvel smiled. "Well now, we've got a man educated in the politics of our home territory, gents, at least in the most rudimentary fashion. In case you haven't heard, friend, our governor's a Democrat, appointed by Mr. Cleveland himself."

"Yeah, yeah, Cleveland might just as well be a filthy Republican. Nigger and Indian lovin' bastard. I got a cousin serving time at Yuma. That's a shithole, and boy there's plenty a men in there'll be happy when you lot are run out of business."

Arvel raised his glass. "Shithole. You can say that again. But then again, I don't know too many prisons that aren't."

The laird interjected, "Or prisoners who are fond of law men."

Dick spoke up. He didn't want trouble and could see Arvel was in a mood for some frivolity. The combination of frivolity and Arvel's incessant teasing of jackasses never turned out well. "We're just passing through. Heading down to Mexico on the next ship. We'll be out of your hair *and town* as soon as we can, mister. Until then." He nodded. "Just get my men what they want, put it on a tab." He dropped bills on the bar. There's fifty, you tell me when you need more."

Dan George no sooner stepped over the threshold when he was tersely ordered to get out.

"What's this?" Arvel smiled.

"No niggers, Mexicans *or* Indians, pal! My saloon, my rules!" He waved his hand with a flourish. "He's barred."

"Well, that's not very Christian-like."

"Don't care." He stared at Arvel. "You Arizona bastards can go as well, far as I'm concerned, you can all get the hell out."

A dapper man stepped forward, introducing himself as an official of the town. "Sorry, gents, Sam's a drunk and an ass." He glared at the man behind the bar. "We, well, we just don't cotton to a lot of darkies . . ."

"Darkening your doorstep." The laird commented as he took a long drink of his beer.

The official nodded, pleased with the laird's clever play on words. "That's right."

Arvel pointed. "Dan there's an Arizona Ranger and a member of our party. He might look dark, might look like a dirty injun, but, just to let you in on a family secret"—he winked and lowered his voice to a whisper—"his mother was Scandinavian, on her father's side. You wouldn't want to eject a man for a little mixed blood now, would you? After all, it's not *his* fault." He grinned as he patted Dick on the shoulder. "Hell, Captain Welles here, he's half German, half Irish and you know what they say about the folks of the emerald isle. Some have argued, and frankly sometimes rather convincingly." He hesitated, taking note of the barman's name, O'Malley, mounted on a placard above the big mirror behind him. "That they're not fully human, by God."

The laird raised his beer as a toast. "To Bridget McBruiser, God bless her pea-picking simian heart!"

"Pre-cisely!" Arvel raised his glass and took a drink. "Or should that be potato-picking simian heart?"

Dan George piped up. "Or rather potato-*digging* simian heart."

"Bullshit!" The barman's face reddened. "Enough of this nonsense!"

Arvel cocked his head. "You are very rude for an Irishman. Most I've known have had a rather pleasant disposition."

Dan spoke up. "Except of course for Hennesy."

Arvel raised his glass again. "Hennesy, you're right. He's dour, though, not really rude. Just old and dour."

"Well, I don't know who the hell Hennesy is, but I do know you can go to hell, law dog. You all come struttin' in here, flashin' badges, flashin' guns, you bunch of goddamned carpetbagger Yankee bastards! Can tell by your accent you're a bunch of northerners. You ruined the goddamned south with your miscegenationist ways, now you're trying the same in the West." He pointed a finger at one of the Ranger privates. "There's another goddamned darkie. Didn't even see him till just now. Get his pepper belly ass"—he pointed again, this time at John Stokes—"and that nigger wearing the Union suit, get 'em all outta here, now!"

Arvel shrugged and sipped his whiskey. He frowned at the glass. "This stuff tastes like iodine." He dumped the remains on the floor. "Especially after beer." Pointing to an uncorked bottle of store-bought stuff lined up on a shelf, he said, "Leave this garbage for your normal clientele. Give us the good stuff, and make certain the seal's unbroken." He turned to his companion and winked. "That's an old frontier trick, laird. Put rotgut garbage in good bottles, pass it off as the real stuff."

The barkeep regarded the dapper man as a child would a parent who'd not gotten his way. He whined. "Make 'em leave, Frank! You're the goddamned town manager, make 'em go away. Send 'em all to the nigger side of town."

Arvel pointed a finger skyward. "I've got an idea!" He looked about at the subdued crowd. "Jesus, boys, it's somber as a funeral parlor around here. So damned boring, let's have a little excitement. A little entertainment, by God."

The town manager was enjoying the strange lawmen. "What did you have in mind?"

Arvel unfastened his gun belt, handing the rig to the laird. "Since you boys are so fond of boxing, I'll fight the biggest man you got for the right to stay here until our ship sails. No guns, no knives, just good old fisticuffs." He winked. "Bare knuckles fisticuffs." He glanced accusingly at a pair of gloves hanging over his head. "Just like the good old days, before all that Marquees of Queensberry nonsense." He smiled at Dick who did not find one bit of Arvel's shenanigans amusing.

The terse lawman whispered in his partner's ear. "Arvel, have you *completely* lost your mind?"

"Calm yourself, Dick," he whispered back. "I looked them all over when we came in. Not a man over a hundred forty pounds who's not a grandfather in the joint." He winked and nodded. "I got this!"

The barkeep beamed. "You're on!" He turned, calling out toward the stockroom in back. "Angel!"

The Negro emerged, ducking to clear a doorway large enough to accommodate a tall man.

"This here's Angel. He's won fifty-seven bouts. He weighs just shy of three hundred pounds."

The crowd awakened, quickly placing bets, a few on Arvel at a hundred and fifty to one.

The floor cleared and Angel stood, like a mountain, peering down at his adversary. He stretched the muscles of his neck, first left, then right. He rubbed his hands together as if warming them at a bonfire.

Dick laughed out loud as he patted Arvel on the back. "Nice knowing you." He turned to walk out when he had a thought. "Oh, just to let you know, Arvel. If you die, I'm going after Chica." He gave a lurid wink. "And, Arvel?"

"Yes, Dick?"

"I'm not half Irish." He walked out.

They circled each other for a long while and Arvel took three right jabs to the head. He fell twice, each time the laird helped him up.

The Scotsman looked worried. "Mr. Walsh, I think the next time you should just stay down."

Arvel held up a hand. "Got him just where I want him." He spit, emptying his mouthful of blood.

At the Negro's next swing Arvel ducked, connecting with a left jab to the solar plexus. The mountain winced, dipping long enough to accommodate Arvel's reach. His uppercut landed with a thud. The big man went down. He was out.

They all stood silently for a while, Arvel pondering his fist. The barkeep, disgusted, harrumphed and went back to cleaning glasses.

Rubbing his jaw the Ranger captain grinned again. "How about some of those nice gulf shrimp for supper?"

My dear wife Dorothy:

I take my pen in hand to tell you we are leaving on a ship to go to Tampico, Mexico, on a ship out of Texas. The weather is holding nice. The spirits are high and Robert Craster and Sam are safe and well. We found them in the desert at the camp of a trapper who died. Gold Hat's men chased him down and shot him in the rump. The wound got mortified and he died. Sam almost died from the sunstroke but is fine now. Robert Craster said it did not cure his stutter. He is right about that. But Sam is fine. They will probably be home before this letter gets to you, so you will know this already. Captain Walsh boxed a giant fellow at a saloon in Port Isabel, Texas, and won. It was touch and go for a while, and Captain Welles said that he would take Miss Chica for his wife in the event of Captain Walsh's demise in the boxing ring which was not really a ring but just the place in front of the saloon bar. That is right funny because you know that Captain Welles and Miss Chica do not like each other too much. It would make for a right ticklish wedding and marriage I expect. But the captain knocked the fellow out and did not die, so that turned out all right. We have a suspicion that the man gave up and threw the fight, but it was an agreeable show just the same. It right pleased us to watch it. The horses and mules are all right. Tell our babies I am all right and give them kisses and hugs from their papa.

Your husband,

John Stokes, Volunteer Scout, Arizona Rangers

CHAPTER 20

Billy bathed Francis and gave him a fresh shave. He polished his boots and retrieved the suit given to him by Hugh Harvey from the young Ranger's bedroom at the ranch, along with a fresh white shirt and high celluloid collar. He found a red tie which looked damned well against the gray-wool suit fabric. He polished the lad's badge and cleaned his six-shooter and the new Winchester that had made him so proud.

There were a few scuffs on the new gun belt and holster which Billy carefully polished out. He replenished the empty loops with fresh cartridges, bright and shiny as a new penny, taken from a box in the Walsh arsenal. He stepped back to survey the results.

"Now you look just fine, mate."

He turned his attention to Margarita who'd been cared for and dressed in the same loving manner by Chica and Pilar. A mantilla veil of white framed the lovely face which even in death bore the countenance of a sleeping angel.

His mistress squeezed him by the hand. "They look beautiful, Billy." She kissed his cheek and turned to Pilar.

The housekeeper had put together a bouquet, which she placed in Margarita's hands. The women prayed over them.

"Now they will be married in heaven, and live together in peace and happiness, Billy."

Lori read over them, specifically in tribute to Margarita. It was something Billy had helped pick out from the Book of Proverbs. It was especially significant, as the retired prostitute was all but illiterate. She struggled over each word, practicing again and again until she'd gotten it right. It was the least she could do out of respect for the sacrifices the couple had made on her behalf.

"Who can find a virtuous woman? For her price is far above rubies. The heart of her husband doth safely trust in her, so that he shall have no need of spoil. She will do him good and not evil all the days of her life. She seeketh wool, and flax, and worketh willingly with her hands. She is like the merchants' ships; she bringeth her food from afar. She riseth also while it is yet night, and giveth meat to her household, and a portion to her maidens. She considereth a field, and buyeth it: with the fruit of her hands she planteth a vineyard. She girdeth her loins with strength, and strengtheneth her arms. She perceiveth that her merchandise is good: her candle goeth not out by night. She layeth her hands to the spindle, and her hands hold the distaff. She stretcheth out her hand to the poor; yea, she reacheth forth her hands to the needy. She is not afraid of the snow for her household: for all her household are clothed with scarlet. She maketh herself coverings of tapestry; her clothing is silk and purple. Her husband is known in the gates, when he sitteth among the elders of the land. She maketh fine linen, and selleth it; and delivereth girdles unto the merchant. Strength and honour are her clothing; and she shall rejoice in time to come. She openeth her mouth with wisdom; and in her tongue is the law of kindness. She looketh well to the ways of her household, and eateth not the bread of idleness. Her children arise up, and call her blessed; her husband also, and he praiseth her. Many daughters have done virtuously, but thou excellest them all. Favour is deceitful, and beauty is vain: but a woman that feareth the Lord, she shall be praised. Give her of the fruit of her hands; and let her own works praise her in the gates."

Billy read for Francis. "This is a poem I have always been fond of. It reminded me of Francis. 'I Died for Beauty' by Emily Dickinson."

I died for beauty, but was scarce
Adjusted in the tomb,
When one who died for truth was lain
In an adjoining room.
   He questioned softly why I failed?
"For beauty," I replied.
"And I for truth–the two are one;
We brethren are," he said.
   And so, as kinsmen met a-night,
We talked between the rooms,
Until the moss had reached our lips,
And covered up our names.

He put Lori to bed and now sat with Chica at the clear pool by the cabin. She held his hand as she poured him wine from a bottle she'd brought, as funerals would never be a time of lamentation for Chica, but rather a celebration of life. She stuck a cigar into Billy's mouth and lit it for him and then one for herself. They blew smoke at the stars.

"Do you remember, Billy, the first time we met?"

"Yes, Chica. You threatened to kill me if I didn't heal Arvel."

"I did." She grinned. "I am sorry for that."

"No worries." Billy regarded the glowing tip of his cigar. "Thanks, Chica, this is a good smoke."

"A lot has changed in our lives since then, eh, Billy?"

He looked at the cabin. "They have, Chica. They most certainly have."

She looked to the bedroom window, the one that offered a beautiful view of the pool and beyond. "How is she, Billy?"

"Oh, fair enough." He looked about. "If there's such a thing as a good place to die, I guess this is it, Chica. At least she'll have some peace and a pretty setting the last days of her life."

She squeezed his hand. "And a good friend to share it with."

"I hope so." He spoke to the water running through the pool. "I'm all right, Chica." He turned to face her. "I know you're worried about me, but I'm all right. Want you to know that. I'm all right."

She swished her feet in the pool as she lay back, staring skyward. Billy joined her, holding tightly to her hand.

"Did you know, Billy, this is where Arvel and I made Rebecca?"

"I didn't."

"It is why we made the cabin there"—she pointed—"and why we fixed the cave. It is why it is called Rebecca Place, for both our little girl and Arvel's poor dead wife."

"That's mighty fine, Chica. Mighty fine."

She pulled his hand to her mouth, kissing him on the knuckle. "I am glad you are here with her. I am glad, Billy, that she will die in such a good place, with such a good man."

CHAPTER 21

Angel stood, like a colossus at the dock the morning of the Rangers' departure. Dick Welles gripped his six-shooter. He didn't want to kill the Negro, but could think of no friendly reason for the man's presence.

His fears were allayed when the pugilist smiled. "I wanted to thank you men."

Arvel took his proffered hand, turned and smiled at his companions. "Feels like trying to wrap your hand around a cured ham." He felt his jaw. "You pack a wallop, Mister . . . ?"

"Angelo. My name is Maurice Angelo, but they all call me Angel."

The laird interjected, "Angel? More like the angel of death."

He flashed a boyish grin. "Wish I could say the same of you, Mr. Walsh, I mean, about your ability as a boxer." He patted Arvel on the head as one would a freshly weaned puppy. "You had better stick to law work, sir, you might get hurt boxing." He winked to the others who laughed.

Dick spoke up. "You going to be all right, Mr. Angelo?"

"Oh, fine, sir, fine as frog hair." He shrugged. "They all think I'm addled. No one pays me any mind. After this, they'll probably stop asking me to fight, which suits me well enough. Tired of it. I just want to thank you gents for what you've done." He nodded at Dan George, John Stokes and the Mexican Rangers. "And what you said back there. I just wanted to thank you for that."

It was a well-worn but seaworthy vessel, used mostly for hauling goods, mail and cargo up and down the inner coast between Louisiana and Mexico, stopping at points in between. The captain was a pleasant man as was his crew, and the Rangers had the place mostly to themselves except for a contingent of nuns fresh from Ireland, heading to bolster the convent staff at San Luis Potosi.

Arvel tipped his hat to them. He elbowed the laird, speaking under his breath. "Hope they're not planning to sew another flag."

He wandered alone to the bridge, as Arvel was an enthusiast of sea travel. In a little while he called out to his partner. "Dick, bring the laird and Dan up. Got something to show you all."

They did and soon crowded the bridge.

"Look here, boys. I'm steering."

Like a schoolboy, he grinned and was indeed steering the ship under the watchful eye of Otto Schüssler, captain of the *Sea Harvest.*

"Captain, these are my pards, Arizona Rangers. That's Dick, Dan, and the laird."

"Pleased to meet you gentlemen."

Arvel grinned at the laird's confusion over the captain's accent. "He's as Mexican as Chica, laird. *Deutsch Mexikanische.*" He winked. "They're the reason why the beer's so good in Mexico." He nodded again at the captain. "Among other things."

"Thank you, Mr. Walsh. I presume you gentlemen are finding the trip satisfactory thus far?"

"Fine, sir."

"We have only two stops. We'll arrive in Tampico by noon tomorrow, barring no squalls." He nodded to his first officer. "Now, if Mr. Walsh has sufficiently nourished his childhood fantasy, we should retire for dinner. My men will take the watch."

They followed him out.

Dick grinned as he patted Arvel on the shoulder. "I believe the captain's put his finger on the source of your condition, Arvel."

"And what's that, Dick?"

"The quest to fulfill your childhood fantasies and desires. Explains a lot, my friend. It explains an awful lot."

"Dick?"

"Yes, Arvel?"

"Go to hell."

"I am, Arvel. I'm heading to old Mexico."

They drank beers and watched the coastline pass them by. The laird was in a talkative mood. "Mr. Walsh, tell me about your wife. She's the most intriguing human being I believe I've ever known."

Arvel smiled and spoke at the waves breaking away from the ship's bow. "You'll never actually *know* Chica, Laird, but I get your meaning." He drained his beer bottle, pitching it as far into the Gulf as his arm would throw. "She grew up with an old woman, at least the very start of her life, in a hovel that wasn't much more than a pile of brush." He grinned. "Chica said they were so poor, they didn't even have their own flint and steel. She'd have to borrow fire from the neighbors."

"That *is* poor."

"After the old woman died she was on her own for a while, until she tried to steal candleholders from a church. Even then, her charm pulled her out of a mess, laird. They could have had her thrown in prison, God knows what would have happened to her there, but they didn't. The priest and an old couple took her in."

"Seems the way of the world, Mr. Walsh. The poor are raised by the elderly. Thank goodness for them."

Arvel nodded. "You can say that again. Thank God for the

old people who raise the flotsam and jetsam of the world." He lit a smoke and offered one to the laird. "That's where she learned to ride and shoot and, more importantly than anything else, how to play cards. The old man who raised her was a card sharp and Chica's brilliant. She picked it up like a duck to water. It's really how she came into my life."

"Fascinating."

"Yes, it was." Arvel grinned at the memory of how Chica'd changed everything in his life. "She was traveling, looking for a game and had come to Arizona to seek her fortunes." He took another beer from the laird. "Then our paths crossed in a little hamlet between my ranch and Tombstone. That brigand, Sombrero del Oro had killed a nice family of settlers, and well, the town folk, when they saw Chica, dressed as a vaquero and being Mexican, they weren't kind to her. Ran her out of the saloon, ran her out of town." He laughed out loud. "But Chica's not one to be run out of any place without a fight, as I can guess you'll imagine, laird, so she rode up and down the street shooting off her guns. I can tell you that got them ducking pretty well."

"And you arrested her?"

"No, not as such. Trying to arrest Chica outright would be akin to trying to cull a nest of baby rattlers using nothing but your bare hands." Arvel shrugged. "I wasn't with the law then. Had reported to the posse to follow up on del Oro. I waited for Chica to reload her six-shooters and roped her from behind, pulling her from Alanza. Scared the hell out of me when she fell on her neck. I thought I'd killed her."

"That's an interesting way to meet one's future wife."

"Indeed. Well, the rest is just, I guess, as they say, history. Chica fell in love with me because I was kind to her and the first man to ever best her." He shrugged. "And I fell in love with her for all the obvious reasons." He suddenly felt despondent. Felt that he was too far away from her and his little girl. He missed them desperately. He took another drink to swallow the bad feeling. "And we've been happy ever since."

"I hope one day you'll come to my home in Scotland. I'd love to show it to you and Mrs. Walsh."

"I'd like that, laird. Chica loved Europe and Britain when we visited on our honeymoon. We never did make it as far up as Scotland, though." He turned to face the Scotsman. "So you're planning to return home?"

"Oh, yes. One day. Likely soon. I like to wander Mr. Walsh, but every five or so years I get the homesickness. Go back until the wandering takes hold of me again."

"Where's the next adventure?"

"Oh, I don't know. The South Seas Islands, perhaps New Zealand, maybe Australia." He nodded. "New Zealand more likely. They say, Mr. Walsh, that there are trout in New Zealand that shame the most impressive salmon in my land. I'd like to catch a couple before I'm too old to handle a rod."

Chapter 22

Hugh Harvey sat at his Tampico office desk, well-groomed and clean-shaven. He'd not touched a drop since his visit to the Walsh ranch. He was learning to hold a pencil, his hands as red and swollen as an arthritic boxer's.

"Captain Welles, Captain Walsh." He nodded to the other Rangers. "Gentlemen. I'm the bookkeeper who helped young Francis escape. How is he?"

Arvel replied. "I'm certain he's fine, Mr. Harvey. Where's Gold and his sons?"

Harvey grinned. "Well, Gold senior's somewhere between San Francisco and here. Dennis is about." He looked at his watch. "Comes in along about noon most days. Little wastrel can't get himself out of bed any earlier." He winked. "But I'm afraid you gentlemen are a little late to bring Damian to justice." He nodded. "I'm sure you know by now, he's your ultimate prize."

"Him *and* Dobbs," Dick countered.

"Yes, well, if you can find Dobbs."

"He's not here?"

"No, sir."

"What do you mean about Damian?"

"Oh, he got himself into a bit of trouble down here, gone on two weeks ago. Hurt a little girl. A peon, but the locals didn't find it amusing. They've got the devil locked up"—he motioned south—"in a local jail, next town south, Valle Hidalgo. That's why Gold senior is rushing down from San Francisco."

"How far south?"

"Oh, an hour's ride, maybe an hour and a half."

Arvel looked the men over as he consulted his watch. "It's noon, boys. Enough time to get there. Dick, how about you and Dan stay here, I'll ride with the rest down and straighten this out."

"Not on your life, Arvel."

Dan offered a grin, but Arvel was chagrined by his partner's response. "Why not?"

"Oh, you know damned well why not, Arvel. You'll kill that boy sure as I'm standing here." He turned his head gravely. "I'll not have it. He'll either swing or rot in Yuma."

"Or face the firing squad down here," Dan piped up.

Dick nodded. "Certain enough, and that would suit me fine, save the territory a lot of money and trouble with a trial, but he's not getting a bullet or rope from us." He looked at his men. "Dan, you and John and the Anglos stay here with Mr. Harvey. Arrest Gold and his son and Dobbs if he shows up, we'll go down to fetch this bastard Damian."

But by early evening they'd met disappointment in the form of the jailer, an officious little man with oiled hair and long mustaches in charge of the little prison in the town of Valle Hidalgo. He wore an old army uniform two sizes too large, his Colt tucked in a shiny black flap holster that bounced as he moved around, the whole affair looking as if it might, at any moment, slip to his ankles. He was friendly to the Rangers.

"What do you mean, gone?"

The jailer shrugged. "Gone. He is gone, Capitan. The *federales,* they come, they give me a paper, they take him away. Gone!"

"To where?"

"Back."

"Back where?"

"Back." He pointed in the direction of Tampico. "Back."

"But why?"

Another man approached. "Because he is connected to the rich, señor, because his name is Gold, and because he is a darling of the Porfiriato." He nodded. "I am Ramiro Marut, and I am, how do you say, a local rabble-rouser in these parts."

Dick gave him a suspicious look. "What's all this to you?"

"I was summoned when it was learned that you had come. I have information for you."

Arvel took his hand. "I like rabble-rousers. They are generally amusing. Pleased to meet you, Mr. Marut."

He spoke quickly in hushed tones to the jailer who shrugged again indifferently. "You gentlemen come with me. It is too late for a trip back to Tampico. I will tell you about the troubles you are facing now."

Marut took them to a part of town not frequented by lawmen, at least not on friendly or social terms. Arvel instructed everyone to put their badges away. The place was festive enough and soon they were dining on good peon food and drinking cool lagers.

Dick started the interrogation. "Mr. Marut, tell us what you know."

He looked about and smiled. "They are not used to lawmen, or Anglos, the people here, at least not the kind who do not break things apart, or act like savages, gentlemen."

The laird replied. "For good reason."

"We are anarchists, Capitan Walsh, Capitan Welles, most of us here, but that does not mean we do not appreciate or value law and order. We just appreciate and value the right kind." He nodded to the entourage. "I have heard of you Arizona Rangers. We could live with your kind of policing in our country." He smiled at a pretty woman setting more beers down and observed

Arvel admiring her. "You are fond of the women of our land, Capitan Walsh?"

Dick spit beer across the table. He coughed to clear his throat, wiping the table clean with the sleeve of his coat. "That, my friend, is an understatement." He watched Arvel blush.

"We Mexicanos are not savages, gentlemen. We love justice and fairness the same as every other civilized culture, but"—he looked about as if checking for spies—"it does not exist in the Porfiriato."

"Tell us of Damian Gold."

"He, he is *mal puro.* He did to a little girl, a little girl not more than ten years, what one would do to a grown woman."

"Jesus!" The laird held his hand to his mouth.

"Did the child survive?"

"She did, but she, being a peon, does not, well, gentlemen, I do not know a delicate way to say this, she is a . . ." He touched his finger and thumb, forming the letter O.

Dick spoke up. "A cero, a zero."

The anarchist grinned. "Precisely, sir. She is what the Porfiriato calls a zero. A nothing. The great presidente and his *cientificos* have deemed such people as valueless."

"Cientificos?" the laird asked, as he'd never heard such a term.

"Yes. The cientificos. They are the scientists, the men our leader has surrounded himself with to make Mexico modern, efficient. A good concept, to reduce things to logical, scientific equations. It has worked to make the trains run on time, the electricity run through the wires, the peso strong on the world economy, but"—he shook his head—"when such is applied to human beings, well, let's just say, the little girl who was savaged, she does not count. She is a scientific calculation that amounts to zero. Nothing." He looked about at the customers and staff. "Just as none of the people here count."

"Goddamn it!" Arvel exclaimed with that look in his eye that made Dick nervous more often than not.

Dick interjected, "Well, we've got one of Damian Gold's victims up in Arizona, and she's *not* a zero, Mr. Marut."

Their host abruptly stood, as if he'd been ordered not to speak further on the subject. He shook the captains by the hand and nodded to the remaining Rangers.

"My advice to all of you, go back home. There is nothing more you can do here in Mexico, and if you try, you might well end up worse than dead."

The laird looked on, confused. "Worse than dead?"

"Yes, señor. There are places, prisons and other such hellholes that death would render more comforting than the enduring of them." He turned. "God be with you, gentlemen. Go back *norte,* go back home to your Arizona. Sadly, your brand of justice is neither wanted nor likely to ever endure here." He gave them a halfhearted salute. "At least, at least not until the monster is slain. Adiós."

They stayed that night in a hotel not far from the restaurant where Marut had taken them. It was poor yet clean. It even had electric lights, courtesy of the Porfiriato.

Arvel noticed the laird's reaction to a fan chopping away at the warm air as they stepped onto the veranda off one of the rented rooms. They blew smoke at the street below.

It was a lively part of town and the odors of good food wafted to them. Three different bands seemed to be competing with each other, creating a not entirely unpleasant din. People laughed and called out. Children lit firecrackers. Lights washed over the adobe-walled buildings, reflecting gay colors of blues and pinks and yellows and reds. It created a downright festive ambiance.

"As our anarchist friend said, Porfirio Díaz has done some amazing things for Mexico, laird. He's electrified even the remotest towns, run rails connecting the entire country, even put Mexico on the international map, its economy now compared to those of your Great Britain, the US, Germany and France. In the north he's pulled the riches from the ground in the form of minerals and oil, made it possible for large-scale farming to flourish in the central valley." Arvel turned and looked his companion in the eye. "Sounds like a splendid chap, doesn't he?"

"Indeed."

"Well, he's not." He lit another smoke. "I know my country's not perfect, laird, hell, your country's not either, none are, but this Mexico, this poor damned country, so poor, so pathetic and it shouldn't be. The people are good, the land's good. There's plenty to go around, yet Mexico bleeds and starves and suffers constantly. I love and hate the place so much."

"Mr. Walsh, I don't think I've ever met such a passionate man as you."

"I'll drink to that." He tapped the end of his bottle against the laird's. "And I'll take that assessment as a compliment."

"I sincerely hope you do, it was meant as such."

Arvel laughed. "It's why Dick Welles is so good for me." He leaned over the rail to watch a couple of peon children run by. "I'm *so* passionate, I'm what folks call *bloody-minded.*"

"Oh, you mean, as you were in the desert, with that bandit gang."

"No, no, actually, that was battle, laird. There's a difference."

"How so?"

"Well, sir, in battle, you are engaged in a fight. You're controlling your fear and you're just trying to defeat your opponent. That's your one objective."

"As you were in the war."

Arvel smiled. "Uncle Bob's been telling stories."

"He said you were rather a hero in that."

"I was a kid." Arvel turned and smiled. "Ran off under an assumed name so my folks couldn't find me."

"They did not approve?"

"Oh, God, no. They'd have put me on some general's staff, pushing papers, *if* that. They'd have more than likely sent me off to England to keep me out of it all together, I was so young. Evidently too young in their eyes. Maybe they'd have never considered me old enough. It would have been their one selfish, self-serving act, I guess, had I allowed it. But I wanted to fight."

"And, according to your uncle, you'd gotten plenty of opportunity over the course of the war."

"I had. But engaging in battle's different than what I mean by being bloody-minded, laird. What I'm speaking of is specifically *not* battle."

"I'm not understanding, Mr. Walsh."

"Let me put it this way. Bloody-mindedness is a state of mind. It's becoming incensed, outraged by something so egregious that it causes you to do things you'd normally not do. Engage in activities best avoided by the sane and, frankly, civilized. It's becoming judge, jury and executioner when something gets your bloody-mindedness up."

"I don't see that in you."

"I know. I'm deceiving. I look nice, mild-mannered. Uncle Bob calls me a bully-trap."

"A bully-trap?"

"Yes, you know, one of those fellows a bully likes to pick out. A person the bully assumes he can use to boost his sense of self-aggrandizement. I am such a man, except well, as I said, I'm bloody-minded. That's why Dick keeps me on a short lead as much as possible. Why he wouldn't let me come down here to fetch Damian Gold. He didn't trust me and my bloody-mindedness."

"I'll take your word for it, Mr. Walsh, but frankly you seem too fine a chap to be such."

"Oh, well," Arvel laughed. "Please don't get me wrong. Being bloody-minded does not mean that the bloody-minded are immoral or evil, and a person who is such is not typically a bad person. In fact, not to sound arrogant, but I feature myself a very good person. Know for certain Chica is. But, people like Chica and I, we believe in the concept that some people just need killing, and we are the ones, the instruments for carrying it out." He grinned. "Let's just say, laird, that you've not seen me riled."

"So you were not, as you say, *riled,* when you killed the bandits?"

"Not in the least. Scared maybe, excited, but no, not riled."

"You appeared neither scared nor excited."

"I hide it well." He grinned. "I'm crazy, laird, but not stupid. Not suicidal. I don't like facing bullets, fear it the same as the next man, but, well, it's just never bothered me when it's happening. In the heat of battle, in action. It's why I'm handy in a tight spot."

"Coolness under fire."

Arvel grinned, a little embarrassed. "I guess so. I can tell you one thing, laird. This business with Gold and his son is heading me in the direction of bloody-mindedness. It's heading me, like a runaway train, right in that direction. Just thank God Chica's not on the job."

"Oh?"

"Chica makes me look like a piker when it comes to bloody-mindedness. Jesus, you don't want to get that woman riled, especially . . ." He swallowed hard, as if he was suppressing an urge to cry, his voice cracked and he cleared his throat. "Especially when children are involved."

"Judge, jury, and executioner."

"Yep." Arvel tapped the railing of the porch, drumming

nervously. He turned to the laird. "If Chica were here, she wouldn't be standing around smoking cigarettes and drinking beer. She'd be riding, right now, back to Tampico and likely relieving Damian Gold's head from its body."

He turned, looking the laird in the eye with the countenance of the brokenhearted. "Why do you suppose, laird, there's so much sadness and cruelty in the world?"

Dan George paced the boardwalk in front of the Tampico branch of the Northwestern and Union Mining Company, more out of fear for what his boss Arvel Walsh would do than for any other reason. He could not imagine a positive outcome from this predicament. Visions of rotting in a Mexican prison danced in his head.

The Golds sat smugly in their office awaiting the Arizona Rangers. Hugh Harvey crouched on a high chair, hunched over behind his desk like a cornered rat.

Dick Welles, however, knew exactly what to expect. He checked Arvel who seemed in relative command of his temper. Arvel could be violent, but not uncontrollably so and Dick was confident his partner would not do something stupid or desperate. It was up to him, however, to act quickly and decisively, or bullets would certainly be flying.

He nodded to Dan who could now relax, understanding that his boss had everything, at least in a rudimentary sense, under control. He trusted Dick to keep Arvel from going berserk, especially in light of what had happened to the little peon girl at the hands of Damian Gold, an act so barbarous it would inspire the most mild-mannered to take up the mantle of vigilante.

The elder Gold was falsely friendly, of course. He smiled. "Mr. Welles, it's good to see you again." He waved his hand across the room. "Gentlemen, please, make yourselves comfortable, please sit down."

Dick spoke. "No need for all that. Mr. Gold, we have warrants for the arrest of Damian Gold, you, and one Norbert Dobbs." He handed the papers to Gold who conducted a cursory review of them.

"I see." He nodded to Hugh Harvey who responded with documents of their own.

Gold continued. "There's a copy made out in English, for your convenience, gentlemen."

He lit a cigar as he waited for Dick to absorb the meaning of the communication.

Welles handed it to Arvel who waved him off. "Yes, I know, I know. A notice from your brethren in the Mexican government, the Porfiriato, warning us off."

Gold spoke with authority. "That's exactly right." He smiled at Arvel. "Mr. Walsh, isn't it?" He extended his hand. "We've not had the pleasure." He nodded to Dick. "Of course you'll have learned by now of my generous offer to Mr. Welles, as evidenced by that warrant for my arrest. And I can say, my friends, the original offer still stands." He moved about the room. "Gentlemen, let's be pragmatic, let's be adult about this. I don't want to fight with you. I don't want to be enemies. I don't want to spend the rest of my days avoiding my home country. I love America! I'm a patriot and citizen of the grandest society in the entire world. I'm an American through and through!"

"Shut up!"

Gold cocked his head at Arvel, evidently unused to being addressed in such a manner. "I beg your pardon?"

"You heard me. I said, *shut up.* It's bad enough that men like you exist. Men that don't give a damn. It's stupid for you to run your mouth pretending to be something you're not. Don't insult us with your ridiculous lies and platitudes and false patriotism, Mr. Gold."

"I'm certain I have no idea what you are on about, Mr. Walsh."

"Noblesse oblige, that's what I'm *on about.* You're a wealthy man. You've got so much and you've got the opportunity to do right." He nodded to Damian. "Do right by getting this boy off the streets. Do right by playing by the rules. Do right by acting decently.

"Hell, I'm rich, have known rich people all my life, not ashamed of my wealth, either. But that doesn't mean I and men of my station or men of your station can run roughshod over society. Wealth isn't a carte blanche to run amok like a bunch of wild animals.

"We have obligations, men like us. We're the lucky ones, need to help ease the way of the not so lucky. That's just plain decent, has nothing to do with religion or guilt or altruism, or anything else. And for you to stand there and declare otherwise is an insult to our dignity and intelligence."

Gold sneered. Arvel's comments had angered him. He shot back. "There is absolutely *nothing* comparable between us, Mr. Walsh. Nothing close and no one I've ever known says and acts on any such a platform as yours. You're living in a fantasy world. You're a dinosaur, Mr. Walsh. No, that's not true, you are *worse* than a dinosaur, you are a delusional dinosaur. You really believe in this fairytale concept that governments, societies, communities run on some platform of fairness and justice. That the money men, the movers and shakers of the world operate, are guided by some concept or principal of moral obligation. And on top of that, you actually believe in the silly notion that all men are created equal. That everyone deserves to be treated the same." He huffed as he looked about at John Stokes, Dan George and the Mexican Rangers. "Absurd! It's nigger lovers like you who do more to hurt our society than anyone else. Oh yes, I've heard of your little liaison with that darkie, your so-called wife. The Mexican whore, more a nigger than that buffalo soldier standing there." He pointed again to John Stokes. "You and your silly quixotic quests for justice and equality.

"Wake up, man! It's the eve of the twentieth century, that damned war should have shown you clearly enough that all this equality nonsense is just that. A load of nonsense! A failed experiment. All those good white men slaughtered, *on both sides,* for what? So a bunch of worthless darkies could have their freedom? To do what with it? It's been thirty years and what's come of the nigger? What's come of any of the inferior races? The Jews and papists and Mexicans? Nothing! Nothing! They've done nothing but stand in the way of progress. Done nothing but hinder the forward movement of men like me. But things are finally changing to the way they should be, Mr. Walsh. Changing for the better." He pointed his finger. "And you, and the rest of your kind should start acting like it."

Arvel stood. Eerily calm. So calm it made the hairs stand on Dick Welles's neck. He smiled. "You say you've never known men who think like us? I can understand that, Mr. Gold. You've never known men like us because you've never been with real men, decent men, decent human beings, men of morality and principle." Arvel turned to Damian Gold. "What do you have to say for yourself, boy? Savaging a child! You animal!"

The young man looked into his hands. Walsh frightened him and it was evident that the impact of the lawman's words weighed heavily on him. He had nothing to say. No way to remotely answer for his deplorable actions. His father relieved him of the uncomfortable silence.

"What makes men like you think for one moment you can do anything about men like me?" He looked at his sons, sitting stupidly on either side of him. "Men like us? We will *always* be with you, ahead of you, lording it over you. Always be the ones running society, the government, industry, and there's not a damned thing you can do about it, Mr. Walsh." He shooed him away. "Now, go! Go back to Arizona and play your silly game of cowboys and Indians. Go prop up, entertain, and grovel at the feet of the detritus of society. Leave the real work of progress to men such as us, and more importantly, stay the hell out of our way. It's a new world, a new century, finally a change for the better and men such as I will, with the aid of science and technology, be able to run it properly."

Arvel put his hand on his six-shooter. Dick moved into action, pulling his partner by the arm. "Come on, Arvel. We'll never get beyond the border with these bastards, or with their blood on our hands." He nodded. "You win for now, Mr. Gold, but let me tell you, we'll be waiting. We'll be watching for you and we'll get you sooner or later."

"I doubt it." He turned his head in disgust. "I don't know who's more pathetic, you or Walsh. At least *you're* an ignoramus. You have an excuse. You're stupid. And you should have taken me up on my offer when you had the chance. You believe for a minute that Bryan or my candidate's going to appoint a governor sympathetic to your silly Ranger cause? You men'll be lucky if you're guarding the privy of a local bank by this time next year." He grinned. "Soon you'll have *nothing.* Nothing!" He shooed them again. "Now, take off, I'm growing weary of all this senseless banter and I've got business matters to attend to."

"No you don't!" Hugh Harvey stood among them, his crippled fingers awkwardly holding a gun. He turned to Arvel and Dick. "I want to thank you men. For years I've groveled at the feet of this bastard." He looked David Gold in the eye. "For years I've watched you, watched your sons behave so shamefully. For years I've listened to your silly theories on this new *master race.* This race of men such as you who will finally take over the world." He grinned at the Rangers. "The great thinker, David Gold! Great thinker! Bah! A great horse's ass! The great joke!" He nodded. "There's nothing more pathetic than a dullard's feeble attempt at understanding philosophy, of that I can assure you, gentlemen." He faced Gold. "My God your arrogance makes me want to vomit."

Gold spoke as if he were commanding a misbehaved bird dog. "That's enough, Harvey. Go on and sit down. You're drunk again and for that reason, we'll forgive the indiscretion."

"No, I'm *not* drunk. Not drunk, in fact, I've never in my life been more sober. Thanks to these men and men like Francis O'Higgins. They've opened my eyes, restored my confidence in humankind. You say there's a new world and a new century. I say bunk! There's nothing new under the sun and thank God for that. There have always been monsters like you and there will always be heroes like these men. And the play will go on and on until the gods or providence or, or *something* occurs to make this godforsaken species cease to endure. But until then, Mr. Gold, there will always be good men and evil men, and I just pray to God there will be more of the former than the latter. That's our only hope."

Gold stepped toward him. He was losing patience with them all.

Harvey held up a hand. He was ready now. Ready to put an end to the drama.

"Detritus. That's what you called people like me. People like us." He pointed at the dark men around him. "Well, here is one piece of detritus that *will* have an impact on bastards like you." He fired, hitting Gold in the heart. He turned, putting a bullet in Damian's brain, and another into Dennis's neck. The three flopped about on the floor like freshly landed trout.

"Jesus Christ!" Dick Welles approached the little man who fended him off. "Now, now, Captain. I have no intention of hurting a good man like you. Please, stay back." He smiled. "None of that." He pointed the gun toward his desk. "In the top drawer is a confession made out in my hand for the murder of the Gold clan. Give it to the Mexicans and everything should be all right. There are also checks I've written out to several persons, aggrieved parties to these sons of bitches, and more blank ones with an official signature for anyone I've overlooked. Please, please make good use of them. See that they're delivered to the appropriate parties. There's plenty of money in the account, I've made certain of that." He nodded to Arvel. "Mr. Walsh, please tell Francis I was a good soldier. Tell him I did the right." And with that Hugh Harvey straightened his back, saluted and, pressing the smoking revolver's muzzle to his temple, fired once.

My dear wife Dorothy:

I take my pen in hand to let you know that we are coming home from Tampico, Mexico. A clerk in the employ of the Gold men shot them all dead. It was a sight. He shot himself as well and is now dead. We did not know such a thing would happen and the Mexican authorities held the captains for questioning for two whole days and a night. It was touch and go for a while, but we are back at the docks waiting for the ship again. This time Captain Welles has got us a nice steamer ship going all the way up to Corpus Christi, Texas. We will take a train from there to home. The horses and mules are traveling all right. They seemed to like the ship going down. I hope they will like the one going back and the train all right. The captains have written every man jack of us a check from the mining company owned by the late Mister Gold for three hundred dollars which is payment over top of the normal Ranger pay we will have got for the whole adventure. Do not worry dear heart because Captain Walsh says he will go to the bank personal for us and make sure the bank makes the checks good and give us hard cash money for them. I know you were not happy for me leaving the roof job, but dear heart, know that I have received more pay than I would make for fifty roof jobs in just this little short time. It was easy enough work and I am now safe and will be home to you and our babies soon. The blackhearts are all dead. The captains are the best of men. Tell our babies I love them.

Your husband,

John Stokes, Volunteer Scout, Arizona Rangers

Chapter 23

They got a late start and rode all day and into the next morning. It was another bright and clear night and the road was easy to navigate. Craster took the lead in Pike's wagon, Sam drove the circus cart, and to keep him company, the teamster made the dog ride with the old man.

He thought a lot about Alice Tomlinson as he rode. He thought a lot about dying as well, probably due to, more than any other reason, the fact that he had to sit in Pike's dried blood. He could see where the bullet had traveled, through the seat and then through Pike's ass and it ended up lodged in the footrest on the far side. It was a sad state of affairs. It made him miss Pike, even though he hardly knew the man.

He thought about Sam and how all this had affected him. He was an old fellow and the sunstroke and the battle with the bandits, and the death of Pike likely stripped years from his life, and all this due to Craster's own hubris. He had to go and lose his temper and hit that dude's men. That was so stupid. All because they said rude things about the ladies. The ladies, two wonderful pure spirits who could have handled that fool with the cheap ugly suit easily enough without his help. They would have put the dude in his place and none the worse for wear. They could have humiliated him and he would have gone away with his tail tucked between his legs and that would have been an end to it.

He regretted all that. He'd hurt Sam and he'd of course hurt

Alice and Ellen, and all the men who relied on him for their livelihood, all because of his damned bad temper. He might have even been responsible for Pike's death, as maybe, just maybe, if Pike had not had to have been troubled by their rescue, he would have checked his traps days before, then he would not have been at the watering hole when the bandits were there. It all gave Craster a terrific headache to think about that.

Close to midnight he saw a light and picked up the pace. Sam followed suit and Craster knew this by the quickening of the squeaking of the circus wagon's poorly fitted wheel.

Soon they were waking up the liveryman and his wife on the outskirts of Carlsberg. The proprietor lost his gruffness when he saw it was Craster, as evidenced by the garish red wagon following him.

"You're the teamster who went missing in Tombstone, ain't you, mister?"

Craster grinned as he helped Sam down. "Yes sir, but how'd you know that?"

"Oh, everyone knows that. Seems a pair of ladies have put out the word, all over the region. Big reward to discover you. Find your whereabouts. Guess that's a reward won't be collected. Hell, you found us!"

"Well, mister, I'll tell you what, you give me a fair price for all these traps, all them Mexican horses, and that'll be a good reward for you, how's that?"

The old-timer held up a lamp, walking down the line and looked everything over. Craster put an arm around Sam and walked him into the liveryman's house. The wife served up some eggs and bacon. She poured them beer and went about fixing them a place to lie down.

He nodded as the old woman moved around. "We thank you ma'am. Sorry for the late arrival. Them Mexican horses didn't want to cooperate much. They kinda slowed us down."

She smiled. "I'm just glad to see you alive, Mr. Craster. All of Tombstone is going to be pleased to know you're fine." She topped off his beer and opened another bottle. "Tomorrow we'll get you men on some fast horses, I know there's a lady anxious for your return."

He felt a little silly being such a celebrity. He looked at Sam and smiled.

"We're goin' home, my friend. Goin' home tomorrow." He scratched his head and muttered under his breath. "Goin' home to Miss Alice."

Robert Craster arrived in Tombstone just before seven in the evening. He got Sam to the old fellow's boardinghouse and put him to bed. He commanded him to not report to work for another week.

He made it to what remained of his shop and picked through the debris. Nothing survived. He sat down and had a quick cry, then recovered. He looked at the dog who sat down next to him, waiting. Craster patted him on the head. "My pride fell with my fortunes." He turned and smiled at the dog, as he wiped his eyes dry. "That's Shakespeare. A very fine lady taught me that."

He got up, dusting his dirty pants clean of the soot and ash. "Come on, boy. Let's get this over and done with."

He waited in the parlor as the landlady's husband fetched him a glass of water. He looked the place over and remembered back to his first visit, it seemed a lifetime ago. The irony hit him that the terrible scene where this whole adventure had started, the whorehouse that was once home to the cut-up prostitute was just across the street, and as he waited he could look through the window into the parlor and see the very piano he'd delivered that fateful night. The remembering of it made him dizzy.

He turned his attention to the room where he waited, to the nice wallpaper and the heavy Persian rug and the piano where Alice likely sat and played of an evening, could not resist and checked to see if it was in tune. It sounded good. He took a deep breath and realized that he had nowhere to go but up.

He'd go ahead and proclaim his love, not in his newly affected way, the way Ellen had taught him, but in *his* way, the way that was all Craster, and he'd show her his ragged clothes and unkempt hair and scruffy beard and he'd tell her he had not even a clean shirt to cover his back and then she could send him on his way and he could start all over again without her, without the preposterous fantastic notion that she could ever be his wife.

He derived great satisfaction from this epiphany. Perhaps the revulsion in her countenance, when she got a good look at him, perhaps his confession that all of this, losing his business, losing Pike, having Sam nearly killed, all due to his own foolish pride, well, perhaps it would make her hate him and he'd be purged of her. Perhaps she'd look at him with disdain and he'd be released from the spell of those beautiful jade eyes. Maybe she'd even laugh in his face. He could only hope for that.

He looked down at the dog, lying on the fine carpet licking itself in a most uncouth manner, and he was glad. The dog looked like hell, scruffy and dirty, an ugly worthless cur, and it was just the kind of animal Craster rated and deserved. The canine was the symbol of what Robert Craster had become and he hoped the dog would go on licking and looking horrible and disgusting when Alice Tomlinson came in to greet him. He deserved that.

He reclined a little and rested his head on the chair back and drifted off. He dreamed of her again, back at the pool up at the red rocks from his previous dream and she was drizzling water on his hands and again the dream became too real and he awoke to Alice Tomlinson sitting before him with a wash basin of warm soapy water and a sponge. She washed his dirty and injured hands and when he was awake she reached over and kissed him on the mouth. She smiled and he sat up straight in the chair.

"Your hands are a sight! We've got to get them cleaned up and dressed to avoid an infection." She pulled out a strip of clean gauze, preparing to bind them.

He worked hard to resist the urge to cry as those beautiful jade eyes made him so happy and yet so emotionally spent to the point where all of it, all of the terrible things of the past days had come cascading over him like a tidal wave, a great wall of water, a force great enough to destroy him instantly.

He reached out and grabbed her hands in his calloused fists. "I've got nothin' to offer you, ma'am. I've lost my business. I've lost everything. Can you ever forgive me?"

"There is nothing to forgive." She washed his face and then thought better of it. "Robert, you are too dirty for a sponge bath." She took him by the hand, leading him to the bathroom upstairs. She ran him a tub of hot water and hushed him when he tried to protest. She left him to soak for a good while.

Afterward, she put him in her bed. He tried to protest again, and again was silenced. She kissed him on the cheek. "Tomorrow we'll talk all about it."

He slept until noon and awoke to the sight of one of his tailored suits, from Nicholson, the Leading Tailor of the West, hanging on the drawer pull to the chifferobe. Next to it, on a chair, sat new shoes, socks, new underwear, a crisp clean shirt, high collar and tie. He remembered buying them with Ellen all those many weeks ago.

He trimmed his beard and shaved his neck and combed his hair and dressed. He did not feel so terrible today. He went down to see them as they had their luncheon.

"Well, you look much better!" Alice rushed to him, leading

him to his chair.

He nodded a thank-you.

One of the boarders, a Dr. Goldwater stood up. “Mr. Craster, welcome home. I believe all of Tombstone will breathe a sigh of relief at your return.”

Craster nodded. He looked for the dog. Agata, the Mexican housekeeper, responded. “I have put the beast in the backyard, señor. He would not stay away from your bedroom door, and we did not want him to wake you. The creature is good.”

They all pushed the food at him. Everyone smiled and waited for Craster to say something, anything. He could not find the words.

Ellen stood. She went to the buffet and rummaged around. “Mr. Craster, this is for you.” She handed him an envelope.

He opened it and read: “Pay to the order of Robert Craster, one thousand dollars, the Northwestern and Union Mining Company.”

He scratched his head.

“It’s for your trouble, and to rebuild your business, Robert. It’s from the Arizona Rangers, Captain Welles and Captain Walsh. It was delivered from the bank this morning. Your landlady delivered it here. It’s not much, not nearly enough to compensate you for your trouble, but at least it’s something. It’s a small attempt at undoing the evil perpetrated by the Gold family. They seem to have written a lot of these checks on behalf of that scoundrel and wastrel of a son.”

He was alone again with Alice as they’d all taken their leave to give the couple some privacy. She waited for him to say something, to react to all that had transpired since his arrival.

He looked her in the eye. She still maintained that beautiful countenance. That beautiful happy smile.

She finally spoke. “I thought I lost you.”

“I’m sorry.” He could not stop the tears. “I’m sorry, I’m

sorry." He had to look away.

"For what?"

"For ever loving you. For ever thinking such a stupid thing. I ain't nothing, I'm a nobody and you are well, just far above me. I've acted the fool and caused all this trouble. I had a stupid idear that I could get polished up and become a gentleman and I'd be good enough for you and I made a mess of it all. I'm sorry, dear, dear, Miss Alice, I'm sorry." He stood up, placing his napkin on the table, as Ellen had taught him. "I'll go now, I'll leave you alone."

Alice smiled again. "Don't I have a say in any of this?"

"What's there to say?" He searched those loving eyes. "I've nothing, Alice. A thousand dollars, less than you likely make for performing one play. I've nothing and I'm thick as a damned newborn calf. I'm about as coarse as the bristles on a hog's chin. I'm nothing, have nothing. Nothing to remotely offer you. What's there to say, Alice? Tell me, what's there to say?"

"That I love you, just as you are, and that I've loved you from the moment you walked through that door and told me my freckles were as pretty as a turkey egg's."

He blushed at the silliness of such a compliment.

Alice continued. "That I don't want you to change and I don't care that your business is destroyed, or that you don't have a great fortune, I don't care that you say ain't or that you might eat with your hands from time to time, or that you don't know which fork to use at which course of the meal."

He looked into her eyes. He was speechless.

"That's right, Robert. I don't care. I love you, *you,* and not your manners, or not manners or your elocution, or common talk. I love the way you love me. I love the look in your eyes when you look at me. I love your gentleness and your kindness, and your toughness. I love the fact that you fought, or at least beat a man to protect, to defend my honor. I love the fact that you clobbered those men for me. You are *my* ideal, Robert, and I love you and I want to be your wife and the mother of your children. I want to grow old with you and be with you for the rest of our days. That's what I want, Robert. Will you give that to me? Because I promise you, I promise you, you will get all of me in return."

He, as if awakening from a dream, understood. He kissed her and held her in his arms. "With all my heart, Alice. I swear, with all my heart."

Arvel found his partner in an uncharacteristically relaxed state, reclining on a chaise overlooking the ship's stern.

"You have found a dandy spot, Dick."

"Pull up a seat." He patted the deck chair next to him. "Beats the hell out of a room in Belem, eh, Arvel?"

"It does, my friend." He grinned. "That was about as close a shave as I've ever had. Those *federales* were mightily damned pissed, with all those dead Golds lying about, weren't they?"

The laird finished a lively piece on the piano and the Rangers cheered and laughed in the smoking lounge behind them.

Dick listened, then nodded to his friend. It was all as it should be.

"Touch and go for a while, wasn't it, friend?"

"That it was, Arvel. A hell of a ride." He turned to face his partner. "Thanks for not losing your senses, I mean, back there. Thanks for not killing the Golds. I know how hard that was for you, Arvel. You showed some grand restraint."

Arvel blushed. "Oh, like I told the laird. I'm crazy, but not stupid, Dick. I will not deny that I was close, damned close, but I knew more than just you and I would have been in a world of trouble. I'd never do that to you or the boys, never risk you for my own acts of hubris."

"Hubris?"

"Sure. Playing God. If that's not hubris, don't know what is, Dick."

They were once again interrupted by the men's laughter. "Glad we could put the boys up in something nice for a change, thanks to you. A nice break after such a hair-raising adventure."

"Not me, Dick." He winked. "Thanks to the late Gold and company, or at least, their money. In the realm of writing blank checks, I do not mind playing God."

"Sons of bitches."

Arvel lit a smoke and regarded Dick. "Resting suits you."

"What do you mean?"

"You look well. First time I've seen you sit still for, well, actually as long as I can remember."

"I rest."

Arvel had a thought. He laughed out loud, as was his wont when he'd conjured up a funny thought.

"What the hell's so funny?"

"The idea of you and Chica, married."

Dick could not help but be amused by the idea. Images of being intimate with Arvel's Mexican beauty quickly came and went. He gave a sly look and nodded pensively. "It could happen."

"Yeah, it could, I guess." He opened another bottle of beer and handed it to his partner. "So you are warming up to Mexicans?"

"Never had anything against Mexicans from the start, Arvel. You and Dan are the ones who keep that damned myth alive. I like Mexicans as much as I like anyone else."

"How's Michael?"

"Fine, I suppose."

"Have you seen him?"

Dick wouldn't answer.

"How about his new bride? What a looker, and sweet as can be."

"I know, you've told me that before, Arvel."

"So, why won't you see them? I mean, now, with your new love, or should I say, your new affirmation of love for Mexicans, I would think you'd welcome her with open arms."

"Her being a Mexican's got nothing to do with any of it, Arvel, and you know it."

"Oh, oh. I see. The whole retired prostitute angle." Arvel stroked his chin.

"Take it easy, Arvel."

"Sorry, Dick. Seriously, I'm sorry. I don't want to fight with you, my friend. Thing is, I've seen them. Seen Michael and Salvatora, seen their little son. They've got a nice life going. A nice life and it might be good for you to be part of it." Arvel peered at his beer bottle. "Sober as a judge he is."

"What sort of judge, Arvel? Johnson up in Flagstaff, he's inebriated more than he's not."

"You know what I mean." He shrugged. "I think you ought to go visit them."

"Maybe." He lit a smoke and blew a cloud toward the flag fluttering off the stern. "Maybe once all this is settled. Find out our fate, find out what's to become of us, I mean, as Rangers. Maybe then, Arvel. Maybe then." He turned to look his partner in the eye. "I don't hold it against her, really I don't. Been forced into all that when she was so young. She's *still* a child, really."

He paused to collect his thoughts. "You know, despite what you think of me, I'm not a heartless stick in the mud, Arvel. I appreciate what it's like for these girls, appreciate what it must be like to have your back against it. Nowhere to turn, nowhere to get any relief or help out of the poverty. I mean, well, I've never been without means, without food, without a place to put my head, but I can imagine what it must be like. Goddamned terrifying." He turned his head. "That goddamned Mexico. I just don't understand it, Arvel. Don't understand how such a place can be the way it is. Hell, it's not much different from our own land, Christ almighty, in many ways, it's a lot richer. Half the time, I can't tell when I'm in Texas or Arizona or New Mexico or old Mexico. Why the hell's it got to be so damned hard down there? I just don't understand."

"Me neither, my friend. I don't know." He took a swallow of beer. "But one thing's certain, we will know our fate soon enough about the Rangers, and I'm glad you're taking all that a lot better than you had been."

"I am indeed, Arvel." He shrugged. "Just don't care really, anymore. Of course I want it to endure. Of course I want to keep doing what we're doing so well, but"—he shook his head—"you were right back when you said it, back on the trail. Can't worry over things we can't control. And another thing, Arvel, you made me realize something. If I can't be a Ranger, well, damn it, I'll do something else. I've learned a lot rangering and I know, I'm old, but not decrepit. I've got a few years left in me."

"And something more important than all that, friend."

"What?"

"You are a great man, Dick. There's greatness about you. You are the kind of leader, the kind of man our country needs, will always need and there aren't enough of you." He stood up, patting his partner's knee. "Not enough by a long shot."

"Arvel?"

"Yes, Dick?"

"I still say, with all your bullshit, you'd make a hell of a politician."

He took another drink, draining his bottle. "And I still say, Dick." He gave his best Cheshire cat grin. "Go to hell."

"Back to old Mexico?"

"No, Capitan Welles. Tombstone."

"I'll drink to that.

Arvel understood fully the seriousness of the attack as he watched Uncle Bob puzzle over the right words to convey it.

"They even cut the lines, Arvel. That's why you couldn't get to us when you tried." He turned his head from side to side. "That bastard Dobbs, he was an evil son of a bitch. *And* thorough."

"You said thirty in all?"

"Yep, well, thirty-one, counting Dobbs, and Chica took about half herself. Finished off old Adulio Sanchez out in the desert."

"The drifter we cut loose last winter?"

"The same. He was the reason they went to Rebecca's Place, he and Dobbs. He was a true Judas, certain enough."

"Everyone else all right?"

"Not a scratch on any of the men. The community really came together for us, Arvel. We knew what this gang was doing almost before they knew themselves. It was like shooting fish in a barrel. We sent the women and children to Tucson. Chica's idea. All except Pilar and Rebecca."

"How's Billy?"

"Good, good, Arvel. He's with Lori. I guess by now it's no secret, the poor thing's dying. Not from the attack. Billy says she's got a cancer."

"They've got everything they need?"

"They're good, Arvel. They're as fine as they can be." He nodded. "Though I pity Billy. Chica thinks he's fallen in love. I guess he has. Wouldn't blame him if he did. She's a sweet thing. Poor tortured soul. I have never seen a human being so gracious as that girl."

"Oh well. A little love's good for anyone, even if it won't be for long. I'll run out and see them in the morning."

Arvel worried over him. He looked old, much older than when he'd left him not that many days before.

"I'm mighty sorry for all this, Uncle."

"Sorry? Sorry for what, Arvel?"

"For bringing so much misery to you, to our happy home. Feel responsible, all this Ranger nonsense. First the attack by that nutty anarchist, and that damned boy poisoning me, and now this. If it weren't for me for my, my . . ."

"Your *nothing,* Arvel! Come now, you and I had this conversation years ago, you remember?"

"I do."

"And we're partners, aren't we?"

"We are."

"And we decided together you'd pursue this Ranger path, so there's an end to it." He stubbed his cigarette. "Arvel, I'm so proud of you, words can't describe it. Sure we've had our heartache, fear, danger, but then again, we're equipped to handle it. We're the ones, Arvel, we're the ones."

"The ones?"

"Certainly. We're the ones to move this land forward, lad. To make this place livable for decent folks." He stood up and stretched the muscles of his tired back. "And besides, if you hadn't become a Ranger, we might never have had the most wonderful thing happen, most wonderful thing ever to come into our lives." He nudged Arvel with his elbow, whispering in his nephew's ear. "Don't tell Pilar I said that."

"Where is she?"

"Off at the corral."

He watched her work another mule and waited until she'd worn herself and the creature out. He pulled her into his arms, breathing her in, glorying in the perfection of his perfect wife.

He whispered in her ear. "Is there a reason why you fought

with no clothes on?"

Chica gave him a wink and a sly smile. "I fought like Alasdair's ancestors, Pendejo. There were many bad men and I needed an extra advantage. When they saw me naked, they did not know whether to kill me or make love to me. I never saw men with such gaping mouths. Worse even than you have ever been. It was a good result."

"You at least wore your boots?"

"No, Pendejo, both me and Alanza were stripped. *Nada!*" She winked and gave him a moment to fix the image in his mind.

"Lady Godiva." He kissed her temple. "God's gift."

"Who is this Lady Godiva?"

"A beautiful noblewoman from olden times. She rode a horse with nothing to cover her but her long hair."

"Well, I did have my gun belt and bullet belt, the one I got from the harness maker last winter." She pulled her shirt down, baring a bronzed shoulder. "Look, Pendejo, it made a mark." She waited for him to kiss the spot. "But I rode Alanza with no saddle. She wore only her bridle and I tied my rifles on with a rope. It was a funny way to fight the bad men. I will say that."

"Didn't it hurt you?" Arvel blushed, nodding in the direction of her nether region, "I mean, you know, down there, riding astride Alanza, with no, nothing between you and her?"

"No, Pendejo. Everything is working fine." She winked as she pulled him by the arm. "In fact, I must say, it made me feel kind of, you know, that way, you know, when I was riding so hard." She threw her head back and laughed as he blushed. "Come with me, to our bed. I will show you all about it."

He awoke and remembered where he was. She was praying next to him. "What are you praying about, Chica?"

"I am thanking Dios for everything. Everything, my Arvel. We are blessed and we have been lucky. I only wish that Margarita and the boy had survived. It made me cry when they died."

"I'm sorry for that as well. I've got a big check for them from Gold's mining company. They could have made a nice start."

"Give it to me. We will make a donation to the orphanage in Bisbee. They need lots of help."

"And the prostitute, Uncle Bob told me. She's dying."

"She is better from the savage who attacked her, Pendejo, but yes, she is dying. She has been sick a long time and Billy cannot cure her. They are living out her days at Rebecca Place. I told them to stay there as long as they like. We will provision them. It is the least we can do for Billy." She snuggled against his chest. "I believe Billy has fallen in love with her and I believe she feel the same way about our Billy."

"Rebecca seems to have handled everything all right. What did you tell her about Margarita?"

"Sí. Pilar took good care of her and Uncle Bob defended the cellar. It was a good plan. I told her that Margarita was with the angels. She does not know that she was murdered. She is too young to know such a thing."

"I love you, darling."

"I know you do, my love. I know you do. Now be quiet because I want to make love to you again. And then we shall sleep as long as possible."

"Chica, I just want to say. I'm sorry. Sorry for leaving you all that way. Sorry for running off. I never imagined Dobbs would have tried to pull off such an idiotic stunt. If I'd have known that, I would never have left the ranch. I'm sorry." He held her desperately. "If I had lost you and Rebecca, I just, just don't know. Don't know if I could endure."

"I know, Pendejo. Dying is not the difficulty. It is living that is hard for people like you and me, my love. But you needa stop worrying over things that did not happen. We are all safe. We are all fine, and Dios willing, we will be that way for a long long time."

Like a veil pulled from his eyes by Chica's words, the guilt seemed to melt away. She sensed it. "What are you thinking about, Pendejo?"

"Just remembering something. I met a funny little man with a red face from drinking too much. He wore little oval glasses."

"*Sí*, the little man who helped Francis O'Higgins. He come here to warn us of the bad men. He disappeared. We thought he turned into a coward again."

"No, Chica. Just the opposite. He was a courageous hero and he said things about us, people like us, Chica. It made me feel a little better, a little more hopeful about all the wickedness in the world." He kissed her forehead. "He made me feel very well."

Chapter 24

She smeared the greasepaint on the red puckered lines now defining her face. Looked left and right and wanted to cry at the dreadful result until the sound of Billy's movement in the cabin's parlor brought her to her senses. He knocked as always before entering the room but still did not give her enough time. She smiled sheepishly as would a child caught in a naughty act. She worked to wipe the paste-like material from her cheeks.

"I guess you caught me."

Billy sat on the bed next to her. He'd been taking such a liberty now for a long time and was comforted by the fact that Lori never moved away. Their thighs touched as he took the tin, holding the label to the light so he could read it. He grunted.

"Sorry, Billy, I shoulda asked you first. Is it bad?"

The healer smelled it. "No, not as such." He reached over and wiped the rest of her face clean. "Where'd you get it?"

"Oh," she laughed. "A long time ago. I had a customer when I was down in Corpus Christi, that's a wicked place. Anyways, had a customer he, well, Billy, some of the men I've known, like the Frenchies that did the black mass, well, they are some odd and wicked men, and this one, he give me this greasepaint and wanted me to smear it all over my face and arms and legs. Then he put me in this black shroud and layed me on the bed." She grinned. "He wanted to pretend I was dead, Billy."

"No kidding." Billy stood up and fiddled about the room as he listened. Lori was educating him on the finer points of human depravity, certain enough.

"Yeah, but, when he was, you know, doing it to me, well, I was too warm so he called for a bucket of ice and started packing me with it, covered me all up and even tried to put it up, you know, up there. It was darned uncomfortable. I didn't like it much and told him to stop, told him I didn't want to feel like a dead body and he got mean about it, but Billy, I have to say one thing for the madam of that whorehouse. She were no woman you wanted to cross. She would allow no locks on the doors and when I took to yellin', she come busting in there with a iron poker and I'll tell you when she did that, the only dead body that man was worried about was his own. He run outta there like a cat with its hind parts on fire."

"No kidding."

"No kidding." She smiled. "You say *no kidding* a lot, Billy."

"Do I?"

"You do. I like to hear you say *no kidding.* It tickles me." She pulled her legs to the side of the bed, doing her best to control the pain. "I'm sorry I put that trash on my face, Billy. Should have told you first. Shoulda asked."

"No harm done, Miss Lori." He helped her stand, placing the robe given to her by Uncle Bob around her shoulders. "Some of that stuff has mercury in it, but this doesn't." Billy hesitated. "At least as far as I can tell. I just, well, Miss Lori, I'd like to see that pretty skin of yours all by itself."

He immediately regretted saying that as he watched tears form in Lori's eyes. They ran along the tracks of her wounds. "Do you mean it, Billy?"

With his thumbs he wiped her cheeks dry. "I do, Miss Lori, I really do."

She sat back down. "I feel all woozy."

He helped her back in bed. "Rest a while."

Mercifully, she'd stopped crying.

"One time, when I was a lad, there was this shop in town, they had nice things, come from Germany. Toys, you know. There was this one little dolly, I swear, Miss Lori, the first time I met you, all I could think about was the beautiful little dolly with the real human hair that was the same color as yours and the porcelain skin. Your skin is the same as that pretty dolly's and I watched a little girl, you know, through the window, watched her pa buy her that dolly and when she got it, she hugged it and I was so pleased by how happy it made her. That's what I like to see Miss Lori. I like to see the pretty color of your skin and especially how it pinks up when you laugh or feel happy. Your cheeks are what tells me if I'm on the right track. I like to see 'em, especially when they're glowing so nice."

"Billy?"

"Yes, Miss Lori?"

"Do you suppose it was all my fault that Francis and Margarita are dead?"

"No. Why do you ask such a thing?"

"Because I do." She began to cry again. "If it weren't for me, that man would not have come here and shot them to death. If it weren't for me, none of this woulda happened."

"I don't remotely agree with that."

"Why not?"

"Did you shoot Francis and Margarita?"

"No." She looked self-consciously at her hands.

"Did you cut yourself up like that?"

"No, course not."

"Who did?"

"Them bad men."

"And so, then it's not logical, your line of thinking now, is it, Miss Lori?"

"Guess not." She smiled uneasily. "How do you make everything sound so sensible?"

"Because I'm a sensible man."

"You are at that, Billy. You sure are at that." She looked him in the eyes. "Where were you so early today, Billy? When I woke up, you was gone. Scared me."

"Helpin' Uncle Bob. I'm sorry for scaring you. I did tell you this morning. You must have been too groggy to remember, Miss Lori. I won't do that again."

"Oh, that's all right." She blushed. "We're talkin' like an old married couple, ain't we Billy?"

He smiled. "Bob had a horse with a bad limp. We lanced a cyst, I packed it for him. The vet's not able to get out for another day and . . ." He smiled. "Bob likes me to help doctor the beasts." Billy shrugged. "He can do all himself. I think Uncle Bob could be an animal doctor he knows so much, but we work well together on such things."

"Everyone relies on you Billy, don't they?"

"Yeah, guess so. At least when it comes to doctoring."

"Who takes care of you?"

"I beg your pardon?"

"Who, who takes care of you? Who takes care of the one who takes care of everyone else? It don't seem right that a man like you don't have anybody to take care of you, Billy. Seems you're all alone in the world."

"Oh." Billy sat down beside her, adjusting the robe on her shoulder as it had slipped. "You've got two pretty freckles there." He ran his fingertips over them.

"A man said they was angel kisses."

She turned and touched Billy's cheek. "Who takes care of you, Billy?"

He pressed her hand to his face.

"My ma, before she died, it was right when I was to come here to America. She told me, and well, I already knew it, being a half-caste, she told me that I didn't, never would, fit in any place."

"Half-caste?"

"Yeah, what you all call a half-breed."

"I see."

"The aborigines were not too keen on me because I wasn't one of them, and the whites, of course, never looked at me as one of their own, and that was true in my homeland, and my ma, she said it would be a hundred times worse here, and I guess she was right, but, you know, Miss Lori, she was a good mother. She loved me very much and so did my pa and, well, to be truthful about it, I never was much bothered about having someone take care of me." He looked around the room at his potions and concoctions. "My friends, the Walshes, Uncle Bob, Miss Pilar, all the folks I've healed over the years, or at least helped to ease their suffering, they've given me loads of love. I feel very blessed, Miss Lori, to tell you the truth. Don't feel alone much at all."

"But it seems right lonely, Billy. To live like you live." She reclined, too tired anymore to sit up. She pulled his hand to her breast and held it close. "Maybe, though, when I think on it, Billy, maybe *your* life's been less lonely than mine."

"How do you mean?"

"I've been with so many, Billy, and I ain't goin' to lie to you. It's been quite a party, sometimes, downright fun. But, not one, not one of them men ever been so kind to me as you are. In all my time, men have lusted over me, pampered me, given me gifts and compliments, even took their own life because of me, but I've never known love." She pulled his hand to her lips and kissed it. "Now, I do, Billy. Now I know a little of your world, your life. In a way, it makes me feel both happy and sad all at the same time."

He reached over and kissed her forehead, brushing a lock of

the spun-gold-colored hair from her eyes.

"Wished I'd a met you when I was fifteen. Maybe both our lives woulda been different, Billy." She grinned as if her fanciful notion was too absurd even for her to take seriously. "Maybe not." She winced. "Oh, God, it hurts so."

He poured her some laudanum. She drank and waited for it to take effect. Billy held her hand to comfort her while they waited for the pain to subside. She smiled. "That potion sure does the trick."

"Better?"

"Much better, thank you."

"Come on, Miss Lori, let's get you outside. It's a beautiful morning. I've got a little treat for you."

He scooped her up in his arms. She rested her head on his shoulder, wrapping her arms around his neck as he carried her out.

"You're strong, Billy."

"Nonsense." He grinned. "You're light as a feather."

In a little while he had her sitting under a makeshift awning he'd put up with some canvas salvaged years ago by Uncle Bob from an old army tent. Two rocking chairs placed by the deep pool afforded them a comfortable place to enjoy the pleasant, albeit already hot day. Billy had prepared the angling equipment he and Francis had previously used to keep the young Ranger occupied before the fateful battle.

"What's all this?"

"Fishing. Don't tell me you've never been fishing, Miss Lori?"

"No, never."

He baited a hook, tossing the line in at the head of the pool. "Now, the trick, Miss Lori, is to get that hook as close to the bottom as you can. That's where the big boys live."

He handed her the rod and showed her what to do.

"There now, you're a natural. When you get to the end of the pool, you just pick up the line and put it right back down again at the top. Sometimes the trout, they're a little persnickety. Got to show them the morsel a few times 'fore they bite."

She was pleased. "It's kinda fun, Billy, ain't it?"

"Wait till you get a fish on. That's the most fun part of all."

At the fifth pass she did. "Oh, Billy, Billy, I got one!" She smiled at the dancing rod tip.

"Good, Miss Lori, now, keep that rod tip pointed up, don't allow him any slack or he'll throw the hook. Good, now reel it in, that's good, I'll get the net."

He did and held the fish up for her to admire as he removed the hook.

"Oh, that's grand, Billy, just grand. Look at the colors! It's just too pretty for words."

"Apache trout, Miss Lori. That'll make some good eating."

"No, Billy." Her lip quivered as she swallowed hard. "I don't want it to die. Let's put it back, if'n it's all the same to you, Billy, please. Let it live. Let it back."

"Of course, Miss Lori." He looked the trout over clinically, as if it were one of his patients. "No harm done, he's just lip hooked, he'll be fine." It slipped from his hands. He pointed. "See, he darted right back to his little perch on the bottom."

"Good, Billy. Good." She squeezed his arm. "But it was a thrill just the same. I'm thanking you Billy."

She tired quickly but was not ready to go back to bed. He moved her to the edge of the pool and they sat quietly for a while, allowing the cold mountain water to bathe their legs. She squeezed his hand, looking into his eyes with an expression that broke his heart.

She turned, speaking to the water as it flowed past them. "Never was much for nature."

"Do you not like it?"

"Oh, sure. Like it well enough." She shrugged. "Just never

had much of a chance to see it, be in it. Kind of a city type. One time in Texas, by the sea, there was this one customer, good-looking fellow. He had a yacht, that's a big sailboat, you know. He had this fancy captain's hat, you know a cap, all dark blue, had a gold anchor on the front of it. He was sailin' around the world, he took me and a gal I was friends with, Bertha was her name. She was real fat. They called her Big Bertha, of course. She was real sweet. She laughed all the time. She had a funny thing she'd say, you know, like the way you say *'no kiddin,'* Billy. She used to say, let me remember, oh yeah, she used to say, *'well, that was a letdown,'* she'd say that a lot, Billy, whenever somethin' didn't go right or suit her. She used to have what she called her *fits of melancholy.* That's like when you're in a dark mood, you know. She'd get real sad and then she'd eat. Boy could she eat. She could eat a whole three-layered cake, frosting and all in one sitting. She'd wash it down with beer. It was something to see, sure enough. Doing something like that would make me throw up, Billy. But not Bertha. That girl sure could eat. But anyway, that handsome fellow with the boat took us out on it and it was pretty enough, but all he wanted to do was fiddle around in the cabin. It vexed Bertha something fierce on account he didn't hire us for you know what. It was supposed to be a social call. It was supposed to be a day off for us. She said it was a letdown and, to tell the truth, she was right."

Lori wiped the tears from her eyes. "Don't know why I'm cryin', sorry, Billy."

"No reason to be sorry. Sometimes it's good to have a cry. What happened to Bertha?"

"Don't know. She just left one day. Never said nothin', I woke up and she was gone. Madam said she didn't tell her a thing. Just up and left. No forwarding address or anything."

"She sounded like a good friend."

"I guess. Don't know. I guess so."

"What happened to the sailing man?"

"Oh, Bertha put him in his place. He liked to take photographs and he was startin' to get real pushy, you know, us out in the water and he thought he'd take advantage of that. Started orderin' us around, said if we didn't do what he wanted he'd keep us out there and then Bertha put him in a neck lock. That's what she called it, anyways, a neck lock. Kind of grabbed him around his neck, just about smothered him with her big tit. She had real big tits, Billy, way bigger than mine. And strong. She was strong as a strongman and spent a lot of years with a wrestler named *Strangler.* Guess she learned that from him, the neck lock, I mean. One thing was certain. You did not want to rile Bertha, I can tell you that. Anyways, she got him under control pretty good and soon we were back on dry land. That was my nature adventure. I guess, like Bertha would say, it was a letdown."

"Sounds like you've had a lot of *letdowns* in your time, Lori."

She shrugged again. Sniffed and dried her eyes. "Guess it don't matter now, Billy. Guess I'll be burning in hell soon enough. Guess I'll pay for all my wickedness and then that'll be the end of it." She laughed, "Or then again, maybe just the beginning of it. They say you'll burn in hell for eternity. Eternity. That's a long time."

"Oh, I don't know about that."

"What do you mean?"

"Well, sounds like you're a Christian, I mean, if you believe in hell and all that."

"I am and I do, Billy."

"Well, I'm pretty sure that a good Christian God is a forgiving God and would be happy to welcome a soul such as yours into heaven."

"That's not what the missionaries said. The women who were so angry at us, I mean at us whores, when they'd come around to our part of town, preachin' and shoutin' about us being damned to hell."

"Oh, stuff and nonsense!" He smiled, doing his best to convince her of something he himself believed to be nothing but a load of superstitious claptrap.

She cried hard now. "Do you really mean it, Billy? Do you really suppose so?"

"I do, Miss Lori. I do. God is forgiving and you are not wicked or evil. You just did the best you could with what was given to you in life. No one like you could ever be damned to hell. Look at Mary Magdalene."

"Who?"

"Mary Magdalene. Don't tell me you don't know who Mary Magdalene was."

"No, I don't."

"Oh, well, now, she was the most famous whore in all of history. She washed Christ's face when he was carryin' the cross." Billy knitted his brow, trying to remember. "Or, maybe it was his feet, doesn't matter. She washed *something* on him, I'm certain of that. She became one of God's favorites, and she was a notorious whore. She sits, to this very day, at the throne of God, and what's more than that, she's even a saint. Now tell me, how could she be treated in such a way and you not? It's impossible, just plain impossible for you to be put in hell and the same kind of person be made a saint. I know that, Miss Lori, I know that certain as I'm sitting with you here and now."

He reached over again to comfort her and she pulled him desperately to her breast. She cried hard into his neck as she held on.

"Oh, God I'm scared, Billy. I'm so, so scared."

"Well, I've got you, Miss Lori. I've got you and I'll be with you to the end." He patted her gently on the back. "Now, come on, I want you to calm yourself down. Billy Livingston's got you on earth, and your Lord Jesus will have you for all eternity in heaven. Doesn't that sound nice?"

"I hope you're right, Billy. Dear God in heaven, I hope you're right."

Alasdair Macdonald stood, fingers fidgeting with the brim of his homburg, dreading the arrival of the Tucson train, the train that would carry him south to Texas where he'd take a steamer through the Gulf to Cuba then New York. From there it would be the *Bremen* completing its maiden voyage to Southampton, and finally home.

Arvel handed him a fancy box, covered in red velvet. The laird opened it, admiring the plain steel Ranger badge that he'd so proudly worn through the desert and on to Mexico and back.

He shook Arvel by the hand. "Mr. Walsh, thank you for the adventure of a lifetime." He turned to Chica, radiant in her best city dress, a House of Worth green silk faille with matching parasol and egret-feather-trimmed hat. It was difficult for him to fathom that this vision of feminine perfection could have killed, single-handedly, a dozen or more men. He bowed at the waist, kissing her on the hand. She pulled him into her arms, hugging him around the thick neck, planting a wet kiss on his wind-burned cheek.

"You will come to visit me, Miss Chica? I promise you some good hunting. The greatest stag of my land will be yours."

She smiled, turning to Arvel. "We will one day, Alasdair. One day soon, we will come to your Scotland."

He pulled her one last time into his arms. "I'm going to miss you. I'm going to miss you both so much." He stood back, admiring her. "I have never, in all my life, in all my travels, met such a remarkable person as you, Miss Chica. Thank you for allowing me the privilege of your acquaintance. Thank you for allowing me into your most remarkable life."

She waved as he stood at the observation car, riding off with a heavy heart.

Turning to Arvel she smiled. "I think we showed him a good adventure, Pendejo. I think we made a good show of our Arizona, our home, our land."

Epilogue

Alice and Robert Craster went about rebuilding the freight hauling business, with the constant and loyal assistance of Sam. They took good advantage when the motor vehicle replaced the horse. Alice also started a school of voice and dance. She and Robert Craster lived and loved and raised three girls who learned to ride and shoot and hunt as well as they could converse in French and serve high tea or conjugate Latin verbs. They spent their spare time at the red rocks, near a clear pool off the beaten path. Alice became an accomplished camper. They slept, whenever possible, under the stars.

The Walshes continued to run the ranch, raise mules, and help the territory of Arizona on its path to civilization. Arvel would do less and less with the Rangers, but his friendship with Dick Welles would endure. William McKinley was elected the twenty-fifth president of the United States. He in turn appointed a governor sympathetic to the Ranger cause, sealing the fate of the finest law-enforcement organization ever known in the wild Arizona land, at least for another term.

Chica placed a granite monument just south of the clear pool where the young lovers had lost their lives. It stood, marking the little graveyard where Lori, Francis and Margarita had been laid to rest. Another spot had been reserved for Billy Livingston, though Chica had forbidden the aborigine from making use of it for many years to come.

Sometimes, when the moon and stars illuminated the desert night, a pretty little kit fox vixen could be observed, using the base of the tribute as a lookout.

ABOUT THE AUTHOR

John C. Horst was born in Baltimore, Maryland, and studied philosophy at Loyola College. His interests include the history and anthropology of the Old West.

The Mule Tamer: The Case of the Silver Republicans is part of the Mule Tamer Saga, about the Walsh family in Arizona and Mexico, spanning two generations from the mid nineteenth century to the early days of the Mexican Revolution.

His Allingham series, which includes *Allingham: Canyon Diablo, Allingham: Desperate Ride,* and *Allingham: The Long Journey Home,* is the story of a US marshal in the wild lands of Arizona in the latter part of the nineteenth century.

He resides in Maryland with his wife and daughter.